Yellow Moon Rising

An indie-authored and indie-published work.

Fiction under the pen name JoJo Riley

Yellow Moon Rising – Book One

Yellow Moon Justice – Book Two

Nonfiction under the pen name Pjo Riley

Atheist in Church – on heaven and other mysteries

Postcards from Planet Eldercare – the last frontier

Cover design by Lynne Pierce

Special thanks to cultural consultants Danialle Rose, of the Cheyenne River Sioux, and Thomas Ghost Dog, of the Oglala Nation, for their invaluable insights regarding culture, history, and language; and to Thomas for granting permission to use his hometown of Manderson, South Dakota, nearby to which his grandfather William Ghost Dog sponsored the first rodeo held on Pine Ridge Reservation land.

My gratitude endures.

Know your opponents and you will prevail.
Raymond Yellow Moon

Kansas City, Missouri
1936

Stopping before the entrance of Conboie Undertaking, Raylene smoothed her rumpled brown dress, the most appropriate garment to be had on short notice before viewing the body of her *até*. Her father. The nearby secondhand store had charged her twenty-five cents for the too-large, slightly wrinkled garment, but included a newsboy cap for ten cents more.

She could make out the bank clock on the building at the corner, which read 10:00 straight up. There was no sign of her sister Annie, who must have received a similar letter about their father's death with its invitation to this place today.

Where was that sister of hers, simply tardy or already inside? Before proceeding, they should speak about what Thomas's death meant to the family. They should be together in this. Raylene glanced at the foot traffic around the soup kitchen a few doors up but caught no sign of Annie, which made her wonder how long an undertaker would wait for an Indian's relatives to arrive. Probably not long. She counted out two more minutes, then stepped through the undertaker's door, travel bundle in hand, and advanced slowly through the vestibule's low light.

Of the two men at the far end of the small parlor, one advanced down the center aisle to meet her, saying, "Good morning. I'm Gerald Lambert, Mr. Conboie's assistant." His gaze flicked down her odd costume to her worn western boots and back to her face. "Are you Miss ... ah, Yellow Moon?"

"Little Moon," said Raylene.

"But you've come regarding Thomas Yellow Moon."

Raylene glanced around. Still no Annie. "Your letter left little travel time. Almost two days by train."

"I understand."

She set her bundled jacket on the closest chair, one of many arrayed in rows, and asked, "What can you tell me about my father's death?"

The assistant lifted a hand to his sternum. "What can *I* tell you?"

"Was it a robbery, or a raid of some kind? Your letter said an apparent fight at his saloon." On her journey south to Missouri with the countryside rolling past her train window, she had pondered who would fight with Thomas. If not the police, perhaps the husband of a lover or a disgruntled loser from one of his backroom card games. More importantly — to whom would her father *lose* a fight?

"The language in that letter was provided by authorities. They haven't mentioned a suspect, if that's what you mean." He fidgeted under her gaze.

She decided that her sister, not known for punctuality, was somehow delayed. Raylene would report to her later. "I guess I should see him."

As the assistant led her up the aisle, the second man stepped forward with a sober air. In one hand he held a dark blue purse by its handle. "Excuse me, Miss. I am John Murphy of the Union Pacific Railroad. I understand this is a dark time for you and I would not trample your feelings, but I'd like to ask a couple of questions about your sister Annie. I brought her purse."

Raylene considered this man, whose spectacles and carefully pressed suit suggested a no-nonsense type. "What do you mean, you brought her purse? Why would you have her purse?"

"The police gave me leave to bring Miss Moon's purse when I came to ask if you knew the whereabouts of some jewelry in her possession."

The railroad man might as well have been speaking a foreign language. Raylene was there to see her father's body, not to listen to nonsense about a purse purported to be Annie's. "Please explain yourself."

"I'm working a case regarding some missing jewelry that involves your sister."

"Has she filed a claim with your railroad?"

Mr. Lambert broke in. "Did you not receive our letter about Annie Moon?"

"I received only the one about my father. The reason I've come."

The assistant cleared his throat. "The first letter we posted to you gave news of your sister's passing. You should have received it before the one about your father."

As Raylene's thoughts went spinning, she steadied herself with one hand on the back of the nearest chair. Was it possible for not only her father to be dead, but Annie too? Her sister, her *chuwé*, who had slept beside her in childhood and protected her on the schoolyard. Dead? An impossibility, yet here were respectable-looking men telling her just that as they watched for her response. Not a woman to dissolve from emotion, she inhaled slowly and asked, "When did this happen?"

"We received Miss Moon's body two days before your father's. The authorities obtained your postal address for us."

Raylene's mind wanted to reject the possibility that Annie was dead, yet why would these men fabricate such a story? She drew another silent breath before speaking. "There was no letter about Annie. What was the cause?"

"Natural, according to police,'" said Mr. Lambert.

"So, I'll be viewing her body as well?"

"Well, no. We buried her on Wednesday."

"Why her but not my father?"

The assistant licked his lips. "There must have been instructions and payment."

"But I have only just arrived."

"When Mr. Conboie says bury someone, we do it, but we waited regarding the, ah, gentleman."

"Who paid to bury my sister?"

Mr. Lambert lifted his shoulders as if to suggest ignorance.

"Then I'll ask Mr. Conboie."

"You may do just that, but you'll have to wait 'til he gets back from Denver. Business, you know."

Raylene studied the assistant and decided he was determined to keep her at a distance from any pertinent details. She didn't know why this would be, but he seemed to be in charge of this place so she said, "I will see the body you have not buried."

John Murphy broke in. "Miss — about the jewelry your sister had ..."

Raylene took the purse he held out to her. "Is my sister implicated in a crime?"

The railroad man straightened. "I've only come to ask questions."

She wondered if this stranger suspected Annie of theft when Annie was no thief. "Can *you* tell me about my sister's death?"

His eyeglasses gleamed in the low light. "I cannot, but I do know that your sister's landlady is holding other possessions for you, should you want."

He did not seem an aggressive sort, nor a salesman trying

to get into her pocket, but clearly, he wanted information she could not provide. She said, "I cannot help you and you cannot help me, so I would like to finish what I came for."

Mr. Murphy stepped aside as the assistant motioned toward an opening toward the front of the seating space, saying, "This way."

He strode forward and turned left, but a closed door off to the right caught Raylene's attention. She moved to it and found that the office within was unoccupied, so she spun toward a short hallway beyond and opened the first door she reached, which held stainless steel tables and countertops arrayed with chrome basins, glass jars, coiled tubes.

Mr. Lambert arrived beside her in a huff. "Miss Moon, this room is off limits!"

"You buried Miss Moon. I am Miss Little Moon."

"Fine, but I insist you return to the parlor. Or else."

"Or else what?"

"Or I will be forced to call authorities."

She said, "I would like to ask Mr. Conboie about my sister's burial."

Mr. Lambert drew himself up. "You are trespassing in this hallway."

She glanced into the gloom. "There might be other rooms to check."

His shout nearly deafened her. "Mr. Murphy! Call the police!"

Raylene blinked at him and pointed back in the direction of the office. "You could call them yourself. I saw a telephone."

"Oh, no no no." He narrowed his eyes. "I'm not falling for that. If I step away, you will do as you please."

Raylene had made her point. She did not know the likelihood of finding Mr. Conboie on the premises and an interview with police would not further her cause. She shook her head and retreated toward the parlor, leaving Mr. Lambert to latch the embalming room door. The railroad man stood in the same place as minutes prior.

"Mr. Murphy?" said the assistant.

"Had I imagined you in mortal danger," said the Union Pacific man, "I would have summoned authorities or aided you myself. *Were* you?"

The assistant only frowned in reply, then motioned to Raylene that she should lead the way to the open chamber opposite, which was lit by the glow of small electric sconces. She did so, stopping before a rolling cart that held a wooden coffin exuding the aroma of fresh-cut pine. Mr. Lambert lifted the coffin's lid and backed away.

Sorrow that had traveled a long road bubbled up inside Raylene at the sight of Thomas buttoned neatly into a plain cotton shirt and clean, worn trousers. The sight of him solid but dead seemed unreal, yet she stood now before his silent body. The deep lines of his face looked soft, his scarred hands, perfectly still. She remembered back to her childhood when he had seemed so tall and true. He was a natural on a horse, sometimes buying and selling them. He had not been tender or gentle, was occasionally gruff and a bit distant, but she had always known she had a father. *Annie,* she thought now. *Here is Ate´. You should be here with me, but you are not. Why is it that you are not?*

When the assistant interrupted her reverie, she swallowed her grief before he could perceive it. He said, "Of course, there's no good time to offer this, but should you desire more formal attire for your father, I can arrange it. A suit perhaps, or else something less plain in the way of a casket?"

Raylene had the remainder of Raul's cash — a dollar and change — that her rail ticket had not consumed. Had she arrived with a pocket full of money, would she now spend it on a fancy casket to drop into a hole in the ground? The ground cared not whether it received the dead in painted, pillowed boxes or atop pyres of sagebrush and willow. Eyes on the body before her, she said, "I doubt you bury the dead without a box."

"The coroner pays for these plain ones, but when we locate family members, they quite often prefer something more memorable. We have nice caskets to show you."

Raylene ignored the assistant and gazed upon her father's corpse, its face aged by the life he had fashioned for himself and Annie in a city where they didn't belong and would never be fully accepted. In another time, his body would have been remanded back to the earth in ashes, back to ravens and wolves, to sun and wind and rain. But he was here now, in the city he had chosen, and she was without the means to reverse what others had set into motion.

Leaning in, she inhaled the odor of embalming fluid. Not a hint remained of the honest sweat of a day shoeing horses in the sun, or repairing tools, or driving wagons, or even his work in the saloon. *Father, why you?*

She ran her forefinger into a slit in the front of his fresh-washed shirt and felt the crude stitchwork that had sewn together a slash in his torso. So — the fight had involved a knife. That explained the cuts on his left hand.

She paused. Death was a regular part of life on the prairie and on the reservations. Animals died and people perished. Sometimes one killed the other, or the weather did, or misfortune. She was not a stranger to death, but death in a city seemed a different creature. Once more she imagined various possibilities: a thief had gone for the cash drawer, or Thomas had crossed somebody, a supplier perhaps. Or a drunk, having spent his rent money, had picked a fight.

Each awful option seemed plausible, but the evidence

before her suggested far worse. No one robbing a saloon used a knife because saloon-keepers often kept pistols or long guns. And as wily as gamblers could be, they were unlikely to best a man who had handled knives since his youth. Though her expression gave nothing away, a rising anger joined the sorrow that had taken root within her, bringing her as close to fury as she had ever felt. She knew of only one person clever enough and quick enough to kill Thomas, but *he* wouldn't, would he?

Then the thought occurred to her that perhaps in her grief she had mistaken this oddly waxen man for his twin. It seemed unlikely but ... first she checked behind his left ear. Then she began to unbutton the front of his trousers.

"Ah, Miss?" said the assistant, his voice jumping a notch as he stepped closer. She motioned for him to stand back as she pulled the trousers open to expose the obvious burn scar adjacent to the body's left hip bone, a deformed circular shape with a blunted tail. Her father's scar, she had no doubt. Closing the trouser flaps, she turned toward the assistant. "Where are the shoes he would have been wearing?"

"There were no shoes."

"None?"

"A feather in his shirt pocket but I swear, no shoes."

Raylene's heart dropped. "What sort of feather?"

"A black one, tattered. We tossed it." He spread his hands as if to suggest that a feather was of no consequence, not the sort of keepsake sent with a body to the hereafter.

The mention of that feather began the tolling of a silent bell proclaiming the identity of the killer. Her brain protested, her heart protested, but the sum of all the clues thus far pointed to only one person. She said, "I'm going to take that silver band."

"It won't come past the knuckle."

"Do you have a jack knife? Any sort will do."

The assistant's eyes grew wide. He patted his jacket pockets. "Not on me."

"How about the railroad man?"

"I don't believe I'd ask him."

Raylene paused a moment, then bent to pull a flat-handled knife from a narrow sheath inside her right boot, which she used to begin cutting around the knuckle of Thomas's smallest finger.

"Aw, now," began the assistant before she shot him a look that backed him up.

Soon she had unhinged the joint and slipped the ring from its place, the chamber so quiet she could hear the assistant's breathing. Leaving the severed portion of his pinkie inside the box, she pocketed the band of silver that held two tiny turquoise stones. Her mother's ring. When the time was right, she would pray for Thomas's safe passage to the next world, and also for Annie, who was supposedly already in the ground. Details regarding Annie's death and burial would have to wait, but at least Thomas's killer was no longer a mystery.

"I have seen enough," she said to Mr. Lambert.

The assistant rearranged his features into a hopeful smile. "About that fancier arrangement?"

The undertaker had already profited from burying Annie. He did not need to profit further from Thomas's death. "You have dodged my questions. I might someday discuss with Mr. Conboie the details I seek. As for Thomas Yellow Moon, you have filled him with chemicals for putting him in the ground. You might as well finish what you started."

The railroad man was at the head of the room. He had probably overheard everything, but to his credit, he had not aided Mr. Lambert in bullying her. In acknowledgement, she dipped her chin in his direction as she passed by with Annie's purse.

Just then, a door slammed somewhere down the hidden hallway. She stopped to listen as its echo faded away. The railroad man narrowed his eyes but did not move. When she threw a glance at the assistant, he was studying his shoes.

At the last row of chairs, she retrieved her bundle and in no time opened the parlor's entry door, admitting sounds from the street — clip-clops and rumbles and the distant clang of a streetcar. She knew the men were watching her dissolve into the bright Missouri sunlight. They had failed to get what they wanted, as had she. If she had thought after hearing about Annie's passing that things could not get worse, she had been wrong. There was no dismissing the only conclusion that could follow from the clues pointing to Thomas's killer. To make matters worse, there was no one left but her to locate him and no one else to deliver the reckoning that family justice required. Retribution. The last duty she would ever have imagined facing.

Her father's killer had a week's head start and would be expecting her to pursue him. He knew her and she knew him — her *atéyA*. Her uncle. Her father's twin, Raymond Yellow Moon.

Two

Raylene had only once ever jumped a train, in the company of schoolmates, back when they had been looking for adventure, back when taking risks felt like entertainment. Union Pacific signaled its willingness to let jumpers ride the rails by leaving a boxcar open aways down the line of this freighter headed west. A few down-and-outers here and there were no skin off a railroad's nose. Such travelers had no spare money to spend on tickets anyway, so there was no profit lost to those tycoons who for decades had controlled the movement of people and marketable goods. She wanted to board this open car before it got rolling.

She had abandoned her second-hand dress, and from Annie's purse, had kept only a smallish cornhusk doll tied with narrow rags now tucked into the bundled jacket tied bandolier-style across her chest. She had retied her hair with a leather string and tucked it up under the newsboy cap.

Thus prepared, she gathered herself and sprang to grab the boxcar's door frame with one hand, then the other. Next, an upward swing of legs through the doorway. With a grunt, she scrambled onto her knees.

The car was lit by a few skinny stripes of daylight leaking through its side boards and the slice pouring in through the open door. As it jerked slightly and got underway, its odors of burnt wood, sweat, and urine swirled in the air. Two other riders were just silhouettes at the back. Neither spoke, so she squatted alongside the open door to let her thoughts wander to her sister, found dead only two days before Thomas was killed. So said Conboie's assistant. But where had they buried her? The man had acted like he didn't know, but she figured Annie must have been laid to rest in the public cemetery. She sent her thoughts outward: *Count on me to find you and mourn you.*

She would mourn Thomas properly then too. But first came her duty to avenge his death. She would rather ignore tradition and return to ranch work, losing herself in the physical duties that at day's end left her exhausted in the best possible way. Such would be her preference. If she did not avenge Thomas's death, who would know it? Not the customers of his saloon or the local authorities. Not even the residents of her hometown on the Pine Ridge Reservation. But *she* would know it.

Her throat constricted at the thought of multiple tasks ahead of her — finding Raymond, extracting answers from him, and delivering a fitting punishment. This begged the question: What kind of retribution qualified as not just prairie justice, but family justice for a killing? The question circled round her, its answer just out of reach. She lacked experience at retribution but she knew one thing — by the time she found her uncle, she had better have a plan.

She held to her place as the train crossed the Kansas River and for the next hour as its wheels rumbled beneath the flow of air, slowing its beat on the approach to Lawrence before passing through the switchyard and picking up speed again. At Topeka, the train approached the rail yard at a creep. That's when a man rose from one of the car's corners and came to the open doorway. Raylene returned his silent nod then watched as he tossed his bundle outward before swinging himself out after it.

As the train crawled through the Topeka yard, another man

appeared in the doorway, his meaty hands pulling him in safely. Raylene straightened and took a step sideways.

"Well, well," said the newcomer, loud enough to be heard over the sound of wind and wheels. "They're gettin' younger all the time."

The man was half lit by the doorway light and close enough that she could smell the sweat on him, and something else — a sickness within. He seemed unsteady on his feet as he made his way into the car, becoming a nearly featureless figure within the shadows. After a minute, Raylene squatted again near the open doorway to watch the countryside flash by.

Before long the sick man reappeared beside her. Raylene stood and tried to read his rheumy eyes.

He said, "We got us a brownie." Tossing a look toward the silent form in the far corner, he gave a low chuckle that turned into a wet cough. "You got food on you?" he asked.

"No," she said.

"At's a shame, 'cause everybody's got to pay his way. So happens it's me gonna collect from you." With surprising speed, he grabbed her bicep, forcing her sideways into the doorway's rush of wind. She tried to jerk free but he clutched her other arm and held her tight.

"You a skinny thing," he said. "Sissy-like." Pinning two of Raylene's wrists in one fist, he squeezed the bundle across her chest. When he grabbed at her pants pockets, her legs recoiled. "Sure about the food?" he asked again, his reeking mouth nearly in her face.

"No food," she said forcefully.

"At's another shame, 'cause a man's got to eat. Eat and piss and ... one other thing." He swung her around, one thick arm binding her tight. The flab of his belly and his hardness below pressed against her buttocks. She drew a deep breath and stomped hard on his instep with her boot heel, managing to wrench one hand free before he grabbed her again and bent her forward, pinning her skull against the door frame.

"Haw! I like a little spunk," he cried as he tugged her hips upward. With his free hand he fumbled his britches open then reached around for her belt buckle. In a flash, she found his hand with her mouth and bit down hard.

Britches sagging to his knees, he tried to straighten, crying, "You bastard!" as Raylene pulled her boot knife and blindly plunged it into his right calf. Arms flailing, he screamed and bent to pull at the knife as Raylene skittered away on all fours. At first it seemed he might wrench the weapon free, but then he straightened, backlit by the slice of open doorway. Hands clutching at his chest, he tipped sideways, gasping like a fish for air. The sound of his arm slamming against steel was lost in the wind as he fell outward.

Raylene worked to catch her breath at the close call. Rising, she found her cap on the floor and slapped it against her leg before pulling it on again as she moved further away from the door.

The dark shape in the corner finally spoke in a man's gravelly voice. "You okay?"

Raylene nodded as she checked her belt buckle. When she stepped toward the shape, it became a seated man who said, "Guess he had it comin'." When Raylene didn't answer, he added, "You ain't carrying no food?"

"No."

"In that case I guess I'll share mine with you." He produced a papered packet, which he opened. "You fight pretty good for a kid. That'll wear a person out." He broke a single biscuit apart and held out half.

Taking the offered morsel, Raylene nodded her thanks and pulled a nickel from the pouch she wore on a leather string around her neck. The man took it and rubbed it between his fingers before sliding it into a pocket of his greasy overalls. His mouth was lost in the shadows but she imagined it curling up into a smile as he said, "Guess today's lookin' up after all."

In the late afternoon, the train slowed and with a squeal of brakes came to a halt. Raylene looked at the tramp who had given his name as Harold, but when he remained slumped in the corner, apparently unconcerned, she relaxed her guard enough to hazard a look out the doorway. The shouting and activity were coming from a short row of blue grain elevators alongside the tracks from which workers loaded corn into a grain car up the line.

Not far off stood a farming town washed in the haze of afternoon light. For some reason, small towns exerted a pull on her. Perhaps it was the allure of community. Her own extended community, her *thíospaye*, had fifty years prior been driven from its hunting lands onto reservations that forced tribes to spend every season on the same acreage. The men in particular had floundered without traditional roles or the freedom to pursue plentiful wild game. They became scrabblers, ever reliant upon beef allotments and rations of weevil-y flour, rancid lard, beans, and sugar. Families split, which also split their *thióspaye*. Raylene's nomadic life included some time in one location, a bit more in another, riding fences and troubleshooting for ranching operations where she was often the only woman on the crew. Wherever she went she carried the lessons she had absorbed at the side of her grandmother, who had raised Annie and her after their mother's death. No heavier than dreams were her grandmother's ways of honoring the land and its bounty.

Eventually the train jolted forward into a slow acceleration that became a steady two-hour pull through more rolling plains patchworked with crops and small towns. At Lincoln, it only slowed before gathering speed again after crossing the rail yard. Many hours after leaving Kansas City, it pulled into Omaha where an early evening glow lay gentle upon rail buildings, water towers, and switching signals. Again, those odors of machine grease and the heat of cooling engines, oil-soaked gravel, and the stink of a couple hundred cows shitting in the dirt of nearby cattle yards.

Harold yawned and stretched his arms toward the boxcar's roof. "This is the end of the line for me," he said. "If you get off to take a leak or you wanna stop over, stay away from the main station. Never know when them official types will roust you." He explained about his knees not working right, something about a fall from a window. He would exit when he got them moving. "The Hoovertown's thataway," he said, stabbing his thumb in a northerly direction.

She knew the encampment would contain shelters cobbled from tarpaper and scrap wood, a few lean-tos, a handful of tents, some outhouses.

He glanced away then said, "I don't usually pry, but I wonder why you're travelin' this way."

"I'm on the trail of someone."

"For love or money?"

Raylene thought a moment. "Love, I guess."

"'Bout that fight," said Harold with a one-shouldered shrug, "I didn't see nothin'."

Raylene hoped his word was solid. She had knifed a man for good reason and had no idea how he'd faired afterwards. Probably not well. After the immediate threat had passed, her recollection of the man's rank odor, his invading hands, and her own actions had left an ache inside her. If she ever faced a judge for defending herself, she'd have a hard go of it. Brown-skinned people usually took the rap.

As evening fell in Kansas City, Kansas, on the west side of the river from Missouri, John Murphy paced the sidewalk opposite the Victorian-era boarding house where Annie Moon had lived. Eventually, he ambled down Georgia Street to where the corner streetlamp cast a yellow glow, then back the other direction. Since leaving the undertaker's parlor, he'd been watching for the little sister, as he now thought of her. In the parlor, she had looked underfed, but perhaps that had just been her oversized dress because she had moved with a grace that suggested a certain physicality. She had also deflected Lambert's shady sales pitch, which meant she was no pushover.

He had suggested the little sister come for Annie Moon's belongings, but he had worked this stakeout for hours and she hadn't shown. Now he wished he had not given her Annie's purse. He should have suggested she meet him at the house to claim it.

He had skipped lunch and sat for hours in his Hudson watching the comings and goings of various neighborhood denizens while thinking back to the little sister's behavior in the undertaker's parlor. His position had been such that he had seen only the glint of her knife as she bent over her father's pine coffin. Afterwards, Mr. Lambert had described the way she had cleaved one of the dead man's finger joints in order to remove a silver ring. Mr. Lambert had seemed disgusted by this, but Murphy found her bold behavior intriguing.

Now he'd spent his afternoon waiting, waiting being a good portion of detective work, but he'd seen no sign of the little sister. Running out of patience, he kept moving in and out of the black shadows cast by trees set into sidewalks buckled by their roots. A late-September breeze rattled what remained of leaves overhead. Where was the sister he needed to interview?

The boarding house, whitewashed in daylight, appeared gray at this hour. Beyond the front porch cast in deeper shadow, the lacy front curtains glowed from a light within. Feeling foiled by the sister, Murphy took the house's steps two at a time. His vigorous rap was answered by the landlady, Mrs. Gunther. In a firm but apologetic tone he requested another few minutes of her time, adding, "Have you seen Annie's sister since I was last here?"

"No, and I suppose I'm glad," said Mrs. Gunther. "She will need to mourn Annie and their father."

"If you recall, you said that an Indian had come. I've been thinking he might not be what he claimed."

Mrs. Gunther touched a wrinkled hand to her throat. "Well, he knew to come. If he wasn't a Yellow Moon, how would he have known?"

"He didn't threaten you?"

"As I said before — No. But he had a deathly look about him. I don't mind saying that I locked the door after he left."

"You did say you saw Annie Moon with fancy jewelry..."

"Just that once, when she was headed downtown. A gold necklace with a green stone hanging down. She said it wasn't real but it looked nice as anything I've ever seen. And earrings to match. Pretty classy for a girl of her occupation." Mrs. Gunther put her hands on her hips. "I've been thinking: What's that girl's death got to do with the railroad? When city police came, I told them what I knew, including about the valise that man took with him."

"The Indian man claiming to be her father."

"Yes."

Murphy had not heard about the valise before. He said, "I'll share with you that Miss Moon may have acquired that fancy jewelry from a railroad official under what might be called questionable circumstances."

Mrs. Gunther frowned. "But if it's stolen goods, why aren't the police asking after it? I want you to know I don't brook misbehavior of any kind. I run a reputable house for working women. There's no nonsense under my roof."

"No offense intended. I'm just trying to get to the bottom of this."

In reality, the police had not been consulted about the jewelry because Murphy and his boss knew those goods had not been stolen. His boss had given the jewelry to Annie and now wanted it returned as quietly as possible. Murphy's questions, tinged with the patina of police work, had gotten him this far. He did not want the landlady lodging a complaint about him.

The woman said, "I assure you I found nothing of value after your search and I've packed Annie's dresses and shoes." Her expression suggested she was out of time for him. "Surely you don't care about her dresses."

Murphy flashed her a smile. "You've been a great help. I'm sure there are others awaiting your attention and more lodgers to come for your quality accommodations." As he pulled a calling card from his jacket and offered it to her, he mentally reviewed what he suspected: If an Indian had taken any items of value related to Annie Moon, the little sister would likely know that person. She might even be in cahoots with him, sharing the proceeds from selling the jewelry. He said, "I work out of the freight office and the secretaries take messages. I hope you'll call if you think of any information that might help us. If the sister returns, for instance, or that Indian man who frightened you."

Mrs. Gunther recoiled, then stood straight and took his card.

Murphy tipped his fedora. "Good evening to you. Oh — I wonder...about that valise. Did you ever see inside it? Was there jewelry perhaps?"

Mrs. Gunther drew herself up. "That was none of my business. Besides, it was locked."

"Did you ever hear mention of what it held? As her landlady, you would have a right to know." The latter was not true, but in his experience, people liked to hear that they were entitled to certain liberties.

Mrs. Gunther narrowed her eyes. "If I remember right, she said it kept important papers safe. Good night, Mr. Murphy."

Papers, thought Murphy as he reached the sidewalk. *What kind of papers would a girl like Annie save?* He could not imagine, and his boss had not asked him to recover papers, only jewelry. He added another proposition to his mental list: Even if that missing valise held papers, it could also hold the jewelry he was after.

Leaving his auto parked curbside in the next block, Murphy began a survey of the nearest diners and inns. This residential neighborhood was bordered by small grocery markets, delicatessens, and laundry shops. Kansas was a dry state. You had to know where to find hidden speakeasies or a brave restaurant owner who served a bottle of beer disguised as ginger ale, or sometimes the hard stuff in a coffee cup. Annie had lived in this area for a handful of years, so Murphy reasoned that the little sister might know it as well. Perhaps he'd find her in a local establishment, partaking of a hot meal, where if she found a lenient (also known as greedy) host, she might also nurse a glass of beer. Since Prohibition's end in '33, you couldn't throw a shoe on the Missouri side and hit a neighborhood dry of beer, nectar of the masses. He himself was a whiskey man, preferably Jameson.

He stepped into each establishment still open at this hour to scan its occupants before moving on. At eight o'clock he gave up and walked back to his coupe. He may have misread

Raylene Little Moon. Perhaps she had no interest in the remainder of Annie's belongings or saw no advantage in burdening herself with extra luggage. Or, she might have gone to stay with friends somewhere on this side of the river or the other, an area too large for him to search in its entirety. His boss would not be happy with his lack of progress thus far. He knew he would have to do better.

On the drive home, his mind turned over which direction the sister in question could have gone. She seemed to have given him the slip, but if he did his job right, she wouldn't do that again.

Making her way out of the boxcar and across the tracks, Raylene watched for any rail marshal who might detain poorer sorts not for riding — but for loitering near their equipment. She sniffed the air and detected smoke. That was farming country for you, someone was always planting something or harvesting something or burning something.

Before long she came to a road that led to Omaha's Hoovertown, which squatted upon a barren swath of land. It was the sort of place that expanded or shrank with the season, dwellings knocked into being as the weather warmed, later dismantled for feeding fires as nights grew cold. Raylene judged it as eighty dwellings strong but many of its occupants would already be moving along in search of someplace warmer.

A campfire here and there delineated the settlement from the wide open beyond. Its dwellings were an assemblage of salvaged lumber and sheets of tin. Some had roofs of waxed canvas, others supported bicycles against their outer walls. Paths trampled by hundreds or maybe thousands of worn boots and shoes led this way and that. Raylene selected a lean-to that appeared abandoned. It contained a thick layer of dried corn stalks and leaves as a pallet.

At the closest campfire, she made the acquaintance of several men and one woman who were passing around tin plates of corn gleaned from nearby fields. Two of the men had found labor jobs but the others had struck out. The unemployed fetched pails of water from the town fountain whenever they went in search of work. Theirs was a sharing economy.

She was the last one lingering at the fire as the night sky glistened with uncounted stars. From the rail yard came the whistle and chug of trains on the move. Lost in thought that was much like non-thought, she didn't at first register a small animal standing near the closest hut opposite. When the creature wobbled in place then folded to the ground, she set aside her plate and rose from the wooden crate where she'd been sitting. Rounding the fire, she recognized the scruffy thing as a coyote pup come in from the fields. It had to be either desperate or injured.

The men in her father's family were part Crow. Now, parts from a Crow story she had learned in her youth came to mind, snippets repeated in various forms by elders who told stories for the children to remember who their people were. Speaking in a calm voice, she recited: *Little crane told the story of one who was always in trouble — Old Man Coyote. Summer's grass stood yellow on the plains. The winds grew colder and the ducks on the water-holes were in such numbers as to turn the water black. All the people were fed. Old Man Coyote lay in a cottonwood grove, singing and beating time on his body. Near the fire where ducks were roasting, he sang of how smart he was...*

Soon she stood where the pup lay panting. She continued: *Old Man Coyote in his foolishness taunts the trees and forgets that they and the people are brothers, and that everything, even the winds, are for sharing.*

She reached a hand toward the pup and felt its ribs and shoulders, avoiding patches where singed fur hung loose. When it turned dull eyes toward her, she lifted it and spoke a few words learned from her grandmother, from way back then.

The pup whimpered as she carried it back to her seat, where she held it on her lap and fed it mashed bits of her remaining fire-roasted corn. Dipping her bandana in a pail of water, she drizzled the moisture into its mouth until it could lap water from her hand. When the pup fell asleep, she held it for an hour while the campfire burned down to nothing. Then she carried it to her lean-to and slept the night with it cradled beneath her jacket against her heart.

Three

In the morning, Murphy drove to Police Headquarters on Locust St. to speak with his connection there, who told him they had not seen the little sister. From his connection he obtained an updated list of all the licensed Kansas City, Missouri, hock shops and the two on the Kansas City, Kansas side. He carried with him a snapshot of Annie Moon given to him by his boss. The photo had been scissored in half so that the only face showing was Annie's. A man's jacket sleeve disappeared behind her at waist level. Though the image was black and white, the necklace at her throat seemed to sparkle and with her hair tucked behind one ear, a glistening earring showed. She looked happy in the photo, and he thought what a shame it was that a young woman's life had been cut short.

Murphy's official cases rarely involved death. Thefts were common, sometimes injuries. Occasionally he uncovered the actions of underhanded rail workers. Just once he led a crackdown against rail riders, hard luck types who moved from place to place. Such crackdowns were the railroad's response when tramps damaged its property or spooked its passengers. Since the stock market crash of '29, most of the rail lines practiced a bit of leniency. He didn't mind leniency, within reason.

Methodically moving about the city, Murphy queried the workers in each hock shop as to whether they'd seen the jewelry shown in the pared-down photo. He also carried a sketch of the missing ring. It was almost noon when in the next-to-last shop on his list he found the earrings. They were being held for an Indian man who had borrowed a cool $100 against them. The man hadn't yet returned, but his loan was good for thirty days.

A hundred-dollar loan meant the shop owner knew the earrings were the real deal. Murphy made the case for the jewels being stolen property and used the shop telephone to call his boss for instructions. Though twenty-four days remained on the loan, Murphy persuaded the owner to sell him the earrings, explaining that the person who had brought them in was implicated in other, more serious crimes. He suggested the shop would be smart to get shed of them.

Daylight was running out as he left the last hock shop on the list. He had found only one of the items he sought. It was a start, but not good enough. Now his search would have to get serious.

Asleep on the floor of her lean-to, curved snail-like around the pup, Raylene dreamed of her father and her uncle, brothers born minutes apart with nearly identical features. They were so alike and both so often present in the early times that Annie and Raylene, children then, had called them both Father. In an earlier era, the Crow of their father's *thióspaye*, would have killed twins at birth, believing them to embody evil sent to harm the tribe, but by the time Thomas and Raymond were born, the Crow had already experienced too many deaths at the hands of others to bring death upon their own. Since being pushed onto reservations, all children, even twins, represented the tribe's survival.

Daylight arrived with the sounds of life rising from other shanties and faint whimpering from the coyote, who still lived. A sign, perhaps, of its strong spirit. "Coh-yoh-tay," said Raylene. "Trickster of the people's legends. You have conned me into helping you." The pup had survived by doing what people did when in trouble — it followed its instincts to seek safety until it could return to the familiar. She too had followed her instincts to reach this makeshift patch of shelters and humanity. North from this place, she meant to locate a married couple long connected to her elders and whom she herself recalled from years past. They knew Thomas and Raymond.

After a breakfast of more corn, Raylene carried the matted pup throughout the shantytown until she located Harold sitting on the ground in front of a tarpaper shack, the sun's glow on his face as he perused a wrinkled, well-used newspaper. He looked different in the light of day, his sparse hair a wiry blond shot through with silver. "Hey, kid," he said when he saw her. "Need a look at Saturday's paper?"

"Not just now. I came with a question. Will you be staying close by today?" she asked.

"Thought I'd rest before looking for work. Travel takes it out of you, you know?"

Raylene nodded. The previous day had been a trying one for many reasons. She asked him to keep the pup safe for her.

"That raggedy piece of fur? What'd you do, dig it up?"

"It chose me and I will see it healed," she told him. When he looked as if he might decline, she added, "I will pay you."

The old man perked up. "What kind of pay?"

Raylene reached into the leather pouch she wore inside the collar of her shirt and brought out a silver dollar coin worn soft with wear. A quarter would have sufficed. Two bits would buy two cheap meals but she could not very well ask Harold to make change. Besides, the pup now seemed symbolic of her own journey from deep loss toward surviving whatever reckoning she delivered to Ray. Yes, she would see the pup live.

The old man's eyes grew round. "S'that for real? How's it that yesterday you had no food but today somehow you have a dollar?"

She considered the horizon beyond the shantytown. "How is it that neither luck nor peace can find me, but somehow this pup did?"

"Alright, alright," he said. "I don't 'spect to understand you Indian types. Give it here."

Raylene began to hand him the pup whose two burnt paws she had wrapped with strips cut from her bandana.

"The money, I mean the money," said Harold.

"When I return to find this pup has had good care, the money will be yours," she said. "First, I will show you how to provide water and bits of corn. Can you do it?"

"Sure I can." The old man looked between the coyote's legs before settling it onto his lap. "It's a male. He gonna be your dog?"

"He does not belong to me. I am just his fellow traveler, for now."

"Don't forget to come back. I don't want no pup."

"My word is good."

Back at Police Headquarters, Murphy accepted a cup of coffee from one of the police secretaries and took a big swig. He had delivered the recovered earrings, sealed in an envelope, to his boss's office, and now, with the help of a wad of cash had persuaded a sergeant to advise his men that a reward existed for the return of the ring and necklace still missing. For an additional bit of cash, he was also granted fifteen minutes to read the police files pertaining to the deaths of Annie Moon and Thomas Yellow Moon.

Opening both files, he compared one report to the other. Neither showed a street address for the little sister, only the

South Dakota post office box he had been told about. In Annie Moon's file he found a statement from a regular patron desperate for a drink, who had reported the saloon locked up when it should have been open for business. Leave it to a drunk to uncover a death of some importance to John Murphy's boss.

The balance of the report included the undertaker's removal of Annie Moon's body. No foul play was suspected, so there had been no autopsy. She had been found reclining in the back room of the saloon her father managed — Down the Block it was called. There was some vomit but no head wound, no bruising from a fight. She'd been dead between twenty and twenty-four hours by the time police were called and her father, the manager of the Down the Block saloon had been interviewed, his answers vague but appearing above suspicion. There was mention of faint traces of formaldehyde, which sounded odd, since she hadn't by then been embalmed. Similarities to other deaths from alcohol consumption were noted, and almost as an afterthought, a brief handwritten mention: "Firm abdomen, possible pregnancy."

Murphy supposed that some special arrangement allowed Thomas Yellow Moon to manage a saloon since technically, federal law still prohibited the providing of alcohol to Indians. Ridiculous in modern times, since almost everyone and his sister drank like fish during Prohibition, continuing through today. Prohibition had probably made alcoholics out of many otherwise good citizens.

In any event, Thomas was found dead two days after the report regarding Annie, and his were different circumstances. He was clearly the victim of a knife wound, the evidence suggesting he'd been deceased roughly twelve hours when found. The coroner's report noted old healed-over scars on Thomas's chest and arms and a crescent scar on one hip.

The report also noted the confiscation of two cases of whiskey. Perhaps the booze had gone to the saloon's proper owner, but why hadn't they simply left it behind since Murphy had checked two days later and found the saloon open again for business.

He wondered what, if anything, to make of Annie Moon's death in relation to Thomas Yellow Moon's. Making something of her death was not his job any more than was determining who had paid for the young woman's burial. His job was to find certain jewels and return them to their original owner, and now he finally possessed details for use in bargaining with the little sister.

As with any of his complicated railroad cases, this one continued to evolve. In this case as in others, questions invariably appeared like weeds before any hint of an answer showed itself. For instance, why had the little sister, Raylene not claimed her elder sister's effects? He had called the boarding house owner today and she had reported no appearance thus far by the sister in question, which meant that his odds of finding her in town might be diminishing. This whole affair might be a waste of his time and the boss's money, but details of the case intrigued him: Raylene Little Moon had used a knife to remove a ring from her father's dead finger; she might have those still-missing jewels; and, there seemed to be an imposter claiming to be the sisters' father. The little sister struck him as mysterious and proud; also, capable. Of what she was capable he didn't exactly know, but he wouldn't mind finding out. Of course, to find out, he'd have to find her.

Murphy returned to the secretary who had brought him coffee and asked to use an office phone. When she offered an unoccupied desk, he called his office.

"Good work finding those earrings," said his boss, who used a cane when his gout flared up and had the habit of thunking his cane upon the floor as he spoke. The sound could be heard like a distant, irregular heartbeat. "I supposed you have guessed by now, the missing pieces belong to my wife, passed down from her mother. If you're making a face about that, don't bother, just come up with an answer to where the other pieces are."

"They haven't been pawned," said Murphy, straight-faced, "so they could be anywhere. I've been talking up a reward for their return."

"God, this whole thing is costing me. You didn't offer much, I hope."

"Enough that the beat cops will check the shops again on both sides of the river."

An audible sigh came down the line. "And if they're not here or across the bridge, where could they be?"

"It's possible that Annie's little sister could lead me to them. By now she might have them with her. There are lots of little towns and wide-open places between here and where she gets her mail in South Dakota."

"Damn it. I guess you'd better catch her," said the boss. "I'd hate to think that jewelry might never surface. I'd be in for it then. Last night I told my wife I'd lent them to the museum on short notice for a traveling exhibit of gowns owned by governors' wives. Quick thinking, huh?"

Murphy suppressed the urge to remark upon his boss having given family heirlooms to his mistress in the first place. Only a man who'd lost his head or his heart would take such a risk.

"Not to sidetrack things," continued the boss, "but there's news out of Onaga this morning. Between there and Marysville the crew spotted a body near the tracks, just off the east rail. We've called it in to the Pottawatomie County Sheriff — what the hell kind of name is that — and they've promised to go out."

"It's named for a tribe. No reports of a passenger gone missing?" said Murphy.

"None so far. We can hope it won't make one of the big papers. The Onaga super checked around and hasn't found anything else amiss. Yet."

"Maybe someone trying to jump on."

"Hmpf — Hang on," came the distracted reply. Murphy could make out someone else speaking in the background. Coming back on the line, the boss said, "Do what you can. I'll authorize some cash at Omaha for you — and Murphy —"

"Yes, sir?"

"I hate to say this but I'm out on a limb here. The museum angle will only work for a while. There's a potentially larger cost to this than the jewelry, if you get my drift."

"I'll do what I can."

The line clicked off and Murphy shook his head, amazed at the things people got themselves into. Not that he was mistake-proof regarding women. He had chosen poorly his first wife, his first-and-only wife, who had beguiled him with her dreamy, ethereal manner. A reader of poetry with a preference for frills and tea cakes and classical music. So delicate and in need of a capable husband, which at the time he felt ready to be, but the fates had not been with them.

Over time, Catherine had grown constitutionally and mentally unfit for marital life. Afraid of common social interactions and repulsed by sexual coupling. Fearful of ordinary efforts such as attending a picture show, and terrified of the germs carried on a summer breeze. When she became unhinged at the sight of puddles oily with rain, even those on the street beyond their home, she quit leaving the house. Eventually her doctor prescribed retirement to a sanatorium in Colorado's high country. Each week he wrote her letters containing observations that he hoped would seem to include her without causing upset.

He sometimes wondered who would dare claim to know the magic combination for a happy marriage or a satisfactory life. He could not, would not, make such a claim. Adult life, he had found, was fashioned on an uphill slope that required the circumvention of obvious outcroppings and recognizable fissures concurrent with interpreting nearly-invisible signals and signs. Even then you might lose that which you thought unassailable.

Annie Moon had lost her life. He had to wonder whether Miss Moon had truly cared for his boss, who was a red-faced, cigar-smoking, profane man. Had she loved him? Once again, he felt a twinge at the thought of a young life snuffed, perhaps by drink. Life, it seemed, defied prediction.

And now, a choice to make: he could travel swiftly by rail to Omaha and places north, or drive his automobile and interview U.P. staff in small towns between here and Sioux Falls for signs of the little sister. Either way, there would be a lot of ground to cover. If she had already left town, she had a good head start on him.

The largest portion of Omaha lay south of the rail yard whose eastbound tracks ran north out of Nebraska through Iowa and up toward the Great Lakes. The rails running westward crossed Nebraska's heartland, sliced through Wyoming then Utah and Nevada before ending in sight of the great blue Pacific. The plains on which the town was built were once the hunting lands of the people called Omaha, but now their reservation lay far to the north, almost touching Lakota country. Raylene scanned the horizon until its contours revealed themselves as familiar. Out beyond the tracks and the shantytown lived a trader and his wife who had taken up farming. They knew her family. She had first been to their home in 1916 and again in '25.

With her bundle tied across her back, Raylene set her cap to shade her eyes and began walking the road whose designation as "75" was as familiar to her as the dry ditches on each side filled with wild mustard and many-headed sunflowers gone to seed. Vehicles rumbled by sporadically, farting exhaust and sending tan grasshoppers whirring away. The sun floated above acres of late harvest wheat planted to benefit from proximity to Missouri River groundwater. Even so, much of those stalks showing looked brittle. Dead ahead, more rolling land. From a fencepost on her right, a meadowlark trilled. *Let me find them still on their land,* she said to the sky.

When the sun was nearly overhead, she came to a small stream that ran through a culvert under the road. Beyond the ditch bank stood giant cottonwood trees holding glossy black birds speaking their own language. Raylene stopped to listen. This tiny stream and the trees rose as landmarks in her memory.

Worming her way between the fence wires she knelt at the stream to cup her hands in its clear water. After drinking her fill, she rinsed her torn bandana and ran it across her face then draped it around her neck.

The stream was flanked by a narrow trail on its north side. This she followed west, grasshoppers clicking away from her heels, until a boxy shape took form beyond the closest desiccated fields — a modest wooden house, its whitewash worn thin by frigid prairie winters and wind-whipped summers. Other shapes were a derelict automobile and a rusting tractor. A nearby tree held wormy apples puckering in the sun as a stand of poplars shed crumbling leaves.

As she drew closer, a pack of skinny dogs came charging

round the house to bark at her. Raylene stopped where she was and waited. In a minute, a burnt-brown Santee man appeared on the slanting front porch. When the screen door slammed shut behind him, the dogs settled into growling. As if Raylene hadn't halted at a respectful distance, the man lifted a long-barreled gun and pointed it in her direction. "Stay where you are," he called out.

Though the man's voice cracked when he spoke, Raylene knew he meant what he said.

September 27, 1936

Dearest Catherine,

As always, I assume that some kind soul will read this missive to you in spite of the unpleasantness of cases I mention here. You were always interested in my work, perhaps out of duty, but I would not write about such matters if the staff there were to counsel me otherwise. Lacking such objections, I will summarize below the excitement of my week.

There were the usual activities and examining of incidents pertaining to missing personal effects (two suitcases, one trunk, one handbag, and a pickpocket loose on the K.C./St. Louis stretch). I long ago ceased marveling at the creativity of thieves.

And then came a deliberate death and a second one of a different type in Kansas City itself. They appear related but without similar cause. Neither seems of consequence to local authorities. Nor does the U.P. involve itself, for the deaths did not occur on U.P. property, but my boss (whom you never cottoned to) has assigned me to locate jewelry related to the second death.

Because you indulged occasionally in reading A.C. Doyle with me, I'll venture one of his assertions that two deaths in one family over a brief span of time is rarely coincidence. Also, the location being a saloon does not cast the deceased in a favorable light. Authorities have closed the cases.

That said, this week I observed one of the deceased's living relatives and found that person most curious, hard to read, and as it turns out, unconventional. It appears I will need to travel for a week or so in order to satisfy the boss's needs, plus for other U.P. business. If my next letter is less punctual, you will know why.

The weather has been fine here, though I have spent little time enjoying it. As always, your peace and health are on my mind.

Faithfully yours,
John

Four

Raylene studied the man on the porch with the long-barreled gun. His aim looked a little off, but she stood within range of his buckshot. At first, she wasn't certain the thin, scruffy figure was Billy Horse, but she could make out that his left hand was missing half its thumb and forefinger. It was Billy, alright, which meant his wife might be inside fixing their noon meal.

"Uncle," she called to him. A greeting of respect.

"Who is it?" he shouted back.

"Raylene Little Moon, daughter of Thomas Yellow Moon and Helma Longman. We buried her twenty years ago.

"Annie's sister?" He clearly remembered Annie. All the men did.

"Yes, but Annie is gone."

"Not Annie." He lowered his gun.

"Ten days ago, in Kansas City."

"Was she attacked? Or too much shine?"

"What makes you say 'shine?'"

"Back in spring, Thomas came on his way north to pow-wow, hustling booze that someone had cooked up and he could sell cheap. I bought a few bottles."

Raylene thought a moment. Annie had been practiced at holding her drink. After all, she tended bar and sometimes drank while working, though not in front of customers. A disgruntled customer could have reported her for that. She had one time told Raylene that alcohol made her blood sing and helped her forget things that needed forgetting. But with legitimate distilleries back in business there was no reason for Annie to drink moonshine.

"She liked to drink," Raylene told Billy, who had not moved a muscle, "but why drink could kill her so young, I cannot guess." She had already reluctantly acknowledged this to herself.

"I am sorry to hear your news," he said, "but I am not sorry you have come. What is it you need? I will share what I have." He called off the dogs, who retreated to the edge of the house to glare at her with yellow eyes.

Raylene advanced until she stood before the porch steps. She spoke without looking into Billy's face. Another gesture of respect. "If you are still trading, I am in need of supplies, but my main task is looking for my uncle Raymond."

"What has he done now?"

Raylene would not lie to someone who had been good to her family, sheltering them and feeding them when they traveled home with the ashes of a mother and wife struck down by tuberculosis. Even as a five-year-old, she had recognized the goodness in Billy and his wife Mary. She said, "He has wronged our family." Without perfect proof, she knew this as truth.

Billy ran one shaky hand through his silvered, shoulder-length hair. "A serious claim. Are you certain?"

"As much as I can be until I question him myself."

Billy set the butt of his gun down with a clunk. "Raymond was here a few days back. Or maybe a week. I am losing track of days. I thought it was Thomas at first, they sound the same."

They sound the same? Raylene kept her voice calm. "Thomas is gone too. Dead from a fight."

Billy seemed to deflate. "And now you seek Raymond..." He turned to a nearby chair and lowered himself gingerly, his gun crosswise on his lap.

Raylene tried to think what it was about Billy's recent words that should mean something to her. "My father loved attending pow-wow. Raymond too."

"As did I before them, when I was young enough to travel. I danced too. It is good to wear your finery and move to the thundering drums. They had their differences, those two. Raymond — when he came, he brought cans of food, a surprise much appreciated."

"Did he name his destination?"

"I did not ask."

To pry into another's affairs would be unseemly, and Billy was nothing if not respectful of those he considered family. She would pry anyway. "Were they labeled, those bottles Thomas sold you months ago?"

"Mm ..." Billy wagged his head a little. "If I recall, they had the name of his saloon. Supposed to be bourbon, but ..." He shrugged.

"You drank them?"

"Over time."

Raylene's thoughts swung back to her bachelor uncle stopping in Nebraska to assist Billy after leaving Thomas for dead. She could feel Ray's gravitational force, pulsing like electricity along invisible threads, beckoning her. She ventured a glance at Billy. His eyes held no spark and rather than looking at her, he gazed outward toward the distance. Like the portions of his farm that she had seen, he looked weary. She said, "The corn fields do not look well this year. I am thinking that when the corn suffers, people suffer."

"You speak truth. There has been little rain this summer and the grasshoppers eat what little comes up in the fields. Many farmers have left for other places. And I am...grown old. I feel death approaching."

Raylene knew how this could be. She herself felt all manner of forces in the world. Some helpful, some deadly. She asked, "What keeps you and Mary on this land?"

Now the old man bent his head. "I do not own this place, but Mary is buried here. Eight years now."

His news was yet one more sorrow. Raylene recalled a plump, quiet woman who cooked meals for all travelers. She had once wrapped Raylene and Annie in blankets for napping in a corner when their family came through.

"She had taken the Christian ways," continued Billy, "but I could not bear to let them bury her in town. This way I have kept her near me. Only now..." He swallowed hard before finding his voice again. "Perhaps you can tell, I can no longer tend this place."

The heels of Billy's boots were worn thin, his hands bent and knobby. He held himself as if beset by other ailments that worked their way outward from the inside. Platitudes, even from someone benign, could not redress a failure of crops or a loss of mate or home. Instead, she said, "Uncle, let me fix you something to eat."

"A kind offer. There may be a tin left from those brought by Raymond, and I would be pleased to share it with you."

Raylene took two steps up the ruptured wooden stairs. When Billy failed to watch her progress, she lifted a hand up and out to one side. That he did not seem to notice was a sign of trouble too big to overcome. A farmer with failing eyesight would struggle to succeed, especially a farmer without children to work the land alongside him.

"Do you still keep chickens?" she asked as she reached his side.

He turned his face toward her. "The rooster got loose but the hens stick close. I think."

"I'll ready the stove," said Raylene, "then I'll fetch eggs if there are any, and we'll eat."

Inside, chairs and counters held pieces of clothing and empty food cans with flies and gnats tracing circles in the air above them. The kitchen sink and short run of counter were stacked with what might have been every dish and cup in the place, all of them dirty. After scrubbing a small pan with sand and rinsing it with water from the hand pump outside, she brought a single egg from the henhouse and slipped it into a little simmering water. When the egg was ready, she opened a tin of pears and called Billy into the house, watching him navigate the front room by touching random furnishings. She gave him a spoon she'd wiped clean with her bandana, set the food before him, and pulled a second chair up to the table.

"You found eggs?" he said, digging in. "They've been rare."

"I can imagine."

"How do you like yours?"

"I'm going to pass."

"Did you find more tins? Maybe one for later."

"I think that's the last of them."

"A shame. The peas were as sweet as these pears. I could go for more peas." His spoon rattled in the can.

Raylene glanced across the tiny kitchen space carved out of the main room. This place was a step up from the shantytown where she'd spent the night. It would be cozy with a fire on the grate during winter.

When Billy had taken his last bite, Raylene filled his fruit tin with clean water and drank from it before filling it again and setting it before him. "I'm wondering if you have any goods for sale," she said while he drank. "Supplies for a bit of travel."

"Where will you look for Raymond, at fall pow-wow?"

Raylene pondered pow-wow. Its purpose was people, their rituals, and their connections to each other. Pow-wow was where her parents had met, and her father's parents. Symbolic, but not where she imagined finding Raymond. "I left my bedroll at the ranch, so I need another, nothing fancy."

"What I have is yours."

"I mean to pay though I may have to send the balance later." Raylene hadn't stopped to check the savings she shared with her sister, hidden where no one else would think to look. In fact, she ought not to bargain without knowing what funds were at her immediate disposal.

Billy smiled wryly. "You will look like an eligible woman at pow-wow, and some of your people might have news of Raymond."

Raylene doubted that her mother's people would welcome Ray. He had not returned for the burial of her ashes. Word was he'd been in the west, working on a fishing boat or else chasing one of his wild notions for making money. But word of mouth was only that, and difficult to corroborate.

Billy scrubbed the back of his hand across his gray stubble. Close up like this, he resembled a man from another century. "It is time for me to live near my own people and you are headed that way. Perhaps we can assist each other." He paused a moment. "It will not surprise you that Raymond is known in some parts as a dangerous man. If he realizes you're following him..." He motioned toward the home's front door, where his long gun rested. "You might need some help."

Billy was right. Raylene had embarked on what might prove a deadly path, but she hoped she would not need a gun. When Billy headed for the outhouse, Raylene examined the cornhusk doll she had kept from her sister's purse. *Their* doll, really. It had been fabricated by Uncle Ray from the green husks of bushel corn, its small shape neither male nor female. They called it *Khéya*, the word for turtle, a creature representing long life. The doll had indeed lasted long, through years of childhood play and all the years since, the sisters repairing and reinforcing it with strips of cotton until it was more rags than anything. Over the years, as the physical distance between the sisters widened, they had passed *Khéya* between them whenever they met, secreting a bit of folding money at its center as a hedge against future, harder times.

Now, the hardest of times had arrived. As long as Annie hadn't used too much of their emergency fund, Raylene could put a bit of it to use while on the trail of their father's killer. The money was important. Money made things happen. It could ease the way out of a terrible fix. But the doll represented more than a place to stash money, to Raylene it symbolized the ties that bound two sisters through the emptiness following their mother's death, and later through the slow disintegration of their family. The doll was all that remained of Annie.

Raylene chewed her lip as she considered the cotton strips, deciding that the newest of them appeared to be of a yellow calico which she untied, worming a forefinger beneath others until she loosened the crackly husks forming the turtle's torso. There, folded tightly, she found flattened paper money.

As she extracted bills and unfolded them, her eyes grew wide. Instead of the three twenties and two tens she had counted last time, there were now three one hundred-dollar bills — many times the amount they had squirreled away during the last handful of years. A magnificent amount that made her question how her sister had acquired the money — how and from where? The money was grand enough to make it seem somehow a sign — could it be a sign? Without planning to, her sister had bankrolled Raylene's journey to find Raymond and exact justice for their father. She had to wonder — Was justice due Annie as well?

In the tractor shed, Raylene stood with Billy before his vehicle, a 1920s truck jig-sawed together with parts of a 30s sedan someone had left wrecked out on the highway. "So, this is it," she said.

"Don't mind the paint or the floorboards."

"What paint?"

Billy chuckled and Raylene smiled to herself. She wasn't about to quibble. If this conglomeration of metal parts, wire, wood, and rubber carried them any distance, she would be glad. When the contraption gave out, she would find another way to follow Raymond's trail. She said, "If you are selling, I would like to buy it, or perhaps rent it."

"I will not sell, not yet. But I am willing to ride shotgun if you will drive. Watch the clutch, though, it's a bugger."

Raylene was reluctant to deny this family friend a chance to leave his falling-down dried-up farm. She didn't relish the thought of traveling with a mostly blind man who had lived alone too long, but he had not even hesitated to offer her what little he had. She was an adult version of a child he hadn't seen in a decade, but he had trusted her enough to welcome her into his home. "Where are your people?" she asked.

Billy rubbed his salt-and-pepper whiskers. "Some are west of Sioux City, on the land."

Raylene nodded to herself. If the easiest way to acquire a vehicle was to drive it with the owner propped in the seat alongside her, she would give it a try. She had no false impressions regarding the nature of Billy's infirmities, but if he remained on his farm, he would likely fail along with it. Leaving him behind would be like leaving him to die. She said, "North seems the right direction. Is there fuel?"

"I didn't run it dry, and there's a couple of fuel cans in the corner by a broken board."

"Then let's get this contraption running."

Raylene fueled the truck and cranked it three times before it groaned to life. She promptly shut it down to save fuel. Back at the house, Billy gathered some useful items and others that Raylene couldn't imagine a use for. Entering the kitchen carrying a cardboard grip, he asked, "Do we have room for kitchen chairs? The others went into the stove, but the two that are left still hold a man."

Billy's pragmatism cut through all sentiment. He had been a trader from back before he took up farming. He would probably die a trader, but she surmised that he might this day be cash-broke, having ridden out the drought years trying to dry farm in a place where the weather refused to cooperate. She didn't know the value of a vehicle that might break down at any moment, but she felt the need to attempt compensation. "For whatever price you deem fair, I will pay for the use of your truck. That way, whatever happens, you'll know I have treated you fairly."

Billy paused, arms at his side. "I have no money but I will not take yours. Today's meal spoke of your character, and you have given me reason to think I might end up in a good place to die."

Grief showed in the set of his mouth and the bend of his back, and now he was leaving his wife's grave behind. Raylene had not even looked for Annie's grave before setting out to find Raymond, a decision that cut her deeply, one she would set right after punishing her uncle. She lifted her head at the sound of distant thunder. "Is there something we can do for Mary before we go? We need to be gone from here."

"Could be dry lightning, or rain," he said as he turned for the bedroom, which he had sorted through while Raylene selected kitchen items. In a moment he was back with a Bible in a worn leather cover. "This belongs with her. I said goodbye at the time and have spoken to her ever since. Her grave is out by the farthest apple tree."

Raylene took the book and went out the back door and across the dirt yard to find a wooden cross surrounded by fallen, shriveled apples. The marker was decorated with carved rosettes and geometric patterns, plus the name Mary Horse and the date of February 20, 1928. Raylene leaned the Bible against the cross as she visualized Mary at rest beneath the cracked earth, dressed in her finery and wrapped in a good wool blanket woven of strong colors and the symbols of her people. In passing to the other side, Mary had left behind a husband who had marked her final rest with honor.

On her way back to the house, Raylene detoured to the chicken coop, latching its wire door open so the one remaining hen would not be trapped inside. The coop would also stand vulnerable to hawks and feral cats, even Billy's yard dogs, but Raylene could not spend time worrying about nature taking its course.

Twenty minutes later under a bruised-looking sky, Raylene shepherded Billy's beast of a truck back toward Omaha's shantytown, one empty fuel can and one full can stashed in the truck bed, which held all the gear they could possibly use, plus extras, the whole of it covered with a tarp.

Between them on the seat lay Billy's sweat-stained hat. Beneath the seat lay his shotgun. His comment about the floorboards had been a warning in disguise. The holes through which the floor pedals jutted were cut too large. Raylene had filled them with old rags so the heel of her boot would not get caught. The dashboard gauges seemed to work fine, except the one for fuel. She wondered how she would know when they were about to run out. "Uncle," she said. "Where will your farm dogs go?"

"Those scroungers. They come over from a neighbor's place a half mile or so west, but they get around, catch some mice, sometimes a snake. When we don't return, they will search out people."

When Billy lapsed into silence, Raylene mentally replayed her discovery of the cash and even more mysterious, a note tucked alongside the money which read: *myup baby.* Though she didn't know the term she harbored no doubt that the note was made by Annie's hand. She would know her sister's scribble anywhere, across a thousand miles, a dozen years, and even in her sleep. It was the same sloppy penmanship that had angered the teachers at the government Indian school where they were made to study as children. The teachers had never broken her of it.

How, she wondered, had Annie saved so much? Who might Annie have known who would have paid, shared, or mislaid money in a manner Annie could benefit from? And what did Annie mean by "myup" and "baby?" *Myup* was unlike any word she recalled their grandmother using. She would have to ask other bloods about it. In English, "baby" could be slang for sweetheart or simply mean a child. Neither reference seemed suited for the sister she knew, but there were a hundred things about Annie's city life that Raylene did not know, that she might never know.

She had tucked one of the folded bills into her leather pouch. The rest of the cash was tied up in *Khéya,* wrapped inside her bundle. Because of its mystery, the money seemed somehow tainted. She couldn't quite envision it being legitimate, yet thought it unlikely she would discover its origins without returning to Annie's boarding house, or to the saloon and its patrons; or to the city where all manner of pursuits and favors were traded for cash. By keeping it a secret, her sister had left the money for Raylene's use. Tainted or not, the fortune would aid her pursuit of family justice.

Ray was surely guilty of Thomas's death, but Raylene

doubted he had harmed Annie because killing women held no honor, not for warriors of old or those who grieved the lost era of warriors. He might, though, have been in Kansas City at roughly the same time Annie died. If so, he must know something about her death. Damn him for fleeing. Not that he had fled white justice, which rarely extended to the unnatural deaths of Indians, but he should have stayed to face *her*. By leaving, he had obliged her to follow until the miles spun outward to touch the stars and the spirits heard her lamentations against him.

Uncle Ray, she thought, just as the sky released a sprinkle of rain upon the windshield, *I have lost much but I will see to it that you lose even more.*

Five

Raylene and Billy arrived at Omaha's shantytown as the evening sky thickened with another wave of rain that would prove too late to save Billy's crops. "Before we travel, I have some business here," she said, stopping the truck in a patch of damp brown grass.

"I'll stretch my legs with you," said Billy, opening the door as Raylene cut the engine. He pulled a carved wooden cane from the floorboard and set his stained western hat on his head. Advancing slowly, Raylene circumvented the deepest puddles, listening for the *thock* of Billy's cane behind her. At Harold's shack she found the tin door closed up tight.

"Harold?" she called out once, twice. Finally, she reached for Billy's cane and rapped it hard on the doorframe. In response, a rash of swearing issued from within. She could make out "Hold your horses!" and other, choicer phrases.

When a disheveled Harold opened the door a crack, he said, "Oh, it's you. 'Bout time. You bring my money? It rained like hell for some while." He scanned the sky over Raylene's head. "No stars showin'. Guess we'll get wet some more."

Raylene pulled the dollar coin from the pouch around her neck. "How is the pup?" she asked, holding the coin just out of Harold's reach.

"He's keeping my cot warm, otherwise he's a pain in the ass, gettin' under my feet, chewin' on the front of my shirt." Harold withdrew from the doorway, returning in a moment with the pup held close like a football.

"Here," he said, thrusting the coyote toward Raylene. "Good riddance. He's fine. If you don't believe me, look him over."

Raylene set the pup on the ground.

Taking the silver coin, Harold said, "By God, I'm rich again. Say —" he squinted at Billy Horse who had stopped a respectful distance back — "That your grandpop?"

"No."

"An uncle maybe? You're the first Indian I seen in some time, and now here's the second. Don't many come around."

"I believe you."

The pup shook itself before limping over to sniff Billy's boots. In no time it lifted one leg and pissed a thin stream on the closest boot without Billy noticing.

"I have a matter to ask your advice about," continued Raylene. "We're going on the road and I need to buy canned foods and such."

"There's been a place at the edge of town, thataway. Jimmy D's." He pointed south from where they stood — "Plus east a couple blocks. Now I've got some money I'll get me a roll of sliced meats and some stinky cheese." His smile was the very definition of bliss. "And a drink."

"Will they be open at this hour?" asked Raylene.

"It's probly too late to walk over. Takes a steady half hour, and that's for folks with good knees. If you go in the morning, maybe you could bring me back some vittles."

Raylene glanced at Billy, who had discovered the pup and was busy scratching its neck. She supposed that it couldn't hurt for Harold to know about the truck since it would disappear with her and Billy soon enough. She said, "I could drive over to see if it's open."

"Drive over? Criminy! First you got a dollar, and now an automobile? What'd you do, rob a bank?"

"It's Billy's truck. He's just letting me drive it." Which was very near the truth.

Harold scratched the crown of his head. "Well, if you're going, I'll come too."

Raylene quickly calculated the benefit of having a white man accompany her to a store where she didn't know the proprietor. Even an unkempt, smelly Harold might lend a certain legitimacy to her shopping. She felt her cap to see that it covered most of her hair. Turning to Billy, she asked if he would stick close while she went for food. "I'll bring us some supper."

"I can give you what I've got." Billy rattled the few coins in his pocket. "Do you suppose they sell beer? Seems a long while since I tasted beer."

"I have enough to cover our purchases," said Raylene. She moved away and returned with a kitchen chair from the back of Billy's truck. After setting it out for Billy and the pup, she led Harold to the truck.

"What the hell is this crate supposed to be?" Harold asked as he climbed aboard. "Don't look like any rig I ever saw."

"It drives, so I don't complain," said Raylene, climbing in. "Point the way, will you?"

From the outside, Jimmy D's resembled a country feed store more than a city market, but inside, Raylene was able to gather a ten-pack of canned foods, a loaf of day-old bread, a sack of apples, a slab of bacon, a small hunk of cheese, a pound of ground coffee, and three aluminum canteens.

At the counter, Harold paid for some sliced meats and cheese and the last two bottles of beer from the cold case. One, he said, was for Billy. He asked the man at the register, "You got any ice cream?"

"Hard Times Sundaes on the weekend. Maybe," came the

answer.

Harold looked at Raylene. "Shaved ice."

When Raylene heaved her purchases onto the counter, the man in charge looked at her accumulation of items and narrowed his dark eyes. "You must have seven dollars' worth of goods here. You got that kind of money?"

"I do," said Raylene, meeting his gaze.

"Lemme see it before I ring everything." The man glanced at Harold then back at Raylene.

She had only a dollar and change left in her pocket, so she pulled the pouch from inside her shirt and extracted one of Annie's hundred-dollar bills.

The man behind the counter looked astonished. "You're shittin me, right? That's not no real hundred-dollar bill." His *hundred* came out *hunnert*.

Raylene bristled as she smoothed it out. "It's real. Why wouldn't it be?"

"Cause nobody round these parts carries that kinda bill around. Where'd you get it?"

Raylene glanced at Harold, who stood there blinking. "Look at it," she said, offering it to the man. "It's real."

Reluctantly, the man took the bill from her and peered at it in the glow of the bare bulb shining down from overhead.

"Have you seen one before?" said Raylene.

The man flexed his neck. "I sure have. In town, not in this store for the kind of goods I sell."

Raylene felt a surge of heat. "I'm here to do business with you, bringing proper money to purchase your goods. A real business accepts real money."

Standing to one side, pockets bulging with bottles and paper-wrapped food in hand, Harold watched with a look of dismay. "Hey now," he interjected, "there's no need to rile each other." He turned toward the market man. "I rode with this kid from Kansas City and got no reason to disbelieve that paper money. Why should you?"

The circles beneath the man's eyes pulsed with purple. He seemed to be calculating the profit he stood to make from Raylene's purchase versus the odds of getting hoodwinked by a stranger.

Harold said, "Here, give it to me." When the market man handed the bill to him, he promptly offered it back. "There. I'm buying. Will that do?"

The man scowled at Harold. "You bum. That's no different."

"Hey, I'm no bum. I worked today and earned that dollar I just spent with you. And it *is* different. You seen me before. I been up this way twice this year and once in '35. When I got cash money I buy from you."

The market man worked his mouth. "Goddamn you people, always wanting somethin'. How do I know it's real? It might not be."

"Well, what're we gonna do?" asked Harold. "We can't stand here all night. You want to sell this stuff or not? We're paying customers and I'm bout to starve to death standing here like this."

"The hell with both of you," said the man. "I'll sell, but I'm taking extra for you insisting on this goddamn big bill. I don't even know it's real. I might get to the bank and they'll tell me it's phony. People pass phonies all the time. I don't wanna be holding the bag on a bad bill and me out all this merchandise. You want this stuff, it's five dollars extra for my trouble."

"Five dollars!" said Raylene. "That's thievery." She looked ready to snatch the bill back.

"You wanna argue, let's make it ten. Take it or leave it. You can get outta my store right now and make me a happy man. I'm going home to supper."

"Damn it, kid," said Harold to Raylene. "You want that stuff or not? I can hear the rain starting up."

Sure enough, a crack of thunder rattled the roof over their heads.

Raylene sucked in a breath. She was certain the big bills Annie had left behind were genuine even if she didn't know how her sister had come by them. And it stood to reason that if the market man had been in business longer than a month, he'd seen a few swindlers. Still, it rankled her to be charged extra for being a stranger. Or a brown-skinned stranger. But ... she and Billy couldn't very well eat their bedrolls. They had a long journey ahead of them and needed these supplies. She could tell without looking through the window of the market door that dark had fallen outside, and here came the sound of rain tapping on the corrugated roof. She told the market man with a shake of her head, "You are sticking me, and I don't like it."

Still scowling, the man rang up Raylene's purchases, extracting an extra ten as he handed back her change.

Raylene said, "I could use a carton," as she counted the change before pocketing it.

Without a word, the market man reached behind him and plucked a paperboard carton from the floor, dropping it on the counter with a bang. Raylene silently packed her purchases into it.

Harold led the way to the door and opened it for her.

"Thief," snarled Raylene as she led Harold out into the night. "Ought to be ashamed."

As dusk fell across the countryside, John Murphy brought his coupe to a halt near the town square in the center of tiny Onaga, Kansas. The sky had been spitting rain for the last hour, dampening the grain-stunted fields abutting the roadway and infusing the air with mineral odors.

He had driven the whole way with his side window open, the damp breeze a liberating force. Not that he disliked city life or his work there. The rail yard embodied an industriousness that spoke to him of man's mastery over steel, over great distances, and over the environment in general. The machinery of commerce hummed a tune containing rhythms he understood and appreciated but the country air had its own taste. It tasted clean.

Onaga was a small farming town where Union Pacific rail cars offloaded implements and supplies necessary for farming — tractors, hay rakes, seed, lumber — and took on the grain grown on what were once vast grasslands, plowed under following a great migration from eastern cities. Thousands of homesteaders had gambled their futures on rising prices for grain. Few had extracted a winning hand. Considering the miles of thirsty crops he had passed today, Murphy would not wager in favor of the farmers. It might be years before the countryside recovered.

The good news was that the railroads always boomed, with manufactured goods dispatched from eastern hubs to western markets followed by timber, grain and beef cattle returning east again. The country's need for rail transport kept Murphy's job secure. There were always passenger or freight disputes to settle, or a theft of some kind.

His task this week did not involve a crime, not to his mind. Annie Moon had not lifted family jewelry from his boss's bank box. That *would* have been a crime. No, his boss had used the jewels as a means of seduction. Or a gesture of true affection. In Murphy's view, the crime was that his boss had temporarily lost his sanity and in doing so jeopardized his marriage and family.

"Well," he said to the view beyond his windshield, "this is

it for tonight." With that he steered toward Onaga's tiny rail station and found its nearby travelers' hotel, with dinner service on the main floor and rooms upstairs for rent. Inside, a long bar spanning one wall held up half a dozen men in low conversation. Three or four of them glanced his way when he came through the door carrying a whiff of the outdoors to mix with the cooking smells from the kitchen. Beef and potatoes and something sugary. The thought of home-baked pie made his mouth water.

Murphy stepped to one end of the bar and caught the bartender's eye. "Can you rent me a room for tonight?" he asked.

"Got one left," came the reply. "Just tonight?"

"Yes, and dinner too, if I'm not too late."

The man said, "I'll have Dora fill a plate for you."

Murphy went out and closed his vehicle's open window, and carried his suitcase back to receive a key to room #3. Upstairs, he washed up and donned his suit jacket once more. Downstairs, he found a white-haired woman depositing a heaping plate upon the table furthest from the men at the bar.

"Coffee?" she asked as he approached.

"Is that for me? Coffee would be great." He sat right down and tucked into the steak and fried potatoes, dabbing butter and salt on both. If there were people in the world who'd never eaten Kansas beef, those were the folks to feel sorry for. He could imagine no better meal to cap a long day on the road than a slab of beef with a good rind of browned fat on it.

After dinner, when he'd changed into pajamas and hung his suit carefully over the back of his room's one chair, Murphy crawled into the brass-framed double bed and lay with his hands behind his head, his mind turned to the little sister. She was either far ahead on a train speeding through the night, or just a day or two ahead, thumbing rides from strangers and sleeping under a field of stars. The northern sky tonight looked stormy as all get-out. The little sister might be getting wet.

Murphy rose early the next morning, eager to advance toward South Dakota and the Pine Ridge Reservation town where Raylene received her mail. Where he would have no authority. Where he couldn't legally confiscate property from its residents, not even stolen property. But if he believed a resident possessed property belonging to an upstanding, respected citizen of Kansas City, Missouri, he might hope to enlist the aid of a Bureau of Indian Affairs agent. Their authority was well established as negotiators, arbitrators, and lawmen of a sort. A deputized lawman could retrieve stolen goods, or, as he reminded himself, retrieve private property in the hands of the wrong person.

Though that goal beckoned, he had an obligation to Union Pacific business, which he would not skirt — specifically the case of the dead man found alongside the UP tracks. Finished with his breakfast of eggs and ham, he asked the hotel proprietor for directions to the Sheriff's office.

"That'd be Sheriff Long, in the courthouse," said the same man who had tended bar the previous night. "Two-story brick, on the town square. Can't miss it."

"Much obliged," said Murphy, pulling out his wallet to settle up.

"You got trouble to report?" The man noted their transaction in a leather-bound ledger and wrote out a receipt for Murphy.

"No," said Murphy, taking the receipt and hoisting his suitcase. He pushed his glasses up on his nose. "I'm hoping any trouble is long past."

Outside, gravel crunching under his feet, Murphy inhaled

the fragrance of rain-washed streets and clean air. Contrary to a big city rife with people hurrying here or there on business, this place gave off an air of measured activity. Not a soul scurrying to catch an electric trolley or beat the traffic. Not a street light or crosswalk or signal light. He could almost feel the pulse of minutes sliding slow as molasses toward the next item to be crossed off the day's list. Here there would always be time for a how-do or a cup of coffee at the downtown diner, which might be Onaga's only other choice for the hungry.

The courthouse flew a flag from a pole to the right of its entrance. An automobile with the county seal sat out front. Inside, lettering on a door identified the Sheriff's office. Before entering, Murphy smoothed his coat cuffs. Clean enough for country business. Inside, he identified himself and asked the woman behind the desk for five minutes with the man in charge. After stepping through a side door, she returned and motioned him in.

"Buddy Long," boomed the Sheriff, extending a hand for Murphy to shake. He was dressed in a western shirt with his badge pinned to a pocket flap, a silver buckle above pressed trousers, and a pair of well-worn western boots. Thick, furry forearms jutted out from turned-back shirtsleeves.

"John Murphy of the Union Pacific. I appreciate your making time for me." He offered his railroad badge, which the other man took in with a glance.

"What can I do you for?" said the Sheriff.

"I'm traveling on a different matter, but I thought I'd ask whether you came to any conclusions about that body found along our tracks recently."

Sheriff Long rubbed a hand across his chin. "The one north of here. It was a white male, in rough shape as you might imagine, out in the sun like that before anyone got to it. I sent a deputy up to Marysville to ask around. There was no wallet.

Haven't heard any reports about anyone missing, have you?"

"Not a one," said Murphy. "Could be someone passing through. A fall like that could kill a person. You find any other clues?"

"Well, the body, from what we could tell, was grimy before it got chewed by scavengers. His pants were practically off. Could have been a fight launched him out of a train car maybe."

Murphy nodded. "What makes you think a fight?"

"We found a knife alongside, and a stab wound in one leg. 'Course the scavengers, they don't make stab wounds like that."

That mention of a knife jolted Murphy. Thomas Yellow Moon had succumbed to a knife wound. Thanks to the chatty undertaking assistant, Murphy knew about it before the little sister did. Then she had used a knife on the corpse, and here was yet another stabbed body.

"*You* get a report about a fight?" asked the Sheriff.

"Not so far. If you have that knife, I'd sure like to see it."

"It's here." The sheriff glanced out his open office window as if considering the features of the Farm Administration building across an expanse of grass next door. "Far as I'm concerned the case is closed. We buried the poor bugger. Your office finds anything, we can open that case again."

"If you found nothing, I'm pretty sure we'll not do better. Still, I'd appreciate a look."

"I don't guess that'd hurt. Haven't sent it downstairs with the file yet. I'm in the habit of waiting a couple of weeks before doing that. Sometimes saves an extra trip to the storage room."

Murphy's curiosity would ordinarily prompt a request to examine a body's wounds, clearly out of the question in this case. The lawman's conclusions were likely accurate, but just when you thought you knew something, a whole other thing had a way of surprising you. "You say the man's pants were down. How about underclothes?"

"None such. Makes me think hobo. You have an idea about that knife?" asked Long.

"Not particularly. Just trying to fix the details in my mind."

The Sheriff turned toward a metal filing cabinet behind him and opened its squeaky top drawer. From a yellow paper packet, he pulled a knife with a narrow steel blade and wooden handle fixed with copper rivets, which he handed to Murphy.

Murphy turned the weapon over in his hands. The hilt showed some wear, as if it had been handled plenty. The blade held scratches, newish ones to his eye. He scraped the blade sideways across his right thumb. Sharp. A man's knife, he thought, though not like a folding knife a fellow might carry for trimming fingernails or scraping tar from his shoes. This one commanded respect.

"Here's a picture of the body," said the Sheriff.

Murphy studied the glossy black and white image. The man's body had not fared well coming off the train at speed. It lay at an awkward angle, half of it bent one way, half the other. Bits of gravel were embedded in its facial skin. Part of the nose had been chewed away. Or pecked.

His thoughts circled back to the little sister and how she'd pulled a knife from her boot to use on her father's lifeless finger. A knife like the one he held now might fit within a boot, but so might a thousand others. Unfortunately, his view of the little sister's knife had only been the glint of its blade and nothing of the handle. He said, "I don't see any maker's mark. Did you find one?"

"I did not. Could be homemade, or maybe altered in some way. Usually it's on the blade."

Murphy agreed, then on a hunch said, "If you have a spare

photo of the deceased's face, I'd like to borrow it. Might pass it around at stops north of here. At Omaha maybe, since he was riding a freight headed that way." He decided to press his luck a little further; no harm in asking. "If you're done with this case, as you've said, can you see your way clear to letting me take this knife for a week or so? It might be related to my other concern."

Buddy Long narrowed his eyes. "The snapshot's no problem, I've got a couple of those. But you're asking for evidence from a case on my books." He hooked his hands in his leather belt and considered the knife in Murphy's hand. "Don't believe I've ever agreed to that before, not with someone from outside of law enforcement."

Murphy stood silent.

"No sir," continued Long, "that's not standard. Not that we don't need to get creative sometimes, but we always follow protocol." He licked his bottom lip. "'Course you *are* a detective." He shifted his weight. "I would expect you to sign for it."

Murphy nodded.

"And return it in the same condition."

Again, a nod from Murphy.

"Technically, it originated with a passenger on your rail line, legitimate passenger or not."

Murphy held the big man's gaze.

"Well ... I suppose I can accommodate ... Since we here have done all we can." He pointed a forefinger at Murphy. "I expect you to tell me if you find anything we ought to know."

"Sure will."

The Sheriff nodded. "I'll have Miss Marie fetch a release form and that'll be that. Where'd you say you're headed?"

"North," said Murphy. Now he had another reason to satisfy his curiosity about Raylene Little Moon.

As Murphy drove north from the town of Onaga, Raylene and Billy headed back along the same asphalt road that had led Raylene to Billy's farm. She wore a barn coat that had belonged to Billy's wife. He had offered it the previous night while they were parked as close as possible to Harold's shack, sitting in the cold truck eating cold food and passing morsels to the coyote. After the squall had passed, Harold fetched Billy's other kitchen chair from the truck and the two sat beneath a clearing sky to jaw a little and drink beer. Later, when Billy returned to the truck, Raylene roused and took a walk to the closest outhouse. By the time she returned, Billy was snoring softly, a blanket pulled up to his chin and the pup in his lap. At daybreak, they ate a quick meal of stale bread, canned fruit, and boiled coffee, then hit the road.

Now, the rising sun cast weak rays, and holes in the truck's floorboard provided intermittent jags of warmish air thrown off by the engine. Raylene watched the road beyond the truck's rounded hood while Billy, in a fit of talkativeness, told tales of his years before leaving the Rosebud Reservation to marry an Omaha woman who insisted they live closer to her people. That was how he became a farmer on land where, as he put it, "The wind could blow like the dickens, sending half your soil into the next county." If not ordinary wind, sometimes a twister, which seemed a test "concocted by spirits from the otherworld." "Sometimes," he said, such a test "found him worthy, other times wanting." Worse yet to his mind were seed salesmen who wouldn't sell on credit when a person — he meant himself — had always paid his seed bill, even if that meant his own suppers were made of dried corn with water and salt to make a meager soup. The worst sort of scourge were certain hustlers who couldn't be trusted to haul a farmer's grain to market without skimming some off the top, their calculations ending short of what Billy knew he had harvested.

Raylene nodded at Billy's stories, sipping now and then from one of the water canteens and stopping the truck when nature called to either of them. During those stops, Billy walked out from the road, keeping his back to her so that Raylene could step down into the roadside ditch, shielded by sunflowers and the truck's cab.

In one of the quieter moments, Raylene asked Billy if he knew the word "myup," the word Annie had scrawled on that scrap of paper. She pronounced it meeoop.

"Myup?" He frowned slightly. "It is not familiar to me, but I have been alone a long time, mumbling to myself in an empty house. Perhaps my people used more water words and this is a forest word or a prairie word with special meaning to your people's people. Where did you hear this, from your grandmother?"

"Someone else." His mention of her grandmother made Raylene smile at the road ahead. "She was wise, my grandmother." Also strong, and gentle when needed, especially toward a granddaughter who rebelled against tradition by running with the boys.

"*Wakan*, perhaps, in her later years?"

"Not holy," said Raylene, "but she had a way with medicines."

Billy nodded. In the time of his own youth, he would have been treated by a tribal healer. Then, "Is myup a word your sister used? Can you say more about her now?"

A lump rose in Raylene's throat, a sorrow longing for release. She blinked back the dampness in her eyes. This was no time for grieving. She had a nearly blind man to deliver north and an uncle to find somewhere up there. "I know little to share," she said, "until I learn more."

"From your uncle."

"Did he mention Annie when you saw him?"

"No. I should have asked about the wellbeing of your family but his delivery of canned foods drove my manners from my head."

So, Raymond had not disclosed her sister's death. What did that imply? Raylene held fast to what the letter from the undertaker had said — that Annie's death had been due to natural causes, which oddly enough gave her a little comfort. Naturally, authorities could be wrong, but she hoped not. She had better not discover that Raymond had harmed Annie. If he was to blame in any way — such a bitter thought — she shuddered at what she might do to him.

Billy asked for a break to make water. Climbing down from the truck in a gravel turnout, Raylene found the breeze from the north turning frigid beneath clouds like purple fists. She was glad to gain the shelter of the truck and resume their travels.

After they had resumed travel, Billy turned the subject to her father's people, pulling Raylene's attention from the undulating land beyond the windshield. "Before I met your father and uncle, I only knew about them by reputation. We all traveled freely between reservations to trade goods and stories. They were beautiful young men, and fierce, everyone said so. Like two halves of one person, committed to warriors' ways when their people had lost the need for making war, except in our minds we were all still fighting to regain the land our people had traveled and hunted."

Raylene's thoughts rode up and out into the clouds on the back of Billy's words. He spoke of a time before she was born, yet it was as if she inhabited his memories.

"Your grandfather was ill by then," said Billy. "A cancer of some kind. But he had taught Thomas and Raymond the ways of riding and fighting. No one could shoot straighter or skin a deer faster. They had fire in their bellies for owning the fastest pony and bringing home the largest deer. When they'd fought all the other young men over card games or insults or the attention of some young woman, they turned on each other.

"They took to stealing ponies from the tribe as if from rivals from another tribe. It was only a competition. The council threatened punishment, but the brothers always returned the ponies, so the elders looked the other way. How well they knew the pressures on young men living under those conditions."

As Billy spoke, Raylene's thoughts floated out to look down upon the land of her father's father. Miles upon miles of grasslands and buttes. Snowy mountains fed by winter storms and lowlands carved by "muddy water," the Missouri River. Traders and trappers and hunters. Homesteads marked by creeks and gullies. Meadows of wildflowers buzzing with insects and bunchgrass that was home to coveys of quail. Colonies of flickertails, herds of mule deer, solitary elk, and brown bears nose-deep in berry thickets.

In her mind, as if driving through the Crow lands, she felt the Montana sunlight warming her cheeks and the winds rustling miles of grasslands once grazed by herds of bison. In the wide open, two young men raced each other through life, competing for a glimmer of recognition among people stripped of their traditions.

Billy continued in the voice of someone dreaming while awake, describing how the brothers learned to forge steel for objects and tools. Thomas was stronger and steadier, while Raymond was faster with his hands, a good reader of adversaries. Also prone to anger and wild behavior. Only those who doubted the stories of their exploits dared to challenge a Yellow Moon. "At riding, wrestling, and the throwing of knives, they were rarely beaten." Billy's chuckle resembled a sigh. "I believe money changed hands over such contests." He paused, his hand upon the pup, and his voice softened in a way that sharpened Raylene's attention. "And then there was the matter of a Lakota girl who was coming of age. A beauty, they said, who meant to make her own choice from the eligible men. One more competition for the brothers."

Changing the subject, Raylene asked, "Did my uncle ever kill anyone?"

"You mean back then? I heard rumors, but it must be understood how stories start and how reputations grow, even in poor dirt." He went silent for a moment. "Talk is easy. Killing is hard. I hope you will not have to find that out."

Raylene looked over at him, thinking how she had never killed a creature for the thrill of it, and never out of spite. Childhood playmates had practiced their marksmanship on animals they would not eat such as toads and lizards. But she had always insisted on fence posts and tin cans, or legitimate targets for consumption such as grouse and mule deer.

The odor of wild pup and the uneven glare of the pitted windshield pushed the olden days from her mind as the road seemed to shift behind swirling air. Not everything about the olden days receded, though. Billy's suggestion of competition between her uncle and father remained. Now planted in her mind was the haunting notion that Uncle Ray and Thomas had vied for her mother's hand.

Six

His morning meeting with Sheriff Long concluded, Murphy drove with the late morning sun glancing off the dashboard and steering wheel, illuminating the powdery road film settled there. A sense of satisfaction ran through him. Though the lawman had asserted his territorial rights, he had also complied with Murphy's request so that Murphy came away with an item that whetted his musings — the flat-handled knife found with the dead body. The more he ruminated about its design, the larger its potential as a weapon to hide in the sleeve of a coat or inside a boot. In the last year he had observed only one person to carry a knife the latter way — Annie Moon's little sister, Raylene.

With the morning's success, Murphy's optimism expanded as did his longing to drive straight away to the little sister's hometown where he might observe her movements at length before confronting her about the jewelry and the dead hobo. Murphy checked that impulse. Why change an approach that had already yielded a look at a knife found beside the tracks? That weapon seemed somehow significant but he couldn't be certain why. Instinct, perhaps. His standard modus operandi was to stay the course, so he would do just that, stopping in towns linked by Union Pacific tracks until he reached a logical place to break toward the southwest corner of South Dakota. The good news was that in even the smallest towns between here and there, he could catch a break for his aching back by stopping for a cup of coffee, or if the town had no restaurant, walking around a bit.

For the rest of the day, he traversed pitted roads, stopping in Marysville and Beatrice to ask the grain operators and station hands if they'd noticed any loiterers around the trains, especially Indians. Just one had caught a glimpse of a dark-skinned boy, so that was no help. As for the snapshot of the dead traveler — it produced no looks of recognition, only frowns, and after glancing at it, one station hand crossed himself.

As the sun drifted westward, shadows grew longer and the sky thickened at the horizon as Route 15 left the gentle swells of Kansas behind. A small road sign read: Entering Nebraska. Other than that, the scenery beyond his windshield rolled on with plowed fields in shades of brown and trees shading toward yellow along streambanks and farmhouses.

At Route 33 he turned east toward Lincoln, crossing over the so-called Big Blue River. He hadn't thought to mix pleasure with this week's work but now he was sorry to have left his fishing gear at home. Dusk was a time that fish rose from the river bottom to feed and a man could hook some action if he knew how to read the water. As a child he had fished the Kansas River below its junction with the wide Missouri, tossing a bobber-rigged line from a weedy spot on the bank, occasionally hauling in pan-worthy striped bass or rainbows, but more often black crappies or sunfish. All of them good eating. Or maybe fish always tasted good when you were a kid with a secondhand rod and for all your casting and reeling and scrambling along the dirt bank, dungarees reeking of weeds and willows and shoes sloppy with mud, you arrived home triumphant, a contribution in hand for the dinner table.

The town of Lincoln came next, capital of Nebraska. At the Lincoln freight yard, four sets of tracks directed U.P. and Central Pacific trains toward heartland destinations. Murphy pulled his automobile to a stop at the yard's headquarters building. After washing up in the men's lavatory he went to the manager's office and explained his mission. The manager escorted him into the yard proper, where Murphy proceeded to query each of the workers, asking if they'd noted any Indian women hitching rides in boxcars, then producing the snapshot of the dead train traveler. None had noticed itinerant women and only one worker thought the dead man looked familiar.

Wiping his hands on a soiled rag, the worker squinted at the snapshot. "Might've seen him," he said. "Some of them go back and forth, following work I s'pose."

Murphy pushed his glasses up on his nose. "Remember anything about this one?"

"Rough looking, but that's nothing if you spend time around rolling stock. You can ask my wife, always grousing 'bout the grease. If I remember right, we rousted someone looked like him from a fight between a bunch of them swinging pretty hard. That one with a stick."

"When was that?"

"July, I guess. Told him not to show his face again. Told them all that. But you know, they come around again once the heat blows over."

"What was the fight about?"

"Hard to say. Can't ever get a straight story and sometimes it's nothin' anyone else would think was worth scrappin' over. This time, uh ..." An embarrassed look came over the man.

"Yes?" prompted Murphy.

"Well, like I said, you can't never be sure. One of 'em was shouting 'Keep your hands where they belong,' only rougher language than that."

"Was it related to stealing?"

Now the man shrugged and looked at his shoes. "Can't say

for sure."

"Have you seen him recently, the man you're talking about?"

"Just that one time, I never saw him working."

Murphy adopted a more nonchalant tone. "Did you ever see him with a knife? Wait. What do you mean by you 'never saw him working'?"

The yard man looked around, as if not to be overheard. "I got this job after someone got fired from cleaning stock cars. Name of Dwayne, that's what I heard. The others was talking about him after that fight. Said it was him lost the job. If you're talkin' knives, lots of people got one. If I was jumping rails, I'd carry me one. Say, we done here?" The man looked over his shoulder at his fellow yard men who stood at a discreet distance.

"What was this Dwayne fellow fired for?" asked Murphy.

Now the worker looked supremely uncomfortable. "Aw well, I don't know it for myself."

Murphy leaned in and lowered his voice. "Okay, tell me the skinny around the yard."

"It was for ... uh, fiddling around with one of the hard luck types that come through."

Fiddling around. Murphy didn't need to hear more about an incident already resolved, so he asked, "What makes you think the one in the fight is the same one as in this photo?"

"His face, partly, but the shirt too. Got the same little squares on it."

Murphy shook hands with the man. "You've been a help."

As the yard man walked away, Murphy thought about what he had gleaned thus far — that the pattern of a shirt could potentially identity this particular dead man. The worker had seemed credible, unwavering in his willingness to assist, except when it came to the reason for the ruckus. He'd resisted repeating the rumor about Dwayne, if that was the hobo's name. Rumors were only rumors, but they could contain kernels of truth. Murphy's portrait of the dead hobo was taking shape: a man willing to fight; perhaps some kind of deviant. This was all well and good, but Murphy's other case was yielding no information. He still lacked a clearer portrait of the little sister.

Without someone recognizing his description of Raylene Little Moon, he lacked a clue to her occupation. She wore boots with the brown dress he'd seen her in, which suggested a country woman, and Oglala was on the Pine Ridge Reservation of South Dakota, big country, but he knew little about occupations there. Farmers, maybe, or ranchers of edible animals. Beef or sheep. On the plus side, he was working his way toward Oglala and could savor each small advance he did make. Heck, the combination of his two cases — a dead hobo plus missing jewelry — was almost as good as a mystery novel.

He had long read for pleasure, countering his extended workdays with a sojourn into an adventure story or a mystery solved through the hero's sheer doggedness. He could lose himself so completely in some stories that when they ended, he found himself blinking against the bright light of regular life and not a little unsettled at how readily he had relinquished awareness of the present moment and place. Back when Catherine's condition was first deteriorating, more and more of his attention went toward interpreting her pacing and the fluctuation of her moods and less toward books. Then had come "the incident," as he now thought of it.

Arriving home one night after a demanding day at work, he found a heap of books on the floor of his modest library engulfed in flames that licked upward toward the ceiling. Catherine knelt nearby, presiding over all with a smile. His books, she said, had become his mistress, which was true after a fashion, given the refuge they offered not only from work but also from Catherine's confusing behavior. She had blamed him and so he had blamed himself. After the fire was out and order restored, he made certain that she did not see him again with a book in hand. With her departure to the sanatorium, their home, his home, was quieter than even he needed in the evenings so he had begun to make time again for reading. Each time he opened a book, however, the image of flames and the odor of burning paper, linen, and glue still came to him, flavoring each story that poured forth from the pages.

The case of the missing jewelry (his current case) contained a plot that seemed to have sprouted tangents involving possible knifings and an unexplained death. The rail rider's death might have stemmed from a fight between two ruffians competing for food or territory — a death like that might come down to nothing but circumstances, one man stronger or faster than the other. No witnesses, no extraordinary causes; bury the dead and consider the matter closed. Instead, Dwayne's death cast a darker shadow, only in Murphy's mind perhaps, and only due to statements made by the rail yard worker. It seemed to Murphy that there must be more to that death than a boxcar scuffle between troubled down-and-outers. Just a hunch, but he knew to give hunches some due until they failed to pan out.

As he started his car and set out from the train yard in search of a traveler's hotel and a hot meal, he thought that like the best novels, this case of the missing jewelry might deliver a conclusion he'd be sorry to reach. For one thing, he was beginning to appreciate that having lived most of his life in a large city, he hadn't much seen these tiny off-rail lands as close as they could be seen through an auto's windows. Second, this assignment shined a light on a race of people he rarely dealt with, and then only at a remove. Thoughts of the little sister floated like whispers around him as he drove, hovering above him when he got out to stretch his legs, as he partook of each meal. She was everywhere and nowhere.

What he knew about Indians came largely from school book references about Indian wars, Custer's Last Stand, Manifest Destiny, and the like. Accounts that painted red-skinned people as mostly uncivilized, rarely trustworthy. What he knew of Thomas Yellow Moon and Annie Moon ran counter to such generalizations. Though the booze business could be a rough trade, it was widely supported throughout the civilized world. He'd never traveled abroad, but the French and Italians were known for making wine and drinking wine. In the United States, whites, Chinamen, and Negroes, all were partakers and all praised the worth of alcoholic spirits. So, if Thomas Yellow Moon ran a neighborhood saloon rather than a fancy drinks lounge, his was still a legitimate business, and Annie, if she helped run such a business, must have had something going for her.

Then there was Raylene Little Moon. Her use of a knife notwithstanding, she seemed a different sort than the saloon keepers of her family. Proceeding cautiously, he would learn about her a little at a time, a prospect he found appealing.

After his miles on the road, and interviews, the rail yards and scenery, the locating (he hoped) of the little sister and the return (if possible) of the missing jewelry, what then? The Little Moon story would be over and he would return to his U.P. office and his badly-behaved boss. Union Pacific investigators operated from the main rail hubs — Chicago, Kansas City, Denver — responsible to station or freight managers and traveling as needed to destinations along the railroad's circuit. Certain benefits came with seniority — a choice of which cases to work, usually the most complicated, perhaps those affecting influential, moneyed customers. His spot was not at the top of the heap, nor at the bottom.

He knew this work did not suit the average man. The job required a certain fortitude for detail work and could demand somewhat odd hours. An investigator needed to be familiar with the impulses of the traveling public, which could include, on occasion, their propensity to steal or damage property or assault others.

Murphy had come to investigative work by way of an accounting degree and time spent working for his father's accounting business. Concentration and an ease at unraveling minute errors in columns upon columns of figures suited his organized mind. He liked the patterns of numbers, their logic and precision. It was the deskwork, which had him hunched over paperwork for hours at a time that proved his undoing in that profession. His back's unnatural curvature, which doctors had labeled moderate scoliosis, rebelled at all that sitting and the poor posture it engendered. He had been willing to fulfill his father's expectations, but had found he could not bend his will to the physical pain that deskwork produced in him. He needed to spend more time upright, moving about at will. Against his father's wishes, he had sought an alternative that would challenge his natural affinity for reconciling details while allowing physical activity throughout the day.

Once he explained his aptitude for balance sheets and the sequencing of transactions, the railroad took him on and taught him the detective trade at the right hand of a senior detective, since retired, who had spent twenty-five years in service to the U.P., a decade less than Murphy had been alive. Murphy did not doubt that he himself had far to go to equal the older man's skill at solving complicated cases, but he had proved a natural at ferreting information from others. Thus far, the most obvious downside to having lived without youthful exposure to thievery, gambling, or illicit activities, was that he had learned about the meaner, coarser aspects of other lives one assignment at a time, one interview at a time.

He checked his pocket watch as he drove through town. He had made slower progress than he'd hoped. Were he to attempt reaching Omaha this evening, he'd spend hours crossing pitch-dark countryside, arriving, perhaps, after the city's restaurants closed for the night. His back argued for not pushing quite that hard. The little sister might already have arrived home with no inkling that he was on her trail. If so, she might let down her guard, the better for him to catch her unawares.

He steered his vehicle toward a string of Lincoln's downtown buildings. Dinner and a soft bed were calling to him. Lately, he'd been reading a chapter of a Dashiell Hammett novel each night before bed, but to satisfy a line of inquiry that had overtaken him while driving, he instead decided to check the town's library before it closed. The knife in his possession begged a bit of study.

Raylene steered Billy's truck north on Route 75 toward the reservation lands of the Omaha people, bounded by the Missouri River to its east. Beyond the windshield, dirty clouds spat mist that froze in the air, turning the view of the road a swirling, ghostly white and the fields to pale swells on a soft sea.

She drove with the headlights on and the wiper scraping back and forth. They had passed through the town of Tekamah, whose one fuel station sported a handmade CLOSED sign. In the gravel side lot, she had poured their spare fuel into the truck's tank. Her best guess was that they would need to find gasoline at Decatur.

Billy slept the sleep of a man exhausted by life and its many losses. The pup lay across the seat between them, its snout tucked against Billy's leg.

For Raylene, there was no shaking the images Billy had spun for her of two headstrong young men vying for the attention of an eligible maiden. A girl, really, for Raylene knew that her mother had married in her sixteenth year and given birth to Annie at seventeen. Raylene had followed three years later, and after her own birth came one more, an infant born dead and by custom sent with the Lakota midwife to be buried. Their mother, already ill, became a spirit when Raylene was six. Their mother's mother, Helma She Walks, assumed the duty of raising two girls so their father could seek work as a farrier and toolmaker. He took all work that paid, even that which broke his hands.

The swirling mist diffused what little daylight breached the clouds. The truck's center wiper slid back and forth in mesmerizing arcs, the frozen fence posts along the road assuming familiar shapes, the fence wires looking like whitish lines. Raylene's mind registered all as she felt the truck's great weight astride tires reaching through the slush to grip the blacktop. To her right there appeared a hump that looked out of place. Her uncle and father still dueled in her mind, so it took her a few moments to glance in her side mirror and brake. "Billy, did you see that?" she said, slowing the truck.

Billy roused with a snort, blinking against the milky, misty light. "Is there trouble?"

Raylene shifted down a gear, looking for a side road in which to turn around. "Something's not right. I think I saw ... on your side. I don't know exactly what."

Billy rubbed his eyes. "Can we stop for a minute, so me and the pup ...?"

"You'll have to wait until — here's one." Spying a pullout,

Raylene wrestled the truck into the turn and got it stopped and backed it out into the other lane, accelerating slowly again in the opposite direction. "It'll be out my window now..." She scanned the mist for the shape that had struck her wrong. Near the downslope it was, or down in the ditch, not a mailbox but — "There. What is that?"

"You're asking me?"

Raylene pulled to a stop half off the blacktop and put the truck into neutral with the hand brake on. Climbing out, she crossed the blacktop to approach the small shape below the level of the road. The pale hump was a person kneeling, or fallen, a threadbare coat covering its head. She braced herself, half sliding in the wet dirt to the bottom of the incline where she touched the figure, which moaned with a child's voice. "Hey now," she said to the child, "are you hurt?"

The moaning figure unfolded into a fair-haired girl whose face was streaked with mud and snot.

"What are you doing out in this weather?" asked Raylene.

The girl, perhaps seven or eight, looked up, wide-eyed, and wiped the back of one hand across her face. "My ma needs a doctor."

"You need to come out of this ditch. Can you walk?"

"My foot —"

Raylene glanced up. The way she'd come down was the best way out. She took the girl firmly by the shoulders and straightened her, then with her back to the girl she half squatted. "Put your arms across my shoulders, up top at my neck, like this. Hold tight and I'll do the walking."

The girl began to cry softly, her face contorting with fear.

"If you want to get out of the mud, you'll have to try. That's our truck up on the road. It's warm." As an afterthought, she added, "And there's a puppy."

The girl put her hands around Raylene's shoulders. With a

grip on the girl's hands, Raylene stood and settled the extra weight upon her back, digging her boots into the slick bank, one foot, then the other, the mud sucking at her boots like something alive. Slowly, up the incline, then onto the gravel shoulder and across the asphalt. At the truck, she squatted again and gently pried the girl's hands loose to let her down. The girl cried out as her feet touched the road. Giving her an arm to lean on, Raylene opened the driver's side door. "Billy, here comes a girl."

Raylene lifted the girl, who huffed and cried out as she scrambled up onto the seat. "Billy, will you hand me your knife for my boots?"

With Billy's jack knife, Raylene scraped the mud from her boots and scuffed them against the wet asphalt until their soles and heels were shed of the largest clumps. She pulled a bedroll from beneath the tarp in back and handed it in ahead of her. Billy opened the bedroll and tucked it around the girl as the pup began licking her face. This brought a small smile.

"He likes you," said Billy. "He doesn't like everyone." Which was not strictly true.

"You have a friend now," said Raylene, "but we need to take you home."

At this, the girl began crying again. Again, the faucet of snot. Raylene chose the cleanest rag from the floorboard and gave it to the girl to wipe her nose. The girl explained that her mother needed a doctor and she had walked out hoping to find him though she didn't know the way. Her plan was to ask at houses.

Raylene glanced up the road and down. *Houses?* The farms along this stretch were a half-mile apart and mostly set back some. There would be no way on foot to ask at each one in this weather. No wonder the girl had collapsed. She asked, "Isn't there someone else at home who can help?"

The girl shook her head. "There's just us. And the baby that's coming." She began to hiccup. "And ... and ..." Her next words held anguish. "It could kill her."

Raylene looked over at Billy. His frown mirrored what she was thinking: Giving birth could kill people. It happened all the time.

With the truck moving again and daylight waning, Raylene and Billy coaxed a bit of the girl's story from her. She went by the name Babe and her mother, Marabelle McCoy, was ill with fever. Directed by Babe, Raylene located a nondescript dirt driveway belonging to a small house set beyond an unplanted field and a windbreak of trees. There, they found the mother in her bed, visibly pregnant. The house was not overly warm, but perspiration beaded on the woman's brow.

"You a doctor?" the woman asked.

"No. My name is Raylene. We found your daughter by the road. She's hurt her foot."

"Oh." The woman tried to sit up but sank back into her pillows.

"How long have you felt ill?"

"I was fine until a few days back."

"Are you due soon?'

"Supposed to be next month." The woman lapsed into silence.

Babe chimed in. "Father will be back. He's gone to sell brushes."

Raylene took the woman's pulse. It seemed slow. She instructed the girl on how to cool her mother's forehead with a damp cloth. To the woman she said, "You must drink water."

"The doctor," murmured the woman.

"There's no phone to call him," said the girl. "That's why I I ..." She looked at Raylene with resignation.

Raylene was already spending valuable time assisting Billy

when she meant to be tracking Ray. Granted, it was Billy's truck that was moving them both along. She had meant to simply deliver Babe home, but seeing her now, perhaps eight or so, she recalled Annie and herself at eight and five, and how girls of that age knew certain things but could never know enough to change the path of what was happening to their parents.

There was no telling what was wrong with Babe's mother. Her troubles might be nature's way of rejecting her unborn child, or due to an external force beyond her control, such as influenza or infection. Internal forces, external forces, causes ordinary or dire, natural but with unsatisfactory results. Raylene knew that she could not leave the girl and her mother without trying to help them.

She asked Billy to make a fire and fetch some food from the truck. With the last of the bacon browning on the stove and a kettle set to boil, she went out and brought her bundle from the truck. From her waterproof packet she pulled a clutch of dried herbs that she broke into a mug she then filled with boiling water. The strained tea she carried to Mrs. McCoy as Babe stood nearby.

"What is it?" asked the woman.

"It's made from horse mint to ease your fever."

The woman licked her lips then began to sip the beverage. Raylene watched her for a moment before speaking again. "I have prepared some food. Babe should eat even if you do not." She went into the kitchen, where Billy sat with the pup at his feet, and took the bacon off the heat before she said to Billy, "I suppose Babe's mother ought to see a doctor."

Babe had followed her. "I know where there's two and a half dollars to pay him."

"If a doctor comes, offer him the money. Do you know an address for the doctor?" asked Raylene.

The girl tore a strip of paper from what looked to be school work. By the waning light coming through the kitchen window, she copied the doctor's information from a paper tacked to a cupboard door. "He's supposed to be the closest one. I wasn't going to make it there, was I?"

Raylene shook her head as she took the note. Back in Mrs. McCoy's room she suggested they somehow mark the turn in to the property's driveway with something bright. After a moment, Mrs. McCoy said, "Fetch my pink nightgown, Babe."

Babe's eyes grew wide. "Oh, Ma. Not that."

Babe's mother nodded ever so slightly. "And something to tie it with." Looking spent, she closed her eyes.

Babe crossed to the room's tallest dresser and from the bottom drawer pulled a pink silk nightgown. Holding it out to Raylene, she said, "It's from their honeymoon in Chicago. She was saving it for me."

Raylene imagined the potential of such a future for the scrawny girl before her. If wind didn't shred the thin, fine garment, it might see another honeymoon. Some day. Babe found them some twine then led the way to a bureau across from the stove. Pulling out a short-handled wire brush, she said, "Here's one of them my daddy sells. Wire ones and straw ones." She thrust it at Raylene. "For you."

Outside, the freezing mist had abated, leaving porch rails, driveway, and everything in sight sparkling like starlight. After checking the ropes holding their gear, the travelers climbed into the truck. Raylene drove them down the driveway. She stopped next to the mailbox and put the truck in neutral.

"Uncle," said Raylene. "I only meant to bring the girl in from the weather, not to prolong our travels."

Billy turned his shrouded eyes to her. "My travels will be over when they are over. And you are young, so you will find sufficient time for the justice you seek."

Raylene alighted to secure the nightgown to the mailbox so it would flap in the night air. Glancing back at the farmhouse, she made out Babe's small shape at the front edge of the porch, one hand raised. She raised a hand in reply then reentered the beast, as she thought of it now, and selected low gear. The clock was ticking on finding the doctor who in coming to a mother's rescue would also rescue a daughter.

After a restaurant dinner of chicken-fried steak and a heap of baked beans, Murphy went to his hotel room, where he kicked off his shoes and sat back upon his bed with a lamp pulled close enough for paging through the slender book he had borrowed at the Lincoln County Library. In his luggage was a copy of "The Maltese Falcon," starring a tough private investigator by the name of Sam Spade. Murphy was far enough along to know that the Spade character was a hit with the women, always touching them somehow, perhaps on the arm or shoulder. Spade was clever, too, at facing off the police dicks who were after him for answers.

Murphy would enjoy reading more of what Spade was up to, but the book now in his hand was "Crafting Knives," by Charles Reine, which he hoped would prove a better use of his evening's free time.

Murphy felt instinctively that the wood-handled knife confiscated by Sheriff Long held secrets to be unlocked. He studied it more closely. The knife had no maker's mark, which would have called it out as a branded item of the sort sold in tackle and sporting goods shops throughout the U.S. The fish cleaning knife he had carried since his teen years was made by Buck. In his thirty-four years of life, he had never given a thought to the making of knives. He knew how to keep one sharp, a skill most sportsmen learned at some point. What he didn't know was how a person (instead of a manufacturer) might produce a handsome knife like this one.

Terms catching his eye as he read for an hour included "brush knives," "Indian crooked knives," and the phrase "such knives are better instruments for killing animals than for use as cutting tools." When he came to the section on making a knife from a saw blade or a file, he thought *Now we're getting somewhere.*

The craft book pointed to no correlation between the case of the hobo found with what looked to be a knife wound in his leg and the little sister, who carried a boot knife and knew how to use it. If only there was a way to know whether or not the little sister had encountered the now-dead man.

Mentally, Murphy tallied the information about the hobo's case: No witnesses had come forward and there had been no inquiries about a missing passenger. If the rail rider had jumped a train and somehow encountered the little sister, it would have been because she had jumped on too. Not one soul had reported an altercation between riders, but such disagreements rarely came to light. And too, based on what he could ascertain from the Lincoln yard crew, the dead man was an unsavory sort and a troublemaker who may have been deviant toward other men.

Even though criminality could not be proved in the hobo's death, Murphy wanted the satisfaction of tying up the loose information he possessed. Not to assign blame necessarily, but to identify cause and effect. Actions and reactions. Logical consequences.

As for the jewelry, for all he knew it might be sitting in some downtown Lincoln hock shop awaiting sale. Or, if not a Nebraska shop, perhaps in a South Dakota shop. Carried by someone on the move, the items might have made it that far. He recognized that finding them in a hock shop would please his boss but remove any reason for his own continued pursuit of the little sister, and that would be ... if not exactly a shame, at least a disappointment. He looked forward to studying her more closely during a contrived but casual conversation, or a more formal interview. He'd be sorry to relinquish what he imagined as a pleasurable bit of cat-and-mouse as he teased information from her. He envisioned her once more as he had seen her in the undertaker's parlor: smooth tan skin and eyes an almost-oriental shape. That feline walk.

Should he find the missing items in a small-town pawn shop, he could still make a pitch for needing to know whether the little sister had been the one to hock them and by what means of travel — by passenger train, freightliner, or automobile. Should he not find the jewels, his boss might still authorize a pursuit of the little sister for information only, but such an effort would necessitate an expenditure of funds without official gain for the railroad. Murphy was not one to take liberties with his employment or employer, but he felt his belt loosening a notch in that regard. He would enjoy the boost that solving those questions would give him. Retrieving the jewels was personal to his boss, but solving the puzzle of where they'd gone and how was becoming more personal to him.

The knife provided by the Sheriff lay on the bedside table. Murphy reached for it and held it aloft, adjusting his eyeglasses in order to inspect it again in light of his newfound knife-crafting knowledge. The shape of the blade, the copper rivets. This knife had been made by a talented individual, not a manufacturer.

He recognized that he had no cause to connect the little sister with the hobo's death or this slender knife. Many investigators might write off as coincidence the timing of her arrival to and departure from the Kansas City undertaker, followed soon thereafter by the discovery of a dead body. But he knew that true coincidences were rare. Everyday life was full of purposeful actions based on conscious decisions. For this reason, he simply couldn't relinquish the notion that the slender steel weapon found beside the hobo was connected somehow to Raylene Little Moon. Experience told him there could indeed be a link between them.

He tapped the flat side of the knife's blade against his right palm then turned it parallel to his fingers. The blade was narrower than his middle finger but just as long, potentially lethal under the right circumstances. For all he knew, that might also describe the little sister. She did not resemble the ladylike women he knew or had once known, three of whom qualified as intimate partners. There was his wife, bless her, and two others before her, all of them dainty, and now he realized they had all been interchangeable, as if cast from the same mold of feminine restraint.

He had long gravitated toward soft-spoken women, indoor types next to whom he felt strong and relatively worldly. But now, the thought of the little sister's potential lethality roused his blood, a pleasant sensation. He ran his free hand down his thigh as he considered this physical response, perfectly natural given that he had been without female companionship for more than two years.

Finally, he set the knife aside and turned out the light. Tomorrow he would make Omaha, where he had much to accomplish.

Seven

The town of Decatur crouched on the west bank of the Missouri River, just below the southeast corner of the Omaha reservation. There, Raylene stopped to fuel the beast before steering onto Route 51 toward the town of Bancroft, a stretch where they should find the country doctor's clinic address.

As the beast split the gathering night, its headlights now two narrow beams on the glistening blacktop, Raylene detected irritation in Billy's posture. "Uncle," she said, "I sense something is bothering you."

Billy sat a moment with just the low growl of the engine filling the space around them before he said, "You are correct."

"If I am the cause, please tell me."

"It is nothing to do with you. I regret that a man's name alone can anger me. I wish it were otherwise. I am too old for anger."

Through the bug-strewn windshield, Raylene watched the black road and the dark fields beyond. While driving this stretch, they had discussed no man, had hardly spoken since leaving Babe and her mother. She wondered now if Billy's thoughts had fled elsewhere and returned to play tricks of shadows and light.

Finally, he spoke again. "The doctor we seek. I know him from another time."

Raylene waited to see if Billy would say more.

Eventually he did. "In 1918, there were Kansas soldiers who fell to the big death. Afterwards, it spread widely, mostly among the forts, and then the bigger town and cities. Many died with little relief." He glanced out his side window. "Our memories were long regarding the deaths of our people at the hands of white soldiers, and we thought these new deaths were simply the spirit world providing justice. But then the illness spread to many states and reservations, punishment, perhaps, for our self-satisfaction."

He went silent again as Raylene watched for an indication of a medical clinic. "And this Dr. Goudy?" she asked.

"Hunh." He resettled his hand on the pup which was licking its unbandaged paws. "He called himself a doctor but he would not treat the native people, even when he took their coins and chickens in payment. He brought no medicine, only stood outside, giving instructions for others to tend the sick and dying, which I did, holding my brother and then his son as they died. Afterwards, the Omaha people sent that white doctor and his white medicine away from the reservation." Billy's voice grew in pitch with his next words. "That man is not to be trusted."

Having no response to Billy's anger, Raylene just shook her head. Before long, she spotted a hand-lettered sign by the road that read:

Dr. E.J. Goudy

Physician

She managed to slow in time to crank the beast into the short gravel driveway fronting a boxy white wooden building. The building's front porch was lit only by the light of dusk, now descended. Parked beside the building was a mud-splattered truck sporting a Nebraska plate. With the beast's engine shut down, Raylene said, "The place looks closed."

There was no reply from Billy, only the engine ticking as it cooled.

Given Billy's earlier comments, Raylene wasn't certain that this doctor was a good choice for a pregnant woman ill with fever, but there seemed no other option. She climbed down and crunched across snowy gravel to the whitewashed porch. Finding the front door locked, she rapped loudly on it. When no one answered, she tried again. There was just the sound of her knuckles meeting wood. The odor of livestock was on the breeze, a scent that brought to mind the ranch job she'd left behind.

She moved to the bare window and peered in at a darkened room and the shapes within it — a reception desk and chairs lining the walls like bachelors at a barn dance. Back at the truck, Raylene told Billy that she would walk a circuit around the building and perhaps find someone belonging to the unoccupied vehicle.

Skirting the east side of the building, she glanced at the muddy Ford. Illuminated by the half-moon above were two lambs lashed together in the truck bed. Catching sight of her, they began a pitiful bleating. Raylene moved past them toward a small house set back on an angle where a black and white dog came out from under the porch to growl at her.

Halting, she glanced between the dog and the house's front door. When no one emerged, she took a few steps forward, which set the dog to barking. *That should bring someone out.* When no one appeared, she advanced again, speaking in a low voice. "Brother dog, you must know the legend of the giant dog who guarded the land when it was new. So fierce was he that none of the people would challenge him. I might heed your warning but for my need to summon whoever is in the house."

The dog gave no sign of giving ground, so Raylene stood before him, speaking of legend and other matters unrelated to the subject at hand until a gray-bearded man appeared in the house's doorway, buckling his belt. "What's the fuss?" he shouted above the dog's bark.

"I have come for the doctor," called Raylene. "A patient needs him."

"You must have seen the clinic is dark."

"I seek Dr. Goudy. Do you know of him?"

"You have found him, but I am otherwise engaged." The man had not quite tucked his shirttail in. He called to the dog, which retreated to the space under the porch from where it kept watch.

Raylene said, "I have come to ask your assistance for a woman with child who has had a fever for some days."

Now the doctor hooked his thumbs into his pockets. "I don't take my practice to the natives. They come to me."

"The woman is white, a Mrs. McCoy."

He stepped to the front edge of the porch. "If she was my patient I'd know the name." He looked at the sky. "If you want to bring her tomorrow, the clinic opens at 8:00."

"If you are concerned about your fee, I will pay you to visit her."

The man lifted his hands skyward as an Indian woman, perhaps forty, appeared in the doorway behind him. His voice rose in volume. "I speak English just fine and have told you what time the clinic opens. I have not yet had my supper so I will not be driving out tonight."

Before Raylene could digest his malice and almost before he had finished speaking, the night air was shattered by a shotgun blast that made them both flinch.

Raylene pivoted to spot Billy with his shotgun. "Billy, there's no need for this," she called, her voice urgent.

"I only shot the sky," said Billy. "Is that him speaking from the porch?"

"That's him, but —" Raylene's words were interrupted by a shout from the doctor.

"What the hell you mean shooting near my medical office or this house — somethin' wrong with you?"

"This man doesn't understand a polite request," said Billy to Raylene.

"You there, with the long gun," continued the doctor. "You'd better back away or I'll call the law."

"Billy," said Raylene. "This won't get us anywhere."

"I might persuade him with this old thing."

"Your arrest will not change this doctor's mind but it might keep you from reaching your family." Billy unshouldered his weapon as Raylene continued, "Let me try something different."

Murphy woke in a sweat in his darkened hotel room. He peered myopically beyond the end of the bed. Was the danger he'd felt still present? In the ghostly light seeping past the window curtains, nothing was clear, especially not the dream that had caused him such palpitations.

He had been lying in this very bed, or one like it, when he sensed a dark figure watching him with malicious intent. The figure's motive had been unclear but the darkness itself seemed to portend danger. Or injury, or something stolen. He had encountered little danger in his detective work. Rough talk from a suspect under scrutiny, a fist brandished in his direction. People were roused when caught in a theft, but the number of times he had known bodily fear were as rare as the number of suspicious deaths he had investigated. He could count them on one hand.

He had known losses, who hadn't? Such a tally would include his role as successor to the family accounting business and his father's good will. One could say he had lost his wife, a cruel blow to which he was slowly growing accustomed. They had barely embarked on their life together, he going off to learn detective work, and she staying behind to...well, those years were behind them now.

What did the menacing figure want? He thought he had seen a gleam at its side. A blade, perhaps, and that's when he'd tried to speak, but his tongue would not cooperate, or his mind would not, so he'd thrashed about enough to wake himself. Putting on his eyeglasses, he blinked the room's dark shapes into familiarity — a curtained window admitting a pinch of light, a chest of drawers, a chair, a wardrobe.

Dear God, he thought. He rarely recalled his dreams, with good reason it seemed, since this one had shaken him. The library book must have fevered his mind. That was it. Multiple chapters describing how to hone a knife to a sharpness perfect for woodsmen and hunters, those who would slice things or skin them. He was neither woodsman nor hunter, only pursuer of a case that now colored his dreams.

He shook himself and consulted the glowing dial of his pocket watch, also on the bedside table. It was early yet, only midnight. Setting his eyeglasses aside once more, he resolved not to dream again. Not if dreams were going to resemble that one.

In the morning, Murphy consulted the hotel's copy of the Lincoln business directory to identify the hock shops in town. After a breakfast of hotcakes and fried eggs in the hotel dining room, he donned his overcoat against the morning chill and set out to locate all five shops, presenting to their owners his photograph of Annie Moon wearing the necklace and earrings. Hitting dead ends in each of those places, he returned his library book, filled his tank with Sinclair, checked his Nebraska map, and headed for the little town of Valparaiso, sunshine casting yellow rays through broken clouds overhead.

Though he would cut away from the U.P. tracks at Omaha,

Murphy stayed his course along the freight route that led to Valparaiso, which had a trackside grain operation. One of the elevator workers there might have seen the little sister. Passing out of Lincoln, he ran his auto up to a cruising speed safe enough for the two-lane blacktop.

For some distance, the road traversed Salt Creek, whose grassy banks were poplar-shaded in places, giving it the look of good water for brook trout, those smallish speckled beauties so perfect for the pan.

An hour later, when Murphy reached his target, his back was ready for a break. In no time he located the grain elevator and parked nearby, climbing out to bend slowly forward before straightening. Two men stood in the parking area conversing over Thermos cups balanced on the hood of a pickup truck. Murphy walked over and introduced himself, asking if they had recently sighted a young Indian woman riding the rails. One worker had once seen a white woman with children, the whole bunch of them climbing down from a boxcar to limp toward town, but neither worker had seen an Indian, so Murphy bid them a good day and went back to his vehicle. After wiping dust from it, he leaned against its driver-side door to soak up the dappled sunshine and gentle breeze while he waited for the next freighter.

Roughly forty minutes later, a train signaled its approach with two blasts of its horn. Recalling the last rail crossing of the route he'd driven this morning, Murphy estimated the engine to be a mile or so out, rolling at a moderate speed, soon to slow and stop alongside the elevator.

He had never performed hands-on rail work, the physical duty of engineers, mechanics, linemen or track inspectors. His work had been relatively cerebral, but he knew the routines performed by the grain elevator operators.

A rumbling 2-8-2 U.P. steam engine seething with power

came into view, dragging a string of cars for animals and grain. This one was fairly short — just a dozen cars total. The great yellow and black engine idled forward at a man's walking speed then with a squeal of brakes came to a halt. The workers from the gravel lot had climbed a ladder to the cantilevered chute at the top of the tall stack. One would take outside duty, the other would take the deadly duty inside. Men were sometimes sucked down into the grain after the wheeled bucket started its rotations. He knew this from the regional newspapers delivered regularly to the U.P. freight office. Each year brought at least one story chronicling a death by grain silo.

Murphy left his auto and crossed the gravel lot to wade through the weedy grasses at the foot of the elevator. He looked at the cars down the line. The door of one boxcar stood partially open. That, if anywhere, would be where rail riders would hunker. He watched for a few minutes, ordinary outdoor sounds of birdsong and barking dogs disappearing beneath the rumble of the idling train and a hundred bushels per minute shooting into the grain car below. A waterfall of sound that wasn't water.

No face appeared in the doorway of the open car, so Murphy walked that direction, crunching along the graveled rail bed and stepping over each tie as he progressed. Standing below the open door, he shouted, "Hello! Anybody there?" Nothing.

He tried another tack. "Anyone need lunch?" This too went unanswered. He supposed he could climb the rungs beside the sliding door, but before he could move to do so, the train bucked in place to the sound of the engine ramping up and then the string of cars began to jerk forward.

Murphy began to jog alongside it the boxcar, timing each stride to avoid the ties set into gravel until the train gathered momentum and he relented, the open boxcar leaving him behind.

He stood a moment watching as the last car rolled past. Just before he turned back toward the parking area, a dark head jutted from the boxcar's doorway, distant enough that there was no telling whether the head belonged to a man or a woman. "Damn it," he muttered, shaking a fist. "Just my luck."

The morning after Billy shot "only the sky," he and Raylene spent the night in Sandy, Nebraska, in a motor hotel so cheap that Raylene splurged and rented two rooms at three bits total, silently thanking Annie as she spent their secret money. Their rooms smelled of stale cigarette smoke but offered hot running water and clean, threadbare sheets beneath warm enough blankets.

She had known better accommodations, but she had also known worse. When driving steers, a bedroll on a pallet of leaves or pine straw was a notch better than a waxed canvas tent containing no pallet. How well she knew that rock-hard ground made an uncomfortable bed.

During the night, Billy, who had taken a shine to the pup, snuck the creature into his rented room. While in the truck, his hand rarely left it, a reason, perhaps, that the coyote now seemed so tame. The last of the pup's bandages had come loose in recent days, and Billy had declared its wounds healed enough to toughen up without further attention. There was still a bald patch on one of its sides where its fur might never grow back. This, said Billy, gave it character.

With a whole room to herself, Raylene slept hard after the drama of recent days. Traveling in haste had left her with few clothing choices, so in the morning she wore her cleanest shirt next to her skin and the dirtiest as an outer layer. For breakfast they patronized a nearby diner. Over eggs and coffee, Billy asked Raylene to clarify her actions of the prior evening.

He said, "I understand that the doctor's woman promised to call upon Babe's mother, but I wonder that three dollars would have been enough to convince her."

"I also purchased medicines from her and sweetened my words with extra money. She is a woman who tends other women, mostly on the reservation."

"She also tends the doctor."

Clearly, Billy did not like the notion of a native woman keeping company with a white man, but Raylene would not denigrate another woman's choice. Women survived in whatever ways they could, whether well-placed or poor.

This brought Raylene to a new subject. "Didn't you say that Ray and my father both wanted a woman's attention? I took that to mean my mother."

"That was my thought as well."

"Did they fight over her?"

"There was talk among the older people. I didn't see any fights myself, but then again, I had moved away with Mary."

Perhaps the rivalry had followed the brothers through the years. She could imagine two men at odds over the love of one woman, yet she had never observed violence between Thomas and Raymond Yellow Moon. Nor had she seen warmth.

"Quite a feat to find that McCoy place after dark," said Billy.

Raylene blinked herself back to the table holding plates smeared with egg yolk and their empty coffee cups. "The moon was fairly bright."

"If she had no vehicle, she might not have gone."

Raylene decided to share the hand she had played. "I explained my view of doctors who care little for women's pain.

And that some fear complications or poor outcomes that might tarnish their reputations. Doctors without ancestors to honor. For such doctors, refusing might be preferable to failing." Now she questioned Billy. "Were you planning to shoot the doctor?"

"You carry Yellow Moon blood so I knew you would understand it if I did. I could not see his eyes. Did he look worried?"

"He looked concerned that you might be crazy enough. You *do* look Indian."

A wry smile came over Billy's grizzled features. "Well...he might have pushed me that far but I resisted shooting him in front of you."

"Why?"

"The law would expect you to act as witness to my actions, and I would not do that to you."

Chuckling, Raylene stood and went to pay at the register as Billy headed for the truck. He carried a bacon sandwich for the pup.

They set out again under popcorn clouds. A breeze had dried the surface of the gravel road that angled away from the wide Missouri. The fields to the east looked more fertile than those opposite, no doubt nourished by proximity to the life-giving river.

Even at a moderate pace, a steady cloud of dust plumed around the beast. The plan was to reach the countryside west of Sioux City before noon. Billy thought he could direct Raylene to his niece's land there. Before long they had driven through the town of Winnebago and crossed the upper boundary of the reservation, arriving in Homer, another hamlet formed around a church, a market, and a dealer of used farm equipment, the basics of country life. For a pound of nails or a roll of baling wire, locals would make a monthly pilgrimage to a bigger town because such items were not readily salvaged from busted equipment kept around a farm.

It took all of sixty seconds to drive through Homer. On the far side, Raylene pulled the beast over and waited while Billy and the pup took a health break. When Billy climbed back in, handing the pup in first, she did not start the engine right away.

"Uncle," she said. "When we part, you would do well to keep the pup."

Billy stroked the shaggy thing that leaned against him like a baby. "I do like him, but *you* found him."

"I never thought of him as mine."

"He is learning to rely on people," said Billy. "In truth, it might not be right to keep a wild thing."

"He seems to prefer you."

"Perhaps my ripe smell."

Raylene did not think that Billy required much persuading, but she said, "I suppose we keep work animals when they are meant to be wild, were once wild."

"People cannot do everything themselves."

"In my company, he will not be first on my mind. If he goes with you, you can choose to return him to the fields. He might leave you then, or choose to stay."

Billy's silence signaled that she had convinced him. As Raylene started up the beast, she said, "While he is with you, he might have a name."

"He is *súnkawakhán*. Sacred dog."

"The term for horse, am I right?"

Billy smiled like life had shown itself to be rich once more with potential. "Or, just *súnka*." Then he pointed to the rough-looking rutted road that led toward Hubbard. Raylene steered them that way.

In this part of Nebraska, they were well east of a deep, wide zone called the Sand Hills, a couple hundred square miles of gentle dunes long since covered in mixed grasses more suited to grazing cattle than farming. Raylene had once worked for a ranching outfit over in Cherry County, west of some marshlands that made for good deer and duck hunting. Rabbits too. In the spring she could sit atop her horse among the emerald hills with nothing in sight but land running out to the sky. A land of water spirits and wildlife. The uninitiated might think such a place bereft of living creatures, but though it was true that the largest prairie grazers such as bison were no more, and the cover for other creatures sparse, a close observer would see a prairie teeming with animals. Voles and flickertails, antelope and burrowing owls. There were elk further west, out Sheridan County way.

A niece to Billy's wife farmed a small homestead with her husband. Billy believed them to still be on the land, which was good enough for Raylene. She would deliver him to his people and return to trailing her uncle without having prepared a plan for when she found him. Not *if,* but *when.*

But first — the safe delivery of Billy and his beast full of gear. The remainder of her own belongings were back at the H-bar-H, as were her horse and saddle. She was picturing the crew there, the cook, the ranch boss and cowhands, when the right front tire blew, yanking the steering wheel hard right as the beast lurched off the road and rammed its nose into a ditch. The abrupt halt concluded with a series of groans and the creak of metal under strain, Billy crumpled where the dashboard met the passenger door, and Raylene bent like a wishbone, her feet against her door.

"Are you alright?" she said, craning her neck to glimpse Billy.

He pushed against the dash to unkink himself. "A hell of a thing," he said. The hand he lifted to his nose came away bloody. His gun had slid from behind his feet to land upon the pup, its barrel pointed at Raylene's legs.

"Heed that shotgun, will you?" said Raylene.

He slid the weapon away from the pup, which shook itself in response.

The beast was good and stuck, its front right corner tipped downward into the weeds. Raylene heaved her driver's side door outward, wedging it open with her shoulder. "Do you want to climb out this side or fall out yours?"

"I'll try this way," said Billy, shoving his door open a crack. It opened under its own weight as he dropped the pup to the ground and climbed out after it.

Raylene's door grew heavy, so she let it slam shut and followed Billy out the passenger side. Straightening, she was surprised to notice a flatbed truck slowing to a stop roughly twenty yards back. An Indian man sat behind the wheel and another stood atop the rectangular hay bales stacked in back. Raylene lifted her chin in acknowledgement.

"You folks okay?" shouted the man atop the hay.

"Guess so," said Billy, squinting upward.

"Looks like you need a hand." The top man climbed down from his post and dropped to the roadway. He was stocky, with skin burnt brown from the sun.

"A front tire blew," said Raylene as the man drew closer. He was about her own age, dressed in worn denim work clothes peppered with bits of hay.

He said, "You carrying a spare?" He waved a hand at the bulge of household items strapped under the tarp and the few that had landed in the ditch.

"There wasn't one," said Raylene. She shook her head. They'd almost made it to Billy's people. Almost.

The other man exited the hay truck and walked over. He was older and bulkier than the first one, somewhat less hay-flecked, but just as brown. "No spare, on *these* back roads?" He went on to say something else about the nature of gravel roads but Raylene's focus had caught on a knife the stranger wore on his belt. Its handle was antler with a bit of burr showing. A half-inch of the handle's decoration looked mighty familiar.

She narrowed her eyes. She had lost her own knife in a needless fight and now this stranger was wearing someone else's prized possession.

Billy gave Raylene's coat sleeve a tug. "A ride to Hubbard is good news. *Wónah' un wasté.* From there we can reach Mary's niece. We'll have to leave the truck here and come back with a tire when I can find one."

Raylene nodded, ignoring Billy's use of "we" since she didn't plan to return to this spot. If he was safely delivered, his family could help him retrieve his beast; she needed to push forward. Her mind cast about for why this stranger wore a knife she recalled so clearly. She could only make out a little of its design, which meant her assessment might be wrong, but the blown tire had not entirely loosened her wits.

Billy was asking the men where they grew hay and the men were giving the name of the ranch they worked for, pointing west toward fields bordering the Winnebago reservation. The men were Edwin and Rocky, who asked if Raylene and Billy were family, which for practical purposes they were.

A minute later, Raylene helped Billy retrieve his bedroll and the cardboard grip. Then she tied her bundle across her chest and carried her own bedroll to the driver who went by Rocky. He seemed to inspect her as she drew closer. Handing him her bedroll, she leaned in close as if to share a confidence, but instead she slipped the knife he carried from its sheath and stepped back.

"What the fuck?" he cried, dropping her bedroll to grab at

empty air as he started toward her. "Give it here."

Raylene motioned with the knife that he should stay back. "It's not yours," she said, "unless you can prove it. This knife belongs to my uncle."

Eight

Omaha. Murphy's last stop on the U.P. line. He made town in mid-afternoon and drove straight for the railroad freight yard. After alerting the yard boss, he queried the workers about whether they'd seen an Indian woman hopping on or off any of the cars. A worker named Jack thought that a week prior he'd caught a glimpse of an Indian male, half-grown, stealing away from a boxcar toward town. A week prior didn't quite fit the facts, though, so Murphy filed the information away.

After thanking the men for their time, Murphy returned to the main office to receive the cash his boss had promised to transfer between offices. The money would replenish what he'd spent out of pocket and, if approved, cover a few days of trailing Raylene Little Moon.

Omaha's main rail terminal resembled Kansas City's, with the constant rumble of trains arriving and departing or idling while passengers embarked. Union Pacific ran both passenger and freight service through Omaha, but so did Central Pacific and Burlington. This made the business offices inherently noisy, with personnel constantly in motion, phones jangling on desks, typewriters and teletypes clattering. The ubiquitous haze of smoke always made Murphy a little hungry for a cigarette. He had given up smoking to please his wife, and though she was no longer present to observe him keep his promise, he kept it anyway.

Rail offices, thought Murphy, probably resembled those of newspaper operations, all that hive-like activity. There were problems to sort out and information arriving piecemeal. Offices and cubicles containing schedulers, publicity people, payroll, and hiring. "Containing" might be less than accurate since the bustle of it looked as much contained as leaves swirling in a gust of wind. Only the secretaries at desks out in the open seemed relatively stationary, answering phones and stabbing the keys of their typewriters before stripping forms from them with a *zzzzip*. A row of wall clocks displayed times zones for the entire U.S., a practice almost fifty years old.

Murphy located the proper secretary and showed her his badge. She suggested he pay the station master a courtesy call while she fetched his cash from the safe. He had met Roger Duncan two years back, but had not communicated with him since.

The secretary led the way to a half-open door, knocked before leaning in to announce Murphy, then retreated so he could enter.

A cigarette smoldered in an ashtray on Duncan's desk, its wisp of smoke headed for the ceiling. After shaking hands and exchanging pleasantries, Duncan said, "I assume you're here on a case."

"I'm following a couple of threads related to a death down in Kansas City."

"Something remarkable about it?"

"Not so you'd notice. Just tying up loose ends."

"Well, if it brought you this far, it's not cut-and-dried."

"True, but I expect to wrap it up in a day or two."

"I understand, but if you find yourself in need of assistance, give a ring. Judith, my secretary, can give you the number." With that he picked up his pen and opened a folder on his desk. Their conversation was done.

Murphy retrieved an envelope of cash from Miss Judith and borrowed her city directory. Granted permission to use a telephone in one of the cubicles, he rang his boss back in Kansas City. "No luck so far," he reported. "I've checked the towns between there and here."

"Damn." Down the line came the sound of a deep sigh, then, "What next?"

Murphy had been thinking about how to phrase the options, casting sufficient light on the one he himself favored. "There are four pawn shops close enough to this station to warrant a closer look. Someone traveling by rail, well, they'd stick close if they were hocking jewelry while traveling."

"The earrings you found, that was a help. I slept a little better that night, but these few days, I've got to tell you, this is giving me heartburn. Gotta shit all the time too."

"We have choices," said Murphy. "If I don't get lucky here, I could close the case ... or, since I know one possible location the Little Moon sister might be headed toward, I could check there. That's in South Dakota. If I catch her when she's picking up mail, I might have a chance to talk her out of the jewels. If she has them."

"Or someone else might have them by now."

"Right. Maybe that unidentified man the boarding house owner mentioned."

"Jesus, what a mess."

Murphy let the options ferment in the silence that ensued. In the background was the sound of his boss's drumming fingers, another fidgety habit that surfaced when stress levels rose. The man could run a freight yard like few others, but with that job came plenty of problems and politicking. Money to be made and money wasted through inefficiencies or risks not fully considered. And then there were risks that weren't of the business variety at all, for instance risks that arose with desire.

"God damn it. Do you think you can find her and convince

her?" said Campbell. "I'd hate to have to buy them back, but I guess that's like buying them out of pawn. I transferred an extra five hundred to you, just in case."

"If she's gone to her home country, I might find her. She might not have the items, though."

"If you find her and she won't hand them over, we're screwed."

Murphy did not state the obvious. *He* wasn't screwed, his boss was screwed.

"Oh, hell. You'd better give that a try," came the decision. "Where'd you say — the Dakotas?"

"I should have an answer within a few days. Also, the dead hobo case looks like a possible dead end. I'll keep asking around, though. It's kind of keeping me on the road, too."

There was a pause on the boss's end. "Well, check in again when you know something about anything. Soon. The suspense is killing me. I wonder if I can get the museum to pretend its own people lost those missing pieces. To make that happen, I'd have to pay them off. Jesus." The line went dead, which was fine by Murphy. He set the handset back on its base and made his way out of the sprawling rail complex.

The nearest hock shops turned out to be a bust. Murphy ran through a mental list of likely scenarios — a person could keep the jewels to pawn later, or use them as trade in some other transaction. Or, should the current possessor be female, she could keep them to wear. Keepsakes from a sister now dead, lovely objects to enliven a life outside the city. His wife had owned a modest amount of decent jewelry. Nothing extravagant, but nice enough for the wife of the accountant he was when she married him.

They had never belonged to the uppermost crust of KC, itself a notch or two below the upper crust of Chicago and far below that of New York City. Kansas City had a sugared, glittery top layer where a person might dance and dine with bankers and rail masters, land barons and politicians. He and Catherine had done little of that sort of socializing. Murphy might not know as much about women as some men, but he knew they liked to dress up and show off a little. Most of them, anyway. So, it would not surprise him to find that the little sister had decided to keep the missing jewelry.

Exiting the Big Chief Jewelry and Loan on C Street, Murphy paused. The freight yard men had not reported seeing any native women riding the rails and there was no way to know if the little sister had ridden as a paying customer. It was as if she had up and disappeared, an exaggeration because he no more believed hocus pocus acts than tales about the man in the moon. Though true disappearances were rare, people sometimes met killers and seemed to vanish. He had read about the Chicago murders of many people around the time of the Columbian Exposition there. Gruesome stuff by a madman. This wasn't that, though. The little sister was traveling somehow, just not in a manner that allowed him a glimpse.

Omaha freight staff had identified the direction of the makeshift Hoovertown where tramps and hobos and the poorer sorts could find shelter and a scavenged meal. Since the national collapse, almost every town of any size had sprouted such a community.

One problem was that he didn't know the identity of the man who had masqueraded as a father and removed the valise from Annie Moon's boarding house. And too, he didn't have a photograph of the man or even of Raylene Little Moon to show around Omaha's Hoovertown. But fortunately, he was still being paid to flush out even the smallest clue relating to either of the two cases that had brought him this far.

Omaha's town of shacks looked like the sort of place where that Dwayne fellow might have stayed while looking for work. With a little luck he might locate a resident who could shine a light on the travels of hobo Dwayne.

Buttoning his coat, but leaving his hat and gloves on the seat of his coupe, Murphy made his way between the outermost shacks, scanning for residents to query. The place looked sparsely populated. Shortly, he came across a group of four gathered close to a campfire whose heat and light danced skyward from broken boards engulfed in flame. He drew closer, stopping at a respectful distance to catch the attention of the men sitting upon mismatched chairs and overturned buckets. He addressed the group at large. "Good evening, gentlemen." Receiving a nod from two of the men, he continued. "I apologize for interrupting you. I'm with the railroad and I have the task of asking around about a ... uh, gentleman who met his death alongside our tracks."

The men at the fire seemed to be studying Murphy, his nice coat and good shoes. He figured they were contemplating whether to speak with him at all, whether he posed a threat of any kind until two of them nodded, granting Murphy leave to continue.

He pulled the photo of the dead man from his pocket and stepped forward to pass it around. The late afternoon glow coupled with the fire's light would be enough for making out Dwayne's likeness. "We're trying to identify this man. To notify his relatives so that they can bury him properly." Only partly true. The railroad would notify the man's relatives should they find them, but his body had already been buried.

The men took the photo and passed it among themselves. The one who sat in a decent-looking dining chair, spoke up. "Can't say he looks familiar. Took a rough fall, did he? That what killed him?"

"We think so," said Murphy. "We see our share of heart attacks and such. It can be hard to tell."

The Hoovertown man held Murphy's eye. "They didn't open him up to check?"

"No."

Murphy pocketed the photo and held his hands out to the fire as if he had all the time in the world. Without a fire to draw close to, this raw place would grow cold indeed. He would not care to sleep so poorly protected. Sure, he had slept out of doors during Boy Scout camping trips, where he learned to tie knots, raise a tent, shoot a bow and arrow, and paddle a canoe. Summer nights had been ideal for a pup tent and a padded bag, the moist night air heavy on his shirtless body as katydids and night birds called to their own. Luckily, he'd had a warm home to return to.

He decided to try his luck with what was truly on his mind. "I have a question about Indians. You men see many come through this way?"

The four he addressed glanced at each other, shrugging.

"A young Indian woman?" added Murphy. "Hair down to her back, perhaps wearing a dress, or suede trousers? Could be traveling with a male relative."

From the one in the dining chair: "You here to arrest someone?"

"Not at all. I only ask questions."

"Is the woman dead too?"

Murphy thought fast. "She's alive. We just need to reach her relatives about something."

The man squinted at Murphy. "I guess we ain't seen anyone like that."

Though none of the others spoke, Murphy wasn't sure he believed the one man whose demeanor had somehow shifted.

He tried a different approach. "I'm also interested in pawn shops around these parts. You know of anyone hocking items nearby?"

One of the others perked up. "Jimmy D's," came the insight. "It's a market, but they hock stuff there. You got sumpin' to hock?"

"Well, no. I only have questions." He thought now that he might have elicited better cooperation or more complete responses had he arrived with food or drink to share. He filed that notion away for future use. "Can you give me directions to that market?"

Three of the men looked over at the man in the dining chair, who didn't budge. "You point him," said the man. "My knees want to sit right here by this fire." At that, the one who had named the market stood and skirted the fire to point across the tracks at distant buildings on the outer boundary of Omaha proper. He said, "Right about there. It's on a reg'lar road."

Murphy shook the man's hand, resisting the impulse to wipe his palm on his coat until after he reached his vehicle. Soon he was headed for the other side of the tracks. A long shot, he thought, but there was nothing to be gained by skipping even one logical step of an investigation.

After a couple of wrong turns, he located Jimmy D's market and pulled into what passed for a gravel lot worn to dirt in places. He patted his jacket pockets. Small notepad, pen, photograph of dead Dwayne, and the one of Annie Moon wearing fancy jewelry. Let the investigation continue.

Standing on the country road between Billy's crashed beast and the hay truck, Raylene squared off against the man called Rocky. Into sharp focus came the sheen of sweat on his face and the odors of damp earth and sun-warmed fields rising all around them. "That's *mine*," growled Rocky.

"The feather design — what color did it start as?"

"Give it here before I take it from you."

Raylene felt the focus of Billy and the one called Edwin. Edwin might be inclined to divert her attention by coming to the aid of his friend, but he hadn't yet, perhaps because he'd heard Billy chambering a shotgun shell — *kachunk*. Raylene knew what the others did not about the old man's eyesight, that he could pepper them all with buckshot or kill one or more with a single blast. She said, "You *stole* it."

Rocky spat his next words. "I won it in a game, just this week."

"Who from?"

"Some old blood. Drunk when he got there. Played okay until he got sloppy." He half smiled, perhaps at the memory of juking someone out of a treasure.

"Where was that?"

"Sioux City. There's a bar has poker in the back." His posture eased a little. He had probably decided that being half again as large as Raylene meant he could take her with only minor damage to himself, as long as Billy didn't intervene.

Raylene held the knife lightly, like the accomplished fighter she was, her family's daughter raised as the family's son. The knife's blade was sharp and fine. Like her boot knife, it would be unmarked. It looked clean, as if it had not recently known flesh, but if this was Ray's weapon, her father had felt its bite. She said, "What did he look like, the one who got sloppy?"

"Long hair, one arm bloody. He held it funny." He smiled slyly now. "At the end he looked like a loser."

Raylene ignored the sarcasm. "Did he give his name?"

"He acted like he couldn't remember." Here, Rocky smirked.

A bloodied stranger carrying Raymond's knife? That

stranger had to have been her uncle, injured from the fight with Thomas, their twinned blood merging beneath the knives in their battling hands. They had been as one from the moment they squalled into the world and through every competition since. The same walk, the same strengths, the same hungers. Two hearts beating in time until parted in anger. Even parted, neither would escape the other.

"A big card game, was it?"

"Started with six. Two dropped out after losing their bank."

"What hand did you win this with?"

Rocky smiled to himself as if recalling a certain bit of luck. "Three tens."

Three tens. Not implausible ... depending. "What game?"

"Uh, stud."

So, the gambler was either luckier or a better player than Ray, or he had used sleight of hand, or was now lying. She asked, "How many hole cards?"

This time he blinked. "Two, no — one."

Raylene frowned. She was beginning to disbelieve his story. "That old man you played against would not have wagered this knife, so let's say you stole it after he passed out. You must have left straight away to avoid a fight."

"Me?" Rocky puffed his chest out a little. He was young and strong and knew it. Before he drew another breath, Billy spoke from close behind Raylene. "You are lucky there was no fight because you would have lost."

Rocky's laugh came out a snort. "Against a drunk?"

Billy's voice again. "If that man was Raymond Yellow Moon, you would have been sorry to fight him, drunk or blind or injured."

Now Rocky's face fell as his mouth dropped open and he fastened his eyes upon Raylene. "Yellow Moon? That was Yellow Moon?"

"My uncle," said Raylene.

"No shit, you're a Yellow Moon?"

Edwin had drawn close enough to punch Rocky in the arm. "You took a knife off a fucking *hombre*. It's yours now!"

Rocky began to shake his head. His mouth appeared to form words that failed to find sound as his shoulders slumped. He unbuckled his belt and slid the sheath from it. "No, no, no," he said softly.

"Yeah, man," said Edwin. "Keep it."

Rocky held the sheath out away from his body, as if it might bite him.

"You don't want it? I'll take it," said Edwin, gesturing for Rocky to give it up.

Rocky shoved Edwin's hand aside with a hiss. "You ass. If he comes back for it — you'd be done for."

Edwin lifted his hands as if to suggest that Rocky had lost his mind.

Rocky shot Edwin a look. "Did we just a few minutes ago tell exactly where we work and live? I'm not losing my scalp over no fucking knife. You think he don't have another?" He held the sheath out to Raylene, who stepped forward to receive it.

She glanced at the fields running for miles and the haze at the horizon. "If you will still transport us, we will pay for your fuel. A square deal."

Rocky narrowed his eyes as if considering his options, then shrugged and waved Edwin to remount the hay truck.

Raylene glanced at Billy, who now had the pup in his arms. She said, "I guess we will make Hubbard after all."

Waiting in the shade of the Hubbard filling station with the pup panting at their feet, Billy said, "I have been thinking on this and it seems you truly mean to challenge Ray. Perhaps you should take this." He held out his shotgun to her, its barrel a steely gray, lightly pitted, and its hardwood stock rubbed smooth by decades of handling.

"He did not use a gun against Thomas, so I will not."

Billy paused. "Will you try to kill him?"

"I am not pleased about what he has brought upon me. I never wanted this."

Billy nodded. "Tradition can be a hard thing. Family honor. Perhaps it is enough that you carry his knife. That you have it and he does not."

"If that were the case, I would gladly return to my life in peace. But it's not enough, and he knows that I know it is not." Raylene looked in the direction that one of the filling station workers had driven to request Billy's kin come to fetch him. "Raymond will meet his knife again. I will see to it."

Inside Jimmy D's market, Murphy removed his fedora and swept the immediate shelves with his gaze. The store appeared to offer canned goods and household items, chicken wire and soda pop. Along one wall sat a meat counter and two iceboxes, one labeled Dairy, one Beer.

From the back of the store came a voice, "Help you?" The sound of footsteps announced the arrival of a man untying a work apron. He said, "It's closing time."

"I was hoping to find the proprietor," said Murphy.

The man eyed Murphy's nice overcoat. "You found him."

Murphy proffered his badge as he explained that he was trying to locate a young Indian woman who might have taken to the road, roughing it.

"This state's full of Indians," said the market man. "And plenty of people living rough."

"Have you seen such a woman come through in the last week? Unaccompanied, or perhaps with an Indian man?"

The market man shook his head.

Murphy glanced around. "I'm wondering if you pawn items for people. Or buy them outright."

"Nope."

Murphy frowned. "Someone told me you do."

"That's a lie, I don't do it."

Murphy let out a breath. He had no reason to think the Hoovertown man had steered him wrong. He was at the right place speaking to the person in charge of the money coming in and going out. This man knew what Murphy was asking. He just didn't want to play ball.

Over the years, Murphy had met plenty of resistant individuals. A few had slammed doors in his face, and more than one had cried. There was swearing, and obfuscations, and digressions. No one liked to implicate themselves and sometimes they resisted implicating others. "Mister," he said, "I'm with the railroad, not the law. I don't care what you buy or pawn or how you conduct your business. I don't arrest anybody. I'm not even armed. I'm just looking for a person and some jewelry."

The market man's posture eased a notch, but he gave no reply.

Murphy pulled out the photo he carried of Annie Moon wearing the earrings he had recovered and the still-missing necklace. "I'm trying to locate this necklace for someone. That stone in the middle is green."

"That the Indian you're looking for?"

"No."

"Must be a valuable necklace if you come all this way for it." The market man paused. "Can't say I seen a Indian girl or a fancy necklace."

Murphy wondered — *can't say* or *won't say*? In his suitcase, he had $200 left of what Campbell had sent with him for incidentals plus the $500 newly transferred. The necklace alone was probably worth most of the cash he had on him, but he would cross that bridge when he came to it. *If* he came to it. He said, "I know where *this* young woman is, and the necklace isn't with her. What I'm hoping you can tell me is whether someone came through here to sell it or if you've seen it, or if you have it. I'm willing to pay the loan with interest on any money borrowed, or else buy it outright from whoever has it."

The market man crossed his arms and paused a beat. "A fair offer," he said, "but I don't have it."

"There's also a ring of rose gold set with a pink stone."

"I still don't have it."

Murphy felt his patience tested, but voicing irritation was a sure-fire way to shut down an interview. "Okay. I hear you," he said. "What about this: anyone flashing money around, like they just got rich?"

Now recognition lit up the market man's face. "Well, yeah. Come to think of it, this Indian kid come in with a white guy. Kid had a goddamn hundred-dollar bill. Damnedest thing. Kind of smart about it too. Made out like I wasn't the kind to ever see one."

Kid? thought Murphy. He needed a young woman, not too girlish, so a raggedy kid did not fit, but the mention of a hundred-dollar bill — *that* flipped a switch inside him. His *modus operandi* was to keep asking questions until answers came out. "What do you mean by 'kid'?"

"Just young, maybe teenager, maybe twenty, how're you supposed to tell when all of them look alike? Had on a brown ranch coat and one of them caps that boys wear."

"Could the kid have been a female, twenty-something?"

The owner thought a moment. "I guess, maybe. Acted smart, though, like a man."

"When was this you saw them?"

"Couple of days ago."

"You recall what they bought?"

"Food, beer, tarp. Regular stuff."

"Did either of them mention where they were staying, or where they were headed?"

"Naw."

Murphy thought a moment. "Did they look like they were traveling, maybe carrying suitcases or bundles?"

The market man shrugged.

"Any other details you can help me with?"

The market man looked into the distance. "They might of driven a truck. One said somethin' about the stuff in the back getting wet."

"You see what model?"

"Nope."

Murphy felt like he'd drained this well dry. He could generally read when a person had given up whatever they had to tell. The market man, whose recall seemed pretty good, was done with sharing. Lots of people you could meet wouldn't be able to say what they'd had for breakfast or who they'd spoken with in a single day. With others, the first things out of their mouths were often the most reliable and the longer they were questioned, the more they diverged from accuracy, embellishing details, sometimes saying what they thought a detective *wanted* to hear. This interview felt finished.

"Thanks for your time," he said, handing over one of his U.P. business cards. "There's still money for the jewelry and I'd come back for it. If you find either piece before I do, there's a bonus in it for you." That last was not direct from the boss, but sometimes you had to speak first and ask permission later.

The market man glanced at Murphy's card and stuck it in his trouser pocket. Murphy went out to his auto and sat in the quiet, thinking about how the "kid" in the market could have been the little sister, except for the hat and the barn coat. And the white guy. Only one detail out of four fit — that hundred-dollar bill, unlikely pocket money for the individuals described. In Murphy's experience, if something seemed out of place, it probably was.

Having met Billy's niece and her husband and watched them load up Billy and his pup and drive away, Raylene hitched a ride with a driver headed to South Sioux City, on the Nebraska side of the Missouri. The town's main street held stores, a bank, a restaurant, three bars, and a beauty parlor. Across the river lay Sioux City, Iowa. Nebraskans counted the river as their own, but so did Iowans, Dakotans, and Montanans. Luckily, the river's shoulders were broad enough for all.

She touched Ray's knife in its sheath on her belt and let the sounds of gentle commerce fall around her as she pondered whether Ray had felt revulsion at killing Thomas. Afterwards, did he feel he had lost a piece of himself? She could not imagine him killing a stranger for no reason, let alone a brother, so what could have caused such a rift? Hopefully not something as obvious as drink. It was no secret that Ray drank, as did Thomas. Had they drunk together in Thomas's saloon and fought to settle some old score? Was it jealousy? Had Thomas's victory of her mother's hand in marriage left a festering wound that decades later turned Ray into a killer?

Raylene felt haunted by what she might not know about Ray, one thing or many things held in the space that circled back upon itself, never aligned to the angles of the world, the spires of trees, the spines of horse brush, the jags of lightning that split the sky on a summer night. Her uncle possessed a secret that had circled round and come out on the tip of his knife. She would not be satisfied until she knew what had made that secret so deadly.

She turned her face to the afternoon sun and let it wash over her, burning away all thoughts but those of Ray — uncle, second father, protector, killer. She saw once more his knife-making hands, the same that had fashioned fragrant corn leaves into the *khéya* doll. He had gentled horses, the hands he laid upon their withers and necks conveying communion and authority. He wore a quickness to anger that fed his wide reputation for winning the fights he started, and those started by others. And there he was, carrying Thomas through the ravines to seek doctoring for a body broken in a terrible fall. He ate her mother's cooking with gusto, each handful, each forkful, as he raged at the loss of the old ways. She knew little of his journeys to find work at the edge of the Pacific or up into Canada's wilds, so she sent her thoughts out toward the land of the Crow, who were the sworn enemies of the Sioux until whites had turned such enemies into allies. Ray had worked on the massive Fort Peck Dam, built to tame the mighty Missouri, with concrete walls reaching skyward through the efforts of uncounted men, their sweat and their machinery. For eighteen months he had tended the project's mule teams by day and cleaned equipment by night until one of the hammering devices had broken his leg. At that point, he came back to the family, for a while.

The sun, all knowing, all seeing, colored her eyelids, bathing her thoughts with a fire that flashed and swirled as if lighting the way for dancers of old, whose stomping and whirling called down the spirits. Within the fiery swirls, she sought her uncle. During the last decade, perhaps more, he had lived as a nomad, in search of a reason to remain fixed in place. To find him, Raylene needed to summon that which called to him. No matter his reputation, no matter his ties to place or people, no matter his need for money or honor or to evade discovery, he was like every person in that he needed at least one thing to turn to for comfort.

When the fire behind her eyes dimmed then vanished, Raylene looked up to find that a cloud had blotted the sun. On a breeze bearing the scent of nearby fields and the ceaseless river, the answer came to her — what Uncle Ray would seek was the comfort of horses. His earliest power had come from riding, racing, and those episodes of stealing horseflesh for bragging rights. He would not be found at fall pow-wow as Billy had suggested, but at a celebration of horses, speed, and racing agility. The flames had shown her exactly that, and she trusted the flames.

Nine

Murphy set out early the next morning for the closest filling station, a Sinclair, where the attendant checked his coupe's oil and tires. Studying his road maps, he calculated the shortest route to his destination, an approximate diagonal across Nebraska's eastern and central zones. Given that the largest roads were one lane in each direction, and sometimes pocked by tractor damage or buckled by ice heaves, a full day's travel lay ahead of him. Perhaps twelve hours or more, but his Hudson coupe, lighter by hundreds of pounds than Chevrolets or Fords, was suited for this very journey.

His pulse tapped a beat at the thought of veering off course from U.P.'s rail routes and driving out through new country. He most often worked directly in the rail towns and cities of Missouri, Kansas, Nebraska, and Iowa, locating passengers and ironing out questions plaguing the cases assigned to him. But here was an opportunity to pass beyond U.P.'s immediate influence and embark on an adventure of sorts on the railroad's dime, or at least his boss's dime.

Someday, engineers would devise a network of quality roads linking northern states to southern, and eastern states to the west. He hoped that would happen before he was too old for the thrill of running his coupe up to its maximum speed.

With his auto ready, he borrowed a clean rag from the filling station owner to wipe the road dust from its seat and dashboard. Gauges too. Returning the rag to the station's service counter, he noticed a small rack of postcards sporting black and white scenes with color tinting to liven them. One showed a road to Yellowstone winding alongside a river. Another, a scene of downtown Omaha with some of Henry Ford's first automobiles parked at the curb. Murphy chose a scene of Indian chiefs in full regalia standing on the wooden platform of an unidentified railroad station. The chiefs wore eagle-feather bonnets, beaded pants and aprons, even decorated vests. No smiles, though. They looked sober, nearly morose. On the back of the card, the caption identified them as Plains Indians posing for tourist photos in exchange for spare change. He left a nickel on the counter. If everything worked right, he'd soon locate the Plains Indian woman who went by the name Raylene Little Moon.

With her bundle strapped across her chest, Raylene caught the westbound morning train that ran passengers and freight out of Sioux City for the Chicago, Milwaukee, St. Paul & Pacific railway. She traveled in a passenger car that had seen better days, but seats beat out boxcars any day.

The H-bar-H spread across land situated west of the Pine Ridge. She'd be glad to get back to check on her four-year-old piebald gelding. The other ranch hands would josh her a little for being gone, as if she'd spent the last week at leisure. They knew next to nothing about her family or its circumstances, but did know her character based on how she comported herself and how she accepted the tedious tasks of riding and repairing fences without complaint. She could repair a lariat or saddle with the best of them and knew which of them were whittlers or readers of a bible or scratchers of letters to be posted in Rapid City when the next supplies were fetched.

Raylene understood she was viewed as someone separate from the men while also aligned with them through the types of work they all performed. She liked it that way. Attending to medical complaints required she spend time hunting the plants she used for remedies to common ailments, including those few that were useful in the right hands but deadly when mishandled. Advancing years had brought modern medicines such as aspirin, which the ranch hands used liberally, and such items as bottled cough syrup and tinctures for calming an upset stomach. She knew those too.

By their nature, cowboys, by whatever name they were called — wranglers, buckaroos, cow punchers, vaqueros — were solitary creatures who preferred the company of a good horse and a day out of doors to any social situation that required them to make small talk with strangers. Outsiders, castaways, drifters, and misfits, they were a largely honest bunch, adhering to a code of sorts that dictated the granting of privacy when another person seemed to want it. She got along with most every one of them.

While away, she had missed her horse, though no one would catch her saying so out loud. Such a display of tenderness would draw ribbing and perhaps derision from the cowhands who maintained a gruff façade under most circumstances. Other stock horses were not given names but labeled "the bay with stockings" or "that ornery yellow one," but Raylene's was her own and as such he had a name, even if she never used it in conversation — Kota. As was typical for a cow pony, he was smallish, just thirteen hands high. Scrappy, hardworking, and possessed of an uncanny intuition for herding and cutting work. Ranch rules required she stable him with the ranch's riding stock, but the others knew to leave him be. He was hers and she was the only one to draw him from rotation.

The H-bar-H was held by relatives of a man named Halt who owned a separate operation near Box Elder. It was said that Theodore Roosevelt had contributed to its expansion by investing in its purchase of another thousand acres of mixed grass prairie, perfect for grazing. There had been rumors about putting bison on the range for Roosevelt's trophy purposes, but no one Raylene knew had ever met Roosevelt to ask him, so there were only stories to go by.

The train carrying her west traveled on tracks that cut across the northeast corner of Nebraska, carving a shallow arc northward into South Dakota, through Yankton, then on to Mitchell and Murdo, ending at Rapid City. As it rolled past miles of golden grasses, she gazed outward, imagining the distant stretch of rugged bad lands where layered formations of corrugated sandstone formed many square miles of deep, shady canyons whose sandy bottoms glittered with bones. Forbidding, inhospitable lands. Also sacred.

Spewing coal smoke and steam, the train gathered speed as it crossed flattish grasslands pocked with homesteads and ranches, its wheels singing *closer...closer...closer*.

At Farmingdale, where the train stopped to take on mail and passengers, Raylene descended to the station platform and made her way three blocks east. When the string of cars moved on, she headed south on the road leading out of town. The day was bright and fresh with the ever-present breeze that in one season or another cooled the landscape or grew into a force that could blow to pieces the stick-built sheds meant to shelter livestock.

She walked for two hours to the musical sighing of poplar trees along Battle Creek, the voice of the Cheyenne River, the rustling of grasses, and songs of birds. These cleared from her mind the residue of city sounds — the squealing of automobile brakes, the snap and buzz of streetcars, and the shouts of workers constructing the next department store or bank. She did not disdain commerce. Even the raising of livestock was a spoke in the wheel of commerce. And like most everyone, she patronized markets and banks, the occasional diner, and hadn't she just ridden on a hulking beast of a train, one of mankind's great inventions? Such enterprises powered the world and she, sometimes willingly, sometimes not, joined in as necessary. When it came to people who thrilled to a city — to each his own. Give her the grandeur of nature and the drama of changing seasons.

Her pace was steady along secondary roads and dirt tracks, the sun a mild presence around her, a sheen of sweat on her brow. About the time she reached the Custer County line, an old rancher slowed his truck to offer her a ride. Raylene was glad to save some boot leather and more hours on foot. After exchanging pleasantries and telling him her destination, she offered him a drink from her water canteen. They rode largely in silence to Hermosa, and then to Fairburn. At Fairburn, he said, "Too far to walk." He meant the remaining distance to the H-bar-H.

"I can walk from here," she said, but as if he hadn't heard her, he drove on.

At the access road pointing toward the ranch, he pulled to a stop. She thanked him and took her leave. In another mile she reached the ranch road, itself roughly a mile long. Thirty minutes later, she strode through the ranch gate.

Immediately following the evening meal came Raylene's quarrel with the ranch boss, although she wasn't quarreling, just stating her truth. At the other end of the worn dining table, three of the ranch hands sat playing cards. "Dammit," said the boss. "You're just now back and saying you're about to leave again?"

"I have unfinished business."

"We're about to move two hundred beeves and you're

fixing to disappear? You know we need all hands." The look on his face telegraphed disgust. "And Cookie needs something done about his tooth."

"I'll have a look."

"And Cleve's got an abscess from those brambles he got into."

"I'll handle that before I go."

His displeasure wreathed him like smoke. "How long you going to disappear for this time?"

It was no use pretending she knew how many days she would need for locating and confronting Raymond. She thought of her uncle now as a wounded animal, dangerous if cornered. His knife at her waist made him feel within reach, but that type of thinking was too simple. Too easy, when nothing about this was going to be easy. The one good thing was that if Ray was headed to a place where he could admire horses, she knew someone who might provide a clue.

"Tell me," said the boss, "haven't I treated you right? Cookie told me you left to see about your family and I didn't fire you over it."

"True enough."

"It's not like I ask you to tend the garden or cook."

"You know I would do any job."

"I don't ask you to ride more fences than the others."

"You don't."

"Somebody been bothering you, one of the hands?"

"No."

"You're putting me in a fix, you know. We've got to cut stock for market."

"I did not wish for this."

"You won't find a better outfit to work for. Aren't many going to let a woman ride with them. Maybe nobody else."

"I know."

"I'm going to have to replace you. Is that what you want?"

Raylene did not want to leave a ranch that felt more like home than any other she'd known. She did not want to be tracking her uncle or planning retribution, but any sort of wanting was out of her hands. These were things that needed doing.

The boss might need to replace her, but she knew and he knew that she was as good a rider as any of the others and had earned the right to ride with them. The ranch needed her as much as she needed the work, but none of the outfits ran heavy with workers. An extended loss of one cowhand at an inopportune time meant extra work for the others when they already faced long days and nights filled with temperamental livestock. Nor would this crew be pleased to take on someone new whom they might not be sure they could count on when things got tough. Even if she promised to return, she was doing no favor by leaving.

Behind his drooping mustache, the boss gritted his teeth. "Dammit. Take your gear. Don't leave none of it behind. If you're going to leave me shorthanded, I don't want none of your stuff left here."

Raylene gave a single nod. "I'll clear out."

When the boss turned on his heel and left, the card players glanced in Raylene's direction then went back to their cards. The Mexican, Raul, known as Cookie, looked past his hand at Raylene then called for three cards. She went out and headed for the corral abutting the stable.

Upon reaching the ranch that afternoon, she had checked on Kota, who had nuzzled the cap from her head and snorted into her hair. Now she whistled low at the corral gate and heard him whinny in reply. A moment later, he came trotting to greet her, first sniffing her outstretched palm then lipping the proffered sugar cubes, crunching them between his big yellow teeth. "As of tomorrow," she said, "no cattle for a while. No fences. Just us." Kota signaled his agreement by fixing her with one brown eye bordered by long lashes.

In the stable's tack room, she took down Kota's two saddle blankets, one of them just a year old, and the saddle bags she had carried to Kansas City and back. There were footsteps behind her, then Raul's hands at her waist.

"Don't," said Raylene.

His words were barely audible. "Don't touch you, or don't whisper?" He had the weathered face of those who had wrangled stock. That bow-legged walk. In a twist of fate precipitated by an instant of inattention while untangling a calf from a broken wire fence, a cow mother had kicked him multiple times, breaking his forearm and crushing his right hand. The way his hand healed precluded his ever roping again, but he had taught himself to favor his left hand for cooking as his right became the helper. The left, grown stronger and more dexterous with pots and skillets, delivered a firm but gentle touch with the round and yeasty forms of bread, their curves like those of a woman.

Raylene felt heat in the back of her throat as she turned, dropped her gear, and stepped toward him. He carried the aromas of man-sweat and the lamb he had roasted for the crew's supper, overlaid with kitchen soap and the peppermints he constantly chewed.

"You are leaving," he said.

"I meant to stay."

"Is it about your father?"

Raul had been the one to bring her the letter bearing news about her father and had driven her to Farmingdale's rail depot. Knowing that on the job, she wouldn't be carrying cash, he had pressed four and a half dollars of his own into her hand. He didn't know the rest, about her sister's death or how her uncle was a killer. She said, "Didn't I warn you about those peppermints?"

"Before you bother my tooth, I have a question. Are you wearing what you usually wear beneath those *pantalones*?"

"Wouldn't you like to know."

"Only if you want me to."

He had been her one indulgence during her time with the ranch, a secret from the crew, she hoped, though secrets on a ranch were hard to keep, at least the physical kind. She inhaled the fragrance of him then gripped the front of his shirt with both hands and pulled him into a kiss so hard that his body responded with surprise before he wrapped his arms around her. They had never kissed before. Kissing had seemed an expression of commitment between sweethearts. He and she suited each other in ways of the flesh and the call of wide-open spaces, but they were not sweethearts. As frustration at the idea of leaving her job rose inside her, she wanted to crush something or bite something.

"Ow," he said, pulling back. "*Dios mío*." He narrowed dark eyes at her. "You are feeling rough."

When he licked two fingers and pulled them wetly from his mouth, her legs went weak. Then he gripped her arm and drew her along to the back stall where the clean hay smelled of sky and earth. There she grabbed his shirt and yanked the snaps of it open. Her northern wind meeting his southern heatwave would produce enough electricity to burn clean through them. She would feel real again. She would feel whole. Just as important — when they were done crashing into each other, he would let her go.

Murphy zig-zagged across Nebraska, flying his coupe past withered fields of corn stubble and open land grown thick with grass and weeds. Twice he sped around a rising corner to encounter a slow-rolling machine of the fields. Each time, heart in his throat, he floored the throttle and swerved into the opposing lane, sending his fedora and overcoat sliding across the seat. As his adrenaline rose with the engine's growl, his adoration spiked for this embodiment of the freedom wrought by man's marvelous combustion engine.

Four times he pulled over in small towns or along a country road to stand out in the late September sun and stretch his back, reminded of why he regularly traveled by rail to distant locations. Rail travel was practical. He could walk the aisles or stand on the platform between cars while the train ate up the miles. But man-oh-man, there was a thrill to motoring the swells of a grassy sea, gravel roads rising and dipping between hills and buttes that boxed the sky.

After hours of turning west and north, and slowing to read bleached-out road signs, he began to worry that he might not make South Dakota by nightfall. He bought fuel in Norfolk and then again in Valentine. The longer he drove, the greater his anticipation for arriving at a place tied to the little sister. She was a compilation of contradictions, a puzzle that begged for an answer.

Somehow, he missed a turn north. By the time he realized it, it was too late to make a correction, so he pressed on, turning up through a corner of Wyoming before circling into South Dakota. By now his back sang a refrain of aches, a portent of what could come — shooting pains in his right leg. That old foe. It occurred to him that he knew little about this countryside of tiny towns beyond the reach of the U.P. Most seemed comprised of a few ranch houses set back from a crossroads or ranch driveways radiating outward from a country church that sat like a beacon for the scattered faithful.

In his drive to follow this northern line of inquiry, he had overlooked the need for information about travelers' hotels or rooming houses up this way. Far north, Rapid City would be large enough for such, but what would he find in Oglala, the tiny town he was actually headed for?

As the sinking sun threw a purple cloak over everything, Murphy's side window began to radiate cold. He steered east again, finally passing a weather-beaten sign marking entry to the Pine Ridge Reservation.

At long last, with stars winking overhead, he reached Oglala, guiding his auto slowly past parched plots of land holding small, weary-looking houses, most of them with a glow of lantern light showing through thin curtains. Some of the houses sprouted corrals containing the shapes of horses standing in starlight.

With his stomach growling at his recollection of the roast pork and wedge of cherry pie he'd eaten for lunch, he realized that he should have purchased a meal for the road at that little Valentine restaurant called Dine Inn. Back then, his meal planning had been usurped by a growing anticipation over gaining proximity to a little sister whom time and distance had painted with a dangerous outline and sensuous colors that pulsed inside him.

Oglala's business district held a half-dozen battered buildings, most with hand-lettered signs and hitching posts. One appeared to be a market, closed up for the night. At an angle across from the market sat a windowless building with two older vehicles outside and a thin line of light seeping out around its doorway. He had been hoping for a place marked EATS open at this hour, but no luck. Instead, he would have to seek sustenance at the market tomorrow morning while watching for the woman he sought.

A bigger problem than supper was a decided lack of travelers' lodgings. Reaching the end of the commercial-looking buildings, he stopped his auto in its lane and gazed out to where the road curved through the eastern outskirts of Oglala on the edge of a great black nothingness. His were the lone headlamps casting pale circles on the two-lane asphalt. Overhead shone uncountable stars. According to his map, this road led to the next town over, which was Pine Ridge, but it too was a tiny dot, which meant another sparse collection of unlit buildings set upon a dark earth.

Maneuvering his vehicle onto the shoulder, Murphy pointed it back toward Oglala's clot of businesses, studying which of them might contain postal services. Not one of them displayed the stars and stripes of an official office, but the little sister held an Oglala postal box, which meant a postal counter was present in town, most likely in the market.

The only enterprise showing signs of life was across the street, and at this hour, likely to be a saloon thwarting federal laws against access to alcohol by Indians. The good news was that it would undoubtedly be warmer than the interior of his auto and offer a chance for a stretch and a gander at some local residents. He could sample a slug of whatever spirits or beer they had available, and if he was lucky, there might be peanuts. He checked his pocket watch — the time was ten minutes to nine. Shoving his gloves and two aspirin into his pockets and his hat onto his head, Murphy exited his auto and stretched a bit before crossing the road.

For a moment, he entertained the notion that he would step through the door to find the little sister in conversation, a payoff for his many days on the road. For an impossibly neat wrap-up of his case, she would be wearing the missing necklace and the rose gold ring. Fantasy, and he knew it. Then came the tug of warning that always accompanied his approach to an unknown. He wasn't familiar with Indian reservations. Small towns, yes, but not this gathering spot with lumber walls weathered to splinters and shards. It looked pretty rough.

He shook off the tingling at the back of his neck. He need not take a seat, but could stand at the bar for two fingers of heat that would quiet his belly and reward his long day of travel. In the silence of the night, he could make out muffled sounds of male voices and laughter. Ten minutes inside would do, or maybe twenty, just long enough to thaw his limbs while deciding whether to drive further in the hope of finding a bed for the night. And there was always the option of attempting sleep upon his automobile's unyielding seat. As he had read in many places and experienced for himself: *Nothing ventured, nothing gained.*

He pulled the saloon door open and stepped into the dark, smoky room. A half-dozen Indian men turned toward him as every note of laughter and conversation died away. From a pool table to one side came the sound of one ball striking another — *Tick*.

Murphy could hear his own breathing. As was his practice, he paused to scan the interior. A wood-fed stove in the corner threw waves of heat.

The man peering across the bar between two rough-dressed men spoke first. "You lost?"

"I could use a whiskey," said Murphy, removing his hat.

While the others remained mute, the bartender gave Murphy a once-over. "Don't get many travelers," he said, "and not this late."

"I probably should have stopped back in Valentine."

"But you didn't."

"No."

"You from the Agency?" asked one of the others. "We don't drink with the law."

Following that remark, Murphy could not acknowledge his actual profession, which nearly everyone mistook for the law.

Having come this far, though, he wanted a slug of liquid heat which might be all he'd get until morning. Also, he was sworn to fulfill his duties to the best of his abilities and he intended to do just that. He rolled his shoulders to loosen them. "Just needed a break," he said, his expression and voice carefully neutral. "Been on the road all day. I'd be glad for a whiskey if you've got some."

One of the drinkers jabbed another with his elbow. "Might be a jobs man lookin' for workers. We could go on the public works."

Murphy had no quarrel with locals wanting a little humor at his expense. Letting others joke sometimes loosened tongues, which could be helpful. He could feel their distrust of him, though, a minor hindrance. He stepped to the bar as the man behind it lifted a brown bottle from a small display.

"One shot?" the bartender asked.

"A double would suit me better, with a water on the side."

"That's six bits."

The price was twice that of the good stuff in the city, but Murphy shrugged to show his acceptance at paying a price for being tagged a stranger. His first sip of cheap spirits brought water to his eyes. He blinked and swallowed hard as the bartender watched. Pulling out his aspirin, he drank them down with the water. "Do you serve any food?" he asked.

"Nope."

"Then here's to liquid supper."

The two men at the pool table had gone back to their game. There was the *thwack* of pool cues and the crack of balls. Murphy thought he'd get the bartender talking about something random. "You know much about the town of Pine Ridge?" That next small dot on his map. If the man said it was larger, he might look for a traveler's hotel there.

"You got business in Pine Ridge?"

133

One of the others broke in, giving Murphy an out. "You going to pow-wow?"

The bartender looked at Murphy, who conjured a tale. "Well, I write for a magazine. You know *Life*? They might be interested in a story about what takes place at a pow-wow."

"So, you brought your typewriter ..."

"Not on the road." Murphy flashed his pocket notebook. "I take notes. The typing comes later."

The bartender narrowed his eyes. "Where'd you say you're from?"

"I didn't, but I'm from Kansas City."

"You been invited to pow-wow by someone?"

Murphy assumed an innocent look. "Uh, no. But I drive all over finding stories that show ... American life. Subjects that might interest magazine readers."

The bartender didn't look to be buying this line, but Murphy held the man's gaze. Finally, the man said, "It's not some kinda curiosity for putting in magazines. It's personal." He picked up a glass to polish.

Murphy took another sip and made like the man had a point. "I'm not saying I force things to get a story, but if I don't ask, I don't get."

The man to Murphy's left leaned toward him. "Seems you got a regular job. How 'bout you stand me a drink and we'll play some pool. Them guys got to be almost done." He turned toward the men at the pool table. "Stoney!" he shouted. "Gimme that table. You had it long enough." He looked expectantly back at Murphy.

Murphy weighed his options as he glanced around. The atmosphere did not encourage questions about the little sister or her dead relatives, even though in a town this size it was likely they knew of her or her family. Another half hour in the place would demonstrate his amenability. After that he'd be thawed out and in need of shut-eye. "I guess so," he said. "Just one though. I've got some figuring to do."

The man swayed a little as he climbed down off his bar stool. "I'll help you. Ask any of these bloods. I'm good at figuring."

Ten

As sunrise smeared the sky with shades of gold, Raylene was already in the saddle, headed east toward Red Shirt Table and reservation land, her possessions tied to her saddle. She rode with her hair in one plait and her Plainsman hat pulled down low, her hands light on the reins. Mary's canvas coat over a denim shirt provided insulation against the chill of morning.

Recollections of Raul's intimate attentions had lingered throughout her preparations, the deftness of his hands as they undid her britches (even the damaged one). His hands and that mouth of his as he ... When they parted, he left the stable first. She waited a few minutes before heading for the bunkhouse for a long soak in the bathing room, an addition made the year before she arrived.

Before taking his leave, Raul had pulled her to him for what felt to her like the very last time, speaking words he'd never voiced before. "Whatever you are doing next, I hope you remain safe." He would never have pledged any feelings for her or asked her to do so. Theirs was not an arrangement aimed toward future togetherness. It existed only for the pleasures possible within the time skimmed from evenings following a work day in proximity to others. He expressed concern the way all the hands did, without fanfare, in carefully neutral words that though he could not know it, boosted her hope of surviving a face-off with Ray.

Kota's ambling gait was comforting in its muscularity and grace. Just before dawn, she had found him standing at the corral gate as if expecting her. Sensitive to her mood, he quivered as she inspected each of his hooves and picked them clean. Running a hand over his withers and legs, she felt for any sign that he needed rest or care instead of a long day's ride. He accepted, as always, the curb bit that was easy in his mouth, his woven headstall, and a blanket topped by her California saddle.

She steered Kota on a familiar route, which left her free to send her thoughts forward to Oglala and Wilma Manheart, whose nephew Leonard raced bareback on a circuit that encompassed small towns in and around reservations. Racing was an event, a celebration really, in which Leonard rode the one racer that mattered to her uncle, sired by the first horse Raylene had learned to ride. Dark Cloud was a racer that her uncle had gentled and trained for the circuit before losing ownership due to a poverty of funds. Ray had sold the steed for not enough to pay the bills he had owed for too long.

When young, she had watched a bareback relay for the first time from atop her father's shoulders. Or had it been Ray who lifted her so high that she looked beyond the waving fields and distant mountains all the way to the seam where the earth became sky? She rolled the recollection over in her mind — had her champion been Father, or Ray? Both had been so fluidly present that where one of them left off, the other began. At the time it had not mattered which was which as long as she and Annie could count on one of them.

Kota slowed as he brought Raylene to a place where a narrow creek ran through a culvert beneath the road. The creek marked the spot for turning toward Oglala and the home where Wilma raised Lizzy, a child more animal than most, whom Raylene had not seen since spring.

Murphy peered through swollen eyes and one cracked

eyeglass lens at the morning light glittering through the moth-bitten curtains hanging at the window. Male voices came from elsewhere in the house, radiating through the walls and into the room where he sat on the floor, hands bound behind him and one ankle roped to a chest of drawers. Cold seeped up through the floorboards, chilling him through.

He recalled how the heat of the previous night's saloon had warmed him, aided by the bitter-tasting booze. The first game of pool had gone fine against a young man named Henry, a fair enough player who steadied himself against the pool table between turns. Murphy was no master with a cue but was smart enough to recognize that he ought not to win any games on foreign turf. Tired and a bit blurry, he had agreed to a second game. The men drinking at the bar seemed intent upon their conversations, but Murphy remained watchful and refrained from brandishing his silver pocket watch. This meant he didn't know precisely, but now estimated the time as before midnight when things went haywire.

Henry had asked Murphy to stand him another round, which Murphy declined. Buying booze for one man in a room full of drinkers seemed a good way to find oneself buying rounds for all. They were finishing their second game of pool, with Murphy losing, when the man who answered to the name Stoney sauntered over as if to claim a game against the winner. Instead, he lifted the overcoat Murphy had draped across a spare chair and began rummaging through its pockets.

"Hey now," called Murphy, moving in that direction, "don't do that."

Stoney flourished Murphy's notebook and pen. Before Murphy could reach him, out came the photo of Annie Moon wearing the missing jewelry. Murphy made a grab for it, but met an outthrust arm. "What's this?" said Stoney, squinting at the image. "Joseph. This looks like your girl Annie. Don't this look like her?"

"Give it here," growled Murphy, reaching for the photo. Someone else intervened, shoving Murphy backwards as two others converged to block his way.

The one called Joseph had grabbed the black and white photo. He turned toward Murphy, his face contorted with rage. "What the hell you mean by this? You coming here pretending you're passing through when the whole time you got my Annie in your pocket?"

Another of the men peering over Joseph's shoulder cried out, "Look there. It shows he's got his arm around her." Five faces glared at Murphy. One of them said, "That why you came here, to show off how you knew her?"

"You've got it wrong," said Murphy to the room.

Someone else said, "Maybe he's the one that killed her," as other voices spoke at once: "Fuckin' *wasícu*," and, "All that bullshit." And worst of all — "Let's fucking show him."

What followed was a blur of fists and arms and elbows. Shouting, shoving, hands grabbing. Murphy got a couple of good licks in before someone clocked him with a pool cue, knocking him to the floor. After that they found his railroad badge and there were more epithets about lawmen. They had it wrong about the lawman part, but by then his own words were coming out sideways, along with one of his teeth and a quantity of blood. He'd bloodied a couple of them too.

Now, here he was at these strangers' mercy, minus his coat and watch and though he couldn't reach his left pants pocket, he was sure his money clip and the wallet with his travel cash was missing. He scanned the room, such as he could through his one cracked eyeglass lens, noting an iron bed against one wall and a wooden chair opposite. Hooks on the wall held a few shirts and a winter coat, all decidedly masculine. He vaguely recalled being dragged from the saloon and shoved into a truck occupied by three others, but not which of the men had driven.

Last night's bar fight was a first for Murphy. He'd never been part of such a melee but could attest that there wasn't much to recommend it unless you came out on the winning side. Every inch of him ached. His head, his guts. His left arm throbbed mightily, probably broken, all because he'd come looking for the little sister and that damn jewelry. All those hours behind the wheel, all those imaginings about sizing up the little sister and studying her up close. All of it, down the drain.

More sounds coming through the wall cut through the fog surrounding Murphy. Through the pounding in his head, he recognized the heated voices of men. They were probably discussing what to do about him.

At Raylene's signal, her piebald stepped off the road and onto unfenced land, his hooves crunchy frosty grass. Here and there came the whirr of a resilient grasshopper or the flicker of a sparrow rousted from its search for breakfast bugs. The air tasted of damp earth. The morning breeze carried a warning of the coming cold season, but bundled warmly with the sun on her, Raylene rode easy in the saddle.

They alternated between walking and cantering, and when they galloped, she gloried once more at Kota's ease on the land, the way he moved as if he were one with the wind and she but a bird upon his back. At mid-morning, the outskirts of Oglala took shape and they slowed to a walk. Kota, ever calm, seemed barely winded as he carried Raylene past wooden houses sprinkled like bread crumbs among the fields. A few of the homes had gardens; almost all sprouted laundry lines made from ropes.

After a little longer, Wilma's property came into view with its tiny house of lumber and barn wood atop concrete blocks set behind a small market that fronted the main road. Two of the house's north-facing windows had been replaced with the windshields of old automobiles, but its best feature was its color — originally painted blood red, it had since faded to the color of a sunset filtered through distant clouds. The north side, which faced Wilma's market glowed reddest, with a patina worn soft by rain, snow, and the eternal wind.

Raylene halted Kota roughly twenty yards out in a patch of grass worth grazing. Tucking her riding gloves into a saddle bag, she left him with his reins trailing while she went to make use of Wilma's outhouse. Afterwards, she drank from the pump and filled a garden pail for Kota, setting it close to where he was already nibbling the tenderest shoots. Only then did she head for the back door.

"Hello," she called into the kitchen recess. "It's Raylene."

"Come in," came Wilma's reply. "We're in the bedroom."

Raylene crossed through the living space, past one small table for eating and another piled high with Wilma's basket making supplies — willow branches resting in buckets of water, tin can lids punched with nail holes, knives for dividing strips into threads — and into the bedroom, where Wilma, roughly forty, plump of figure but strong, had skinny little Elizabeth pinned to the bed with one arm. Lizzy — her late-life child.

The girl wriggled and squirmed, bicycling her legs in the air. "Oof," said Wilma at a kick to the stomach. "It is one of those mornings."

Raylene stepped close to Lizzy and waggled her fingers before the child's face. "*T'élanuwé*," she said soothingly, "little lizard. Have you no mercy for your mother?"

The child turned toward Raylene and gave an animal

grimace, her way of smiling. There was no telling whether she registered voices only, or if she understood the words she could not imitate. Wilma wrestled a clean cotton diaper onto the child and pinned it. She reached for a faded blue skirt and fussed at the child's hair. She had not yet looked at Raylene. "What brings you back so soon? No more mail has come for you."

Raylene shed her boots and crawled up onto the bed, pulling Lizzy into her lap for the buttoning process. "Thank you for sending Henry to the ranch with that letter. It told the news about my father."

"But not about your sister? Oh —" She lifted a hand to her mouth.

News traveled like air among people largely without telephones, but not *that* fast. Raylene could think of only one source for Wilma's knowledge about Annie. Raymond had told her what had transpired in Kansas City.

Pulling on a short coat, Wilma said, "That's why you are here."

"I came to bring you this." Raylene pulled two big bills from her pouch and held them out to the woman.

Wilma blinked at the bills in Raylene's hand. "I thank you but I am flush right now. Ray brought cash and some silver jewelry for me to sell." A long pause followed before Wilma spoke again. "He also bought all the jerked meat I had on hand."

"Did he stay?"

Wilma shook her head. "Something was wrong. He was favoring his arm."

"Did he say where he was headed?"

The woman shrugged. "I would only be guessing. Montana maybe?"

Raylene studied the woman who had at times been Ray's

woman. If she could, she might still try to protect Ray.

Wilma continued. "Will you try to find him? He's not well, I could tell that much."

"I am not well either. He has made me an orphan."

Wilma's shoulders sagged as she spoke to her hands. "I have to check the market. Henry was supposed to open it this morning but he hasn't come yet."

"Doesn't Leonard help out?"

"I haven't heard from him since he talked Henry into telling him about my money box. If he shows up, I'll see to it that he'll need help getting up off the ground. I'll go post a sign for opening late. Then I'll cook you some breakfast."

Raylene waved away the offer. Raul had risen early to fix her a big plate of food and handed her a package of biscuits and ham for the road. They had taken care not to touch each other this morning, not even let their hands brush, because doing so would provide fodder for gossip or complaints. To Wilma she said, "I'll wait here."

Wilma left and there was the sound of her boots crossing the front stoop. Raylene sat holding Lizzy, the girl stroking Raylene's leather trousers as Raylene pictured where Ray might be headed. Though she expected an explanation for why he had killed her father, she wondered what he knew about Annie's "natural" death at only twenty-eight. Would she know if a plague had taken her, or some female troubles? Or had she possessed a heart weakness that no one could have saved her from? Internal forces, external forces, how could a person know?

Lizzy began to fuss and Wilma had not yet returned. Perhaps Henry had arrived and they were talking business. There would be matters of inventory or credit for certain customers or a bit of stock to be unpacked. Like his mother, Henry had a strong back but he had been born sickly, though with fewer troubles than Lizzy. Years ago, Raylene's grandmother Helma had delivered Wilma of her son and instructed other women in how to assist. Too young for school at that point, Raylene had been at her grandmother's side for the births of many of Oglala's children.

Now she pulled one of the bed pillows close. Leaning back into it, she opened her mind to words that needed release. "Little lizard, you are like a sister to me. Perhaps we are even blood, I do not know. But there is another sister, my own, whose hands will never hold you again. She was born under the spring moon which gives a pale light, so she was given her own name. That is because our parents sometimes broke with tradition. Like the moon, she carried her smile with her. People who saw her felt her fair hand with their worries and their feelings, so she was never without friends. When I was born under a slice of moon, I was given a small moon name.

"My sister had many friends, and all who knew her wanted to keep her for themselves. But she grew into a young woman who found the ways of the land and its people were not for her. For her were the ways of cities full of other people, different from us, and with those people she knew satisfaction.

"I saw her at times. My work kept us apart, but each time I saw how she was glad, my heart was also glad. And then ..." Here, Raylene's voice faltered as images of a smiling Annie came to her, full of life and hope — hope that a girl from a reservation tribe could fit into the outside world. "Then suddenly, she left us, with barely a track in the dust to note her passing. And I am the one to look for any tracks she has left."

Lizzy had drifted off to sleep, which gave Raylene the chance to do what she knew not to ask of Wilma. The woman seemed defensive about Ray, which meant she might be reluctant to give up information that could bring him harm.

In Wilma's bureau she located a carved wooden box with silver corners on it, Ray's handiwork. Quickly she sifted its contents to uncover a small folded page with printing. This she unfolded and studied a moment before returning every item to its place.

Back on the bed, she turned her thoughts to Oglala boys — men by now — who might have known Annie well enough to intercept her in the city and do her harm. Had anyone here known her better than Raylene had? There were those who attended the same Indian school in classes strictly segregated by the nuns. To reach across that divide, scribbled notes were passed from hand to hand, but most of the students attending the reservation school lived near enough that personal attractions could be indulged outside of school, on walks or horseback rides along dirt roads and at swimming holes dotting the streams and rivers. Even those who rode in from the unnamed places between towns formed friendships and rivalries, the boys posturing for attention by plucking at the girls' shorn hair or throwing pebbles, the girls granting shy smiles and occasional kisses.

None of the boys who had grown into young men seemed a match for dreamy, hardworking Annie. Raylene remembered their childhood hijinks and escapades. The stolen wallet, the tool shed set aflame. No one paid notice to a little sister at the periphery, a person with the standing of a rock or a bunch of grass. But little sisters had eyes and ears.

One particularly smitten boy, William Talking Bird, might have received the favor of Annie's kisses, but when she left for the city, she took none of the old gang with her. Later, Raylene heard mention of one man or another, city men who had taken her to dinner or a motion picture, new names mentioned each time Raylene visited. None of the names were reservation names, but now she wished Annie had taken along a beau from the rez. Someone who would have watched over her, probably against Annie's own objections. Someone local for Raylene to ask about Annie's city life would be better than what she had now — nobody who could answer anything. At least until Ray provided what he knew, either willingly or under threat.

With a bang, the front door slammed, rousing Raylene from her reverie and waking Lizzy. It was Wilma, out of breath and wearing a frown. "Stoney is outside my market rummaging through a fancy car, and he has trouble written all over him."

The arguing Murphy could hear in the reservation house died away as the front door slammed. One of them, or more than one, thought Murphy, had gone out. He again tried with his roped ankle to pull against the bureau to which it was tied, with no luck, and twisted his hands against their bonds which sent shooting pains through his left arm and brought up what little was left in his stomach so that he turned the best he could and vomited to one side. Exhausted, he slumped once more against the wall beside him.

At some point, he was roused by the stomp of boots vibrating through the wooden floor and opened his eyes as the pool player named Henry came in to stand with his hands on his hips. The young man gave Murphy's shoe a kick as he flashed a gap-toothed grin.

"Hey you," said Henry. "What are they going to find in your car?" When he noticed the puddle of Murphy's vomit, he backed away.

Through the pounding in his head and the stink rising up around him, Murphy marshaled his thoughts and gazed at Henry through his one remaining, cracked spectacle lens. The crack separated Henry into disjointed sections, which seemed a match for the thoughts inside Murphy's head. "Who do you mean?" he asked.

Henry paused as if parsing Murphy's reply. He gave a sigh that signaled Murphy's stupidity. "Joseph mostly. You sure made him mad."

Murphy had known he was in for trouble when the one called Stoney found the photo of Annie and began waving it around. His plan had been to question the little sister as he showed her the picture, but instead of being an aid to discovery, the photo had delivered his own undoing. Perhaps this dull young man could reveal a bit of local knowledge, but a fog had rolled in to envelope Murphy's mind. He swam against it while managing, "You ever see anyone wearing that jewelry in the photo?"

"Sure."

"Who was it?"

Henry wore a *You can't fool me* look. "Anybody can see it's *Annie* wearing that jewelry."

Murphy nodded to himself as opaque thoughts swirled round. He said, "Do you play pool with those others? Regularly?"

"Sometimes."

"They should treat you right. If they're really friends."

Henry kicked at Murphy's shoe. "That's none of yours."

Clearly, Henry was the one left out of important decisions between friends. He'd be the one bullied by the others, who ended up beholden to them for so-called friendship.

Murphy asked, "What happens next?"

The young man hitched up his pants. "They went to get your car. Joseph knows how to drive all the kinds, and he takes them apart too."

Murphy wanted to ask something, a question he ought to ask, but it wouldn't form properly in his mind.

Henry continued. "They can't keep your car unless they lose *you*."

Murphy's head throbbed worse than ever from trying to focus through his broken eyeglasses. His thoughts were shutting down; something was wrong inside his head. But he held to Henry's words as he fought against the murk swallowing his mind. "Huh?" was all he managed.

Henry stood a moment as if watching a distant scene in his mind. Then he said, "There's lots of places to lose someone. Enough nobody could ever check them all."

Eleven

Wilma came back from her market and told Raylene, "That damn son of mine hasn't showed. After I started the market stove to take the chill off, Mazy came for some corn meal, so I let her in and that took a few minutes. When she left, I opened the curtains to let the sun in, and there was a fancy car parked where I could see it just across from the saloon.

"I figured it was broken, maybe someone's friend came to visit and left it there. But who was there but Stoney and another one of that bunch, Joseph. Troublemakers my Henry follows around.

"I went out on to the car. Joseph wouldn't look at me. Stoney smelled like a drunk dog. He said the owner had sent him for it but it wouldn't start. So, I asked for a name and he went quiet until I threatened to call the BIA man from the market phone — you know, the only one close by — so then he said they have a stranger, a man from the city, over at Joseph's, and he's got a photograph of Annie."

Wilma could have hit Raylene with a rock and had the same effect. *A photograph of Annie?*

"The car wouldn't start when he tried it," continued Wilma. "When the sun warms it more, I think he will take it."

To Raylene's mind, *who* had come to town with a photograph of Annie mattered less than the fact that someone — anyone — had a photograph of her sister when she herself did not. She lifted Lizzy from her lap and set her to one side. "I have to see it," she told Wilma.

"It's parked on the road, unless they got it started."

"The *photograph*."

"Oh. Stoney said it's back at Joseph's."

Raylene visualized Wilma's first-born, Henry, and his friends from school days, most of them Annie's age or hers. Stoney, whose proper name was Lyle Stoneman, was the youngest, but he always tried to out-tough the rest. "Does Joseph still live in the house his parent's left him?" she asked, pulling on her boots.

"The one on the east side, with the kitchen added on the back. You know he is full of stories. There might be nothing to it."

Raylene backtracked from the bedroom, past the table of weaving supplies and through the kitchen recess. She had not been to Joseph's house since the year his father died, but she knew the back way to it and had the swiftest means for getting there.

Wilma's words followed Raylene as she pulled the back door closed. "Watch yourself — those boys play rough."

Raylene and Kota flew at a gallop. In no time, the rear of Joseph's family home came into view. Pulling up short, Raylene slid from her saddle, jumped the two back steps and banged in through the back door, startling Henry.

"Hey!" he said. "You're back from ... uh ... wherever it was."

Raylene noted the kitchen's disarray. Cupboards stood open and a whirl of gnats turned circles above a heap of dirty dishes in the sink. Next to the cook stove lay a flea-bitten sleeping bag. The relatively roomy kitchen had been added onto the tiny house during Joseph's parents' days. "I've been speaking with your mother," said Raylene. "She said you were supposed to open the market this morning."

Henry straightened and his mouth dropped open a little as

he glanced away and back. "Did you come on Kota? I think I heard him." He strained a bit as if trying to see around Raylene to catch a glimpse of her cow pony.

"Your mother saw Lyle and Joseph this morning," said Raylene. "She seems worried they'll get you into trouble. Again."

Henry appeared to be registering Raylene's words. "They're my friends," came his answer. "If Kota's here, can I pet him?"

"You can rub him down if you can find a rag for it. He would like that. Lyle told your mother that there's a man here."

Henry's eyes scanned the adjacent front room and stopped on the opening that led to the one bedroom. "Uh, no. No man's here. You should call him Stoney. He wants to be called Stoney." When he turned toward Raylene again, he would not meet her gaze.

Raylene lifted a hand to her chin. "There is no man here? That surprises me. I never thought of your mother as a liar, but if you say so." The blasphemy hung like a challenge in the air between them.

Henry studied the buttoned front of Raylene's coat. "Them guys are not going to like this."

Raylene ignored the warning. "If there's someone here with a photograph of my sister, I want to see it."

Henry's head began to bob in a compact motion, as if powered by a small inner rhythm that only he could hear. Raylene watched him and waited.

"Isn't anyone supposed to know," he said finally.

"Because there will be trouble?"

Henry shrugged. "Yeah."

Raylene stepped into the front room, sidestepping a beat-up couch piled with dirty clothes and skirting a wicker chair that held a heap of gray wool overcoat. Henry caught up to her in a flash as she said, "I guess I'll just look around. If there's no man here, I won't find him."

Murphy's stomach had given a lurch at Henry's suggestion that the other men might take him somewhere far from any town and leave him there, perhaps still bound. Though he didn't know this state's backcountry, he was pretty sure he would not find it hospitable.

The throbbing in his head joined knife-like stabs running down his right leg to become a physical pounding that registered in waves. He tried to decide if the waves were themselves a sound and not his tortured mind. The voice of his coupe's engine, for instance, telegraphed movement. The association sent him drifting through thoughts of motoring along a country road that rose and rose toward blackened clouds until he broke upward through the thunderstorm into a sheet of misty rain. A slap of lightning sounded like a slammed door.

Suddenly there came voices growing closer. He made out Henry saying, "Raylene, you can't — Joseph's not here. You can't just —"

Raylene. Had he heard right? He squinted through his cracked lens at a shape forming in the doorway. His unaided eye saw only murk, which matched the thoughts stuck in the mud of his mind. The figure that spoke with Henry's voice looked too wide, with too many arms. And then it became two figures.

Henry's voice came again. "They said to wait."

A new, female-sounding voice said, "Why is this man tied?" as a figure moved enough to form the suggestion of a canvas coat and a western hat. The shapes sparked a thought in the cotton batting of his mind. *That black hair. The little sister.* Then a knife appeared in the figure's distorted hand, advancing toward him until it became as big as a sword beneath a circle of hat that blocked his view. Disbelief rose up as his sour tongue died in the desert of his mouth. He drew into himself as best he could while thinking he ought to protest — *Don't let her, don't let her...*

"Don't!" cried Henry as the knife closed in on Murphy.

When the rope fell away from his bound ankle, Murphy cried out from pain. The figure took off its hat, *her* hat, and leaned closer, the halves of her face not quite meeting. Murphy blinked to bring his unaided eye into focus, without success. Something told him that he was supposed to have found her, but instead she had found him. Prostrate on the floor, no less. He knew he had questions to ask her. Something about the railroad, or his boss. Something about something, but all he could muster was a scenario in which the little sister proved more dangerous than suggested by facts he'd been able to corroborate. He ought to use her name, a tactic that under the right circumstances could calm an opponent or at least reduce their animosity. This befuddlement was not helping. One word would signal benign intentions. His lips were gummy and sticking together. He wanted to say "sister" so the woman would know that he knew her as such, but what emerged came out a whisper that rose through the air and hung there: "Annie."

The woman turned and shouted something that started with the name Henry. Poor Henry, poor dull Henry, who took instructions not only from the group of thugs at the bar, but from the little sister too. Even without the others, Murphy, hands still tied, was outnumbered by the two now in the house with him. He closed his eyes to blot out the disjointed woman hovering in his fractured view and gave himself over to whatever would be his fate.

A moment later he startled at the touch of cool hands upon

his brow. Gently, they probed the area above his eye, continuing in a circuit around his skull until they found the knot on the back of his head. He winced.

"Ice would help," said the little sister. "But a wet kerchief will have to do. Henry, bring me a jug of drinking water and a glass."

"I might have to wash one."

"Just bring the cleanest you can find before this man fails further."

"There's already going to be trouble with what you've done."

Raylene unfolded to her full, half-cracked, half-blurred height. Her next words came out a growl. "Go. Get. Water."

As if certain Henry would do her bidding, she bent again to Murphy and spoke low. "I'm going to cut your hands free. If you are injured, this may cause further shock."

She was right. When Murphy's shoulders came free, he bugled like a wounded animal and the room began to spin, but her voice brought him back from the edge of his pain. "If you can stand to reach the bed, I'll tend to your injuries."

He rolled to one side and got his legs under him, his injured arm dangling useless. With the little sister's hand supporting his good elbow, he straightened and moved gingerly to perch on the edge of the bed. Before he knew it, a tumbler of water was in his working hand, and with assistance he was drinking from it. The first swallows tasted coppery and sour. His tongue found the empty, tender hole where a tooth had come out. Soon he felt his swollen gums, his tongue, and the cavern of his mouth flutter back to life. As that happened, the liquid, which had no flavor but that of well water began to taste glorious, better than any wine, better than any whiskey.

"Finish that and I'll pour another," she said. "Water is the first cure."

Murphy's innards flared in protest at the influx of fluid, but he held firm and finished a second tumbler's worth. Before long, his thoughts began to form better shapes. He tried to study the woman who had shed her bulky coat. Here she was before him. After all the days since his brief glimpse of her in the undertaker's parlor, she was in the room beside him. He had found her in the town dictated by logic, but now he could not even view her properly. Instead of launching into an interview, a face-to-face on the street or at the postal window, in which he would pursue the truth that lay beneath the tangle of who knew who and what they had done, he was now, wretchedly, at her mercy.

He could tell she was compact, her hair a flow of black — he remembered that from the undertaker's parlor — and dark eyes that he could not just now bring into focus. She had opened the room's one window, through which now poured a fresh breeze. Beneath the prairie air he could still smell his own rank sweat and the odor of boozy bile, but from this close vantage, the woman seemed to smell of grass and wind and something wild. Or else, and he was just lucid enough to recognize this, he only imagined such fragrances for her.

He ran his tongue around in his mouth wondering if it would work now and tried speaking again. "Little sister," is what he said.

Raylene said, "I will bind your arm before the others return. Then the words you speak had better be true." She considered the man dressed in a suit of matching pieces that had seen better days. That suit, that reddish hair. She could detect no pocket watch, but still ... this man could be the same one from the undertaker's parlor, the one who had given her Annie's purse but no information about Annie's death. If this was that man from the railroad, what was he doing here in Oglala, and more importantly, did he possess, as Wilma had reported, a photograph of Annie?

The man before her had spoken her sister's name, the word itself a gem that Raylene carried from her earliest re-membered days along with the knowledge that she had a sister to sleep beside. A sister who demonstrated the ways in which girls walked through the world. When uncertain how to overcome a problem or face another test of cunning, or even simply survive another day with nuns who found so much lacking in each student, she need only repeat the name to herself ... *Annie* ... *Annie* ... and the day was redeemed. They were unalike, the two of them, yet so much like two halves of a whole. Now the memory of that time seemed sharp-edged and black, like obsidian. Still a gem, but one the color of sorrow.

She blinked and set herself to the task at hand. Wetting her kerchief with water, she had him press it to the knot on the back of his head. As she probed his limp arm through his shirt sleeve, he sucked a breath between gritted teeth. Turning up his sleeve, she found his arm swollen below the elbow but no bones poking through the skin. The upper arm seemed sound, which was good. The best she could do was splint his damaged forearm. "Henry," she said, "I need two or three sticks for splints and an old shirt."

He answered from the spot he had taken up by the door. "Aw. I help you at all, they'll give me hell."

"You have already dishonored your mother today. Now is the time to do better."

"I know you know my mother."

"And I also know you. Am I not the one who taught you how to ride without a saddle, and the proper way to circle a rope? And other things before and after that. Shall I name them?" It seemed a shame to wield such words against Henry, but she needed his cooperation.

A moment of silence preceded Henry's exit from the doorway.

Murphy began, "Thank you for the help."

"You are not out of danger yet, nor am I, but I aim for us both to leave this place without further damage." She knew that Joseph and Stoney stirred up trouble when together. Like loose dogs with the wind in their fur and thoughts of mayhem, they would find sport in chasing down a bit of prey. Henry was probably not in any real danger from them. Though he would take their threats to heart, he would hold their secrets close and they would be stupid to renounce the butt of their jokes and foolery. Without Henry, they had only each other to bully and tougher foes to target.

"Tell me your name," said Raylene.

"John Murphy," came the answer, "from Kansas City."

Her instinct had been right. "I remember thinking that you would do well to leave me to my business, yet here you are — oh, good, Henry. Those sticks will do."

Henry handed over an old shirt which Raylene cut into strips, instructing Henry how to assist her in splinting Murphy's forearm. Had John Murphy been an ordinary traveler with a bit of bad luck, one who could stay another day, she would brew for him a drink to reduce the swelling and apply a poultice to the knot on his head. He would be wise, though, to leave this house, this town, and this land before another hour had passed.

"If you want to fuss with Kota, go ahead," she told Henry before turning back to inspect the splint on the detective's arm. "He knows you, but he will still expect you to treat him right." There came the throaty sound of a vehicle growing closer on the road leading to the house. "Now is the time," Raylene continued, "to make yourself scarce."

Henry looked from Raylene to Murphy and back again.

"Are you sure? They are — even with you, they'll be angry as hell."

Raylene smiled so that on the outside she looked calm. "They are not strangers to me," she said, "so if things get ugly, they will get ugly in both directions." She donned her coat and hat and took Murphy by the elbow to lead him from the room. With Henry headed for the back door, she stood Murphy against the living room wall and pulled the wicker chair with the overcoat closer. "John Murphy," she said. "Stand tall for as long as you can. They should see that you are strong in spite of them."

Positioning herself a step closer to the front door, she pulled Raymond's hunting knife from its sheath and assumed an air of casual concentration while cleaning a bit of grime from under her fingernails. Let them come.

In a flash, Stoney burst through the front door carrying a bottle of hooch and a jumble of clothing. "Henry! You should see — Hey!" Spotting Raylene, he pulled up short, so that Joseph nearly rammed him from behind.

"What?" cried Joseph. Suitcase in hand, he squeezed in to stand alongside Stoney.

Eyes narrowed, Stoney looked from Raylene to Murphy and back again. Then his gaze lit on the knife in Raylene's hand. "What the hell? Where's Henry?"

Raylene took in the men before her. Bleary-eyed, bruised, and rumpled, they looked like they had recently drunk the town dry, appearing in some ways worse off than John Murphy. "Hello, Lyle. Hello, Joseph. It looks like you have come into some new clothing."

Stoney clutched the items to his chest, as if to protect them from prying eyes. "It's none of your business." He took a half step forward. "No one invited you."

Raylene pointed Ray's knife at what the men carried.

"Where'd you get the fancy clothes? The suitcase?"

Joseph tossed the suitcase to one side. "You've got no business in my house."

"I have made this my business," said Raylene, "because word is that you have come into a photograph of Annie."

Joseph drew himself up as he scowled at Murphy then at Raylene. "She was *my* girl."

Raylene paused. While tending Murphy she had given some thought to Joseph's possessiveness of Annie and his attachment to a girl who had probably kissed him once, or let him pet her in the way of young people. Because he had tasted her mouth or touched the skin beneath her clothing, she remained lodged in his memory the way bees remember the taste and scent of wildflowers. Women held power over such creatures, rising to their touch but also to the caress of sun and moisture of storms. A flower existed for the bees, but also for its own sake. Annie was not Joseph's. She wasn't even Raylene's, not any longer.

Raylene had no intention of yielding to Joseph and the pollen of his memories. "She did not give you that photograph," she said, "so it is not yours. I have come to see it."

Joseph pointed an accusing finger at Murphy. "The lawman said he was here for another reason, but he lied. The fucker." He seemed to strain against some force within that wanted to have a go at Murphy again.

It was time for the railroad man to speak, but Raylene would do her best to keep from the others the fact that she'd met this man once before. "John Murphy," said Raylene as she held the gaze of the two before her. "What brought you here?"

Murphy cocked his head and cleared his throat to speak. "I work for the railroad — the U.P. — and my boss knew your sister. That's how I had her photograph."

"You lied about being a writer," snarled Joseph. "Drinking like you were some regular guy. But you weren't no writer."

"Fucker," said Stoney.

Raylene spoke to Murphy again. "If your boss knew Annie, why isn't *he* here?"

"Yeah," said Stoney. "She's Joseph's girl."

Raylene pointed her knife directly at Stoney. "She was not his girl when she died, and she is nobody's girl today, but she will always be my sister."

At this, Joseph bunched his fists but stood his ground. Raylene couldn't very well turn away from him or Stoney, so she waited.

Murphy found his voice. "I came for Miss Little Moon, to speak with her about her sister."

"Not to announce Annie's death." This, from Raylene.

"No. Because there are items gone missing," said Murphy.

"What items?" said Raylene.

"The jewelry she is wearing in that photograph has gone missing. I wanted to ask you about it."

"More lies," growled Joseph.

Murphy sighed. "My boss gave the jewelry to Annie Moon, but he shouldn't have. I'm just trying to buy back the items from whoever has them."

A wry smile lit Joseph's face as he reached into one of his pants pockets and pulled out a new-looking wallet full of cash. "I guess you won't be buying anything any time soon."

"Enough," declared Raylene. She had no way of knowing whether someone had taken jewelry from Annie before or after her death, or whether Annie kept such valuables hidden. "I want to see that photograph," she said to Joseph.

Joseph patted his pockets. He glanced at Stoney, who shrugged and said, "You had it last."

"You mean," said Raylene, "that all of this is about a

photograph you couldn't bother to hold onto?"

Joseph's face contorted in anger as he stabbed the air in Murphy's direction. "You weren't there. He was feeding us lies." He made as if to spit. "Writer — bah!" He took a step forward but Raylene pointed her knife at him.

"This ends right now," she said.

"Says who? We might not be done," said Joseph.

"Oh, you are done," said Raylene. "This man is leaving in his automobile and you will not molest him further."

"You think you and that knife are going to stop the two of us?" He waved a hand at Murphy. "He's in no shape."

Raylene held Joseph's gaze as she slowly sheathed her knife then lifted her hands to show they were empty. "I guess you need me to explain. You've got a stranger here who's been seriously injured, probably by drunk Indians, and it's known to people in town that a stranger is in this very house. For instance, one of you told Wilma Manheart that information, and if you told her, you probably bragged to someone else. And even if you didn't, I'm betting you weren't the only two in the bar when this man came in.

"And then there's the matter of a railroad employee being injured on the Pine Ridge, which would be of interest to South Dakota authorities and perhaps the Agency." She pressed her palms together. "Not only that, but word is that the BIA has an unsolved case over on the Rosebud where one of their buildings burned in a suspicious fire. If I remember right, that was ... back in May. Funny thing about buildings that go up in flames and no wildfire nearby, or misfired car. It's people who start those fires. People who may have been up that way delivering, say, a load of last year's hay coming off the Windrow Ranch." She paused for a breath. "I'm betting the BIA would be interested to know who makes deliveries like that."

Joseph threw a glance at Stoney, but for good measure Raylene added, "And then you get me involved by ransacking someone's automobile in the middle of town and mentioning a photograph of my sister, which connects me to all of this. So, I'm thinking you shouldn't feel disturbed to hear that the railroad man is going to drive away and you are going to stand aside while I assist him."

Joseph stared hard at her for a moment. "BIA? You wouldn't."

She flashed him a look that said *Try me* then turned to scoop up the crumpled overcoat, clearly a city coat. She motioned to Murphy before remembering that he wore broken glasses. "John Murphy," she said. "We'll go now." Murphy took a step forward from the wall and she stepped back to catch his good right arm, guiding him toward the front door, which stood ajar. She held the bundled overcoat over her arm and beneath it placed her hand upon the knife at her waist. Joseph gave her a disgusted look but moved to retrieve the suitcase he'd flung aside.

Stoney, standing near the doorway, seemed to tremble with a need to call Raylene's bluff, except that it wasn't a bluff, because she knew he had either assisted Joseph in setting the fire or else knew about it and celebrated its destruction with him afterwards. It was their way — to pick at the scab of the Agency's presence on land that had become their people's unfenced prison. They would also always protect each other, though not always through honorable means. The truth of it was that Joseph had seen the inside of a jail more times than Stoney had, meaning he was growing closer to receiving the sort of sentence applied to those deemed "incorrigible." Longer jail sentences accompanied such a determination, and if jailed for a long time, he could lose his house, for one, and his job delivering hay. Stoney, though, had less to lose, which made him more likely to take a risk against a stranger, or Raylene.

Stoney had her by four inches and thirty pounds. As she drew alongside, he leaned in so that every whisker on his face shone black and his rancid breath poured over her. She knew what he wanted — he wanted her to have to brush against him as she pushed past, giving him license to shove her into Murphy. If she fell, so much the better.

She stopped short of his leading arm that clutched clothing too nice to be his own, and tightened her grip on John Murphy to signal that he should not waver. Staring into Stoney's eyes, she paused and spoke in a near-whisper. Not that Joseph would have overheard; he had stomped off toward the kitchen. "Lyle. I remember attending your birth with my grandmother, who assisted more than three dozen Pine Ridge children into the world. I was only a child, but even back then I knew the parts of a girl and the parts of a boy that are, with the rest of an infant, wiped clean of blood and slime. It is messy work bringing children into the world, and it falls to women. This is how women know plenty about whether all of an infant's important parts are there and how someone like me would know things about you that others would not. Others such as your drinking partners."

Stoney worked his mouth before speaking. He might have been talking to himself, or perhaps he intended for her to hear him. "This isn't the end of it," he said. Then he shifted just enough to open a path for Raylene and Murphy to exit.

Through the doorway and down two steps, Raylene guided the railroad man. Reaching level ground, she turned aside to whistle loudly, then ushered Murphy to his automobile and opened the driver's door for him. "Here is your coat," she said, giving it a shake, at which a square of glossy paper fluttered to the ground — a photograph of Annie with a crease through one corner and dents all over it. She picked it up. The likeness of Annie was a good one, though without the warm smile and twinkling eyes to be noticed in person. "This must be the photograph that started it all," she said aloud. "Who is standing with my sister?"

"I don't know for sure," said Murphy. "It's only shows that bit of sleeve. I'd still like to find that jewelry."

Did this man not give up? thought Raylene. She ordinarily admired persistence but not in combination with unbidden trouble. "Your boss. Is he married or single?"

John Murphy licked his lips. "Married."

"And the jewelry? If it's been given, why try to get it back?"

Murphy tipped his head left and right as if trying to bring Raylene into focus. "It's, uh, complicated. A family matter."

"Then there must be an unhappy wife involved. I have been wondering what you can tell me about my sister's death, but I sense you cannot or will not. I do not have your jewelry and you would be wise to remove yourself from this place where you have clearly made yourself unwelcome." She motioned toward town. "Go that way to the blacktop and follow it back to town, past the saloon and market. At the far end you'll see a small sign pointing north. It's some hours to Farmingdale, but before then you can ask for fuel at the Farm Exchange."

"I am without ... funds."

"The price of poor choices. Also, dishonesty. There will be an old man by the name of Otto Lightfoot who tends the pump. Tell him that Thomas Yellow Moon's youngest daughter sent you. He will assist. Can you see through those spectacles?"

"Not really."

After pocketing the photograph, she reached up and slid three fingers to the inside of the cracked lens and managed to straighten the offset pieces just a little. She handed him his overcoat, which he tossed onto the passenger seat.

As Murphy climbed awkwardly into the automobile, its trunk popped open. "Damn it," he said. "I don't suppose you would assist one more time?"

Raylene moved to the rear of the car. Inside the rear compartment lay a torn map, a postcard turned blank side up, a gentleman's handkerchief, and a book without its paper cover. A gleam of metal caught her eye. Tucked within a fold in the trunk's lining was her own boot knife, the one gone out the boxcar door with the hobo. She slid it into the scabbard in her right boot before taking up the postcard and closing the trunk with a slam.

Back at the car door she handed the postcard to the railroad man, picture side up. Its image showed a band of sober-looking tribal men dressed in regalia. "Had your opponents noticed this card, your luck might have been even worse."

"Why is that?"

She could have explained that though someone paid each warrior a nickel for posing, the warriors would not have profited from an arrangement meant to enrich the photographer and the printer of cards. Instead, she left his question unanswered.

Murphy set the card aside. "I recall now another question I had for you. Did you lose a knife in your travels this week, a narrow one with a fine blade?"

Just then Kota arrived at a trot, followed by Henry, a little out of breath. Henry cast a wary glance toward the house before Raylene signaled that he should remain quiet. She retrieved a waxed paper packet from one of Kota's saddle bags and handed it to Murphy through his open door. "Here is food. You can ask for water at the Exchange. The old man there will give you as much as you need. Once you make Farmingdale, look for the passenger depot. From there, Rapid City lies to the west."

"Thank you for all of this, for your assistance, but it's been on my mind that you misplaced a knife."

Raylene folded back the right flap of her coat. "I am wearing my knife, the one I used to cut you free. Clearly, it is not missing." With that she moved to close the driver's door. The railroad man possessed one cracked lens to see through and one good arm to assist two working legs. With sufficient determination, he would make his way to a city, which was where he belonged.

As Murphy's automobile turned and headed slowly for the dirt lane leading to the main road, Raylene pondered who might have found her boot knife. Since it had been in John Murphy's car, he might have found it himself. Or someone else had, which meant they probably found the hobo too. She shook her head. If the hobo had died, someone might think he had been killed by a knife, but many things could kill. A fall from a train, for instance, or lies.

To Henry she said, "You might let your friends drink themselves into better humor. If we ride easy, Kota will carry us both back to your mother."

The day's battles had been mental ones, but still she felt spent. She would be glad for a cup of Wilma's coffee and a meal to replace the one she had given the railroad man. After that she would not turn toward Montana, as Wilma had suggested with a little too much hope in her voice. She would head the opposite direction.

Raylene delivered Henry to the market, then went to wait on Wilma's front stoop for the trio to arrive, which it did, with Henry sheepishly toting Lizzy and Wilma looking wrung out.

Inside Wilma's house, Raylene asked to examine the

woman's cache of medicinal plants, some received in trade from other women, some having originated with a druggist in Rapid City. From Wilma's supply she chose one preparation to add to those she carried, offering cash, which Wilma refused. One last item: victuals. Wilma still practiced the making of pemmican, a combination of cooked ground meat and berries, which she sold in her market. Raylene purchased a few portions for the days she would be on horseback.

It was midafternoon by the time she set out cross-country for the town of Manderson. She would not get far before dark. The diversion to Joseph's house and her time with the railroad man had cut hours from those available for traveling, but at least she would make a bit of progress before dark.

She was fairly familiar with Manderson, having attended animal husbandry courses there with a visiting veterinarian. If her memory served, there were smallish ranches on the outskirts then a halo of boxy houses closer to a business district somewhat larger than Oglala's. The immediate area was large enough to support the hundreds of fans and revelers who followed the bareback racing circuit, but small enough that such an influx of people would transform its streets and businesses.

The circuit had begun its season in eastern Montana, moving through North Dakota then south again to Rapid City before looping back onto the Pine Ridge. According to the schedule Wilma kept in the box in her bureau, the circuit's final competition would be run in just a few days. Copious amounts of liquor would stoke the betting and inflame the passions of victory or despair. Manderson would become a racing town, beckoning Ray closer. Raylene would simply have to locate him within the racing madness.

As they rode, Raylene gave Kota his head so she could mentally review the strangeness of the previous week: the hollow places inside her left by the loss of father and sister, the ride via boxcar and the hobo who had accosted her. Courtly Billy Horse. Stranger than the coyote pup appearing out of the dark was Billy's and her encounter with the ranch worker named Rocky and his claim to have won Ray's knife in a poker game. That last seemed improbable, and yet Ray had clearly lost his knife somewhere between Kansas City, where Thomas and Annie had died, and the north country. She wasn't sure if the appearance of Ray's knife in Rocky's hands had been due to sheer luck or the intervention of spirits.

Other occurrences seemed odd as well. The railroad man and his story of jewelry gone missing. The photograph of Annie did indeed show her wearing the sort of city finery that no woman in their family had ever owned, lavish looking even in black and white. She had to wonder what kind of man gave his wife's jewelry to another woman. And why to Annie? What could Annie have been to him? Raylene had not misled the railroad man, had not been untruthful about the jewelry. Having no information about it, she had told him nothing.

There had not been time in Oglala to convince John Murphy to tell what he knew, if anything, about Annie's death. To Raylene's mind the man's silence meant one of three things: there were truly no suspicions surrounding Annie's death; or, a railroad man would not be party to such information; or, what Murphy knew, he was not willing to share. She had surreptitiously checked his rumpled overcoat after Annie's photo fell out, but had only recovered one of his business cards. No reports, no notes, nothing of consequence.

Uncle Ray's reported arrival in Oglala seemed both peculiar and ordinary. He knew plenty of people around those parts because their own family had lived in the area for so long, and the town held Wilma, who must still hold meaning for him. She seemed broken-hearted about Ray and at the same time protective, like someone holding a losing hand they want to keep playing.

Traveling the golden-hued prairie, Raylene felt the threads between her and Ray growing shorter and her heart heavier to know that their confrontation was coming soon. The diversions of the previous week had been just that — diversions. Perhaps she had welcomed them because though Ray needed to be held to account, she had never imagined such a task for herself. She would rather be wrangling ornery cattle or delivering salt bricks to outer pastures. She would rather muck stalls or haul supplies from Rapid City or even the unthinkable — help with the cooking. Retribution was a messy business. The Yellow Moon *thióspaye* did not need another killing or another killer. Yet things might come to that.

She knew that Ray could foil her by diverting to the country of his father. Then her search would grow all but impossible. Montana was vast and sparsely populated. Except for supplies and random work opportunities, Ray would not have need of a town for weeks at a time. His old truck could serve as shelter and he could lie low with one of his friends in the backcountry. In that case, she might never find him. A part of her would welcome that outcome, but another part knew that leaving family business unfinished would prove a weight she would carry a long, long time. She had no choice, really. She would do her duty. She had started on this journey and she would finish it.

As light fell away from day, so did the previous week — the arduousness of travel, her encounters with people known to her and those with strangers, including the railroad man, whose determination intrigued her. He seemed the type who had seen a bit of life and was perhaps hard to ruffle. She was always surprised at her attraction to men unlike her own people. In this way, perhaps, she was like her sister. She credited John Murphy for taking multiple risks in pursuit of the jewelry he was after. He had driven into country unknown to most whites. That could be seen as either foolhardy or brave. Perhaps he had a wild streak that even he didn't recognize, or a taste for rural places, or both. She would put him out of her mind.

Raylene watered Kota at numerous creeks that dissected the prairie, threads of water emerging from hillocks or from the creeks Porcupine and Wounded Knee, the latter still running with sorrow. The afternoon breeze prodded the two of them along.

Later, cocooned in her bedroll with a few hearty crickets singing nearby, Raylene breathed deeply the prairie's air and walked her thoughts out among the pinpricks of light in the black above her. Opening one of her mental compartments, she once more contemplated what might have driven Ray to kill Thomas. Was it their old rivalry over her mother, a woman who was content to tend children and family though her beadwork could have provided a bit of extra income? Her mother, twenty years gone, was no longer present to turn her attention to one brother instead of the other. So, would Ray have nursed a grudge over not being the chosen one? Was the killing somehow an escalation of that time in the smithy shop when Ray stabbed Thomas with a hot poker, burning right through the front of his dungarees? She didn't know that complete story, only about the resultant scar, which she had observed on her father's dead body.

Or was their fight about money? Thomas had known success at managing a saloon, while for the last fifteen years or so, Ray had been a nomad, following jobs that kept him in a little cash, never lighting in one place for long. He had even spent time carving wooden animals with a Blackfoot artist by the name of Clarke, but when it came to making money, carving was no match for the money to be made in keeping a saloon. All that booze, all those drinkers. Then again, if Ray had chosen his own path, envy for Thomas's enterprise would seem a waste of energy, at least to her mind.

She had never envied Annie and her choices. Especially now that she knew, if it could be called knowing, about Annie's attraction to a married man. The jewelry he had given Annie must have been valuable, else why send someone all this way to fetch it home? Raylene would no more blame her sister for choosing someone she could not call her own than she would blame her piebald for grazing in a neighbor's garden. Living creatures were driven by need. She held fast to her tears for Annie. Now was not the time for them, but they were there and would arrive some future day.

For some reason, thoughts of Thomas and his violent death brought no tears to her eyes. Anger, yes, but for reasoning that had eluded her, sorrow at his death had drained away. She emptied her mind and watched the moon rising in the east until a reason came to her — Annie's body had been found in Thomas's saloon, which was basically Thomas's kingdom, and Thomas had not saved Annie from whatever danger had befallen her. He had not summoned a doctor in time or carried Annie to someone who could help.

It seemed now to Raylene that their father had somehow forsaken her sister, though Annie was an adult who chose who to spend time with, and Thomas could not have observed every minute of Annie's days. Nor would that have been in character. Still, natural causes or not, Thomas's fatherly duties included protection. She tasted resentment at the recognition of her father's negligence, but his negligence did not erase her own duty. She must still hold Ray to account.

Nearby, Kota shifted in the dark. They had made camp

beyond abandoned property that held a windmill still feeding a water pipe. The muddy ground around the trough held the narrow hoofprints of antelope and the wider tracks of deer. Small dog prints recorded a coyote on the prowl. There, Kota had grazed a nearby patch of short grass while Raylene filled her canteens and stood in the waning light to eat a slice of pemmican. A distant shotgun house was probably known to squatters, so she had turned Kota the opposite direction for another mile until they came to a level area where she stomped flat the late-summer grass and laid out her ground cloth and bedroll.

From within her bedroll, she listened to a distant pack of coyotes singing songs of their hunt. At Manderson, late tomorrow, she would resupply before studying its layout of businesses and nearby ranches. The better she knew the place, the better her chances of using that knowledge to her advantage.

Twelve

Murphy drove with the windows down, everything blurry and cracked through — the northern sky and waving grasses, the narrow blacktop, a line of trees along a river, all of it distorted as if viewed through broken aquarium glass. An odor of spilled booze wafted up from the floor beneath his feet.

If an automobile mirrored the disposition of its passenger, thought Murphy, his coupe was a weary, injured traveler, shuffling into the Farm Exchange atop Red Shirt Table. There, he followed the little sister's instructions to obtain water to drink and fuel for the remainder of his drive. He ate the biscuit sandwiches provided by Raylene before driving north out of the reservation, keeping the veined, gray road in the center of his windshield.

Refreshed by the food provided by Raylene, but still weary, he drove and drove, rehashing, as was his habit, the last few days. After the disastrous bar fight, he had at least come face-to-face with the little sister, just not in the manner he had intended. Owing to his busted eyeglasses, he was denied a clear look at her cheekbones, her eyes, the way she moved. Still, through his obstructed view, she had radiated competency. Also, mastery over her opponents and Murphy's own inquiries. Using some kind of inside knowledge that Murphy hadn't been able to follow, she had sidelined the man called Stoney. Raylene Little Moon would be a worthy adversary indeed, or a person to partner with in a fight.

A flare of exhilaration overtook him at the realization he

had survived a bar fight against multiple aggressors. Three, anyway, given the quantity of hands and elbows. He had not won, had in fact been soundly beaten, but when considered within a balance sheet, he had come out on the right side of it.

He drove for hours through the countryside, distant equipment throwing dust into the air and shorn fields resembling the stubble on an old man's face. Like a dog with no place to bury its bone, his mind worried the notion that the little sister had wielded a hunting knife to good effect on the rope binding his ankles and arms. His memory was not currently in perfect repair, but he did not recall her wearing a hunting knife in the undertaker's parlor. He did recall a dress over western boots and her bending down before a slim knife appeared in her hand. Perhaps her dress had also hidden the knife at her waist, but today she had not revealed the knife in her boot. His head hurt to think about it.

Back to his mental ledger of debits and credits: On the debit side, the long journey without jewelry at the end of it; his broken arm and eyeglasses; the loss of his wallet with all his cash; the boss's cash gone up in smoke; his suitcase and clothing; all were tangible losses which would damage his reputation. On the credit side he had arrived at this point alive, his beloved Hudson intact, his pride a bit bruised, but with the feeling of having wakened from a deep sleep. He had been marching through time doing everything by the book only to discover that the risks he had taken in the last few days and the sensible rules bent or nearly broken, had not totally defeated him. On the contrary. His assessment of the little sister had been generally correct. That she was smarter and tougher than imagined simply left him feeling that she would occupy his thoughts long after he returned to Kansas City.

He had not begged a container to fill with water from the man at the Exchange. Consequently, his thirst grew with the hours until late in the day he somehow arrived on the outskirts of Rapid City without ever reaching Farmingdale. Good grief. Had he not encountered Rapid City, he might have driven through South Dakota to end up out of fuel, perhaps, in the middle of a Montana prairie. Now, following signs, he found the city's rail station and half-tumbled from his automobile, shaking himself like a dog before affecting a gentlemanly aspect to counter his bruised face and lip, broken eyeglasses, smelly, rumpled clothing, and an arm splinted with kindling and strips from a stray shirt. Waiting passengers threw him suspicious looks and gave him a wide berth.

In the men's lavatory, he rinsed dust and blood from his face and drank water from a cupped hand until his stomach signaled him to quit. She had said, *The first medicine.* He would always remember that. After running his good hand through his hair, he sought the station manager's office and following a sufficient explanation was granted the use of a telephone. It was the hour of his boss's after-dinner brandy.

"Good to finally hear from you," said Campbell. "Tell me something to make my week."

"I'm in Rapid City and alive." Murphy couldn't keep a smile from his face. He wanted to laugh at the fact that except for one tooth, he was whole and somehow different. "I did not locate the jewelry and I lost your money. Mine too."

"Tell me you didn't just say what I think you said," cried his boss. "What does that mean 'lost'? You lost my money, or you spent it?"

Murphy sighed. There was no easy way to distill the details surrounding his fiasco in Oglala, not with the station manager lingering nearby. "Some men jumped me and everything's gone."

"You fought someone over the jewelry? Jesus Christ. *Wait!* If you've been robbed, you've got to report it to the local police.

Tell them where it happened, give a description."

Murphy had mulled over a theoretical robbery occurring in a proper city. In such a case he would notify authorities and assist them in finding the perpetrators. But this one was on him. He had bungled the grand finale of his case through hunger, thirst, and fatigue, allowing the men in the saloon to discover his fabrication and the photograph of Annie, his business cards, his U.P. badge. Police involvement might only make the situation worse.

During investigations, truth had always been his ally, allowing for a minor omission here, a bending of small details there. Lies rarely elicited good results, yet he had fallen into that trap. He halfway regretted the whole jewelry affair. It wasn't even his proper job. His boss had caused the dilemma, then he himself had prodded it until — well, he needed to quit dwelling on what had gone wrong. Very few assignments got the best of him, but this one had. Still, he felt the satisfaction of locating the little sister in her hometown. He had gotten close. "It was my fault, plain and simple," he told the boss. "I tried a strategy and it backfired."

"You don't have to sound so goddamned happy about it. You'd better be sorry about losing my money."

Murphy could picture the boss drumming his fingers as his face reddened behind a fog of cigar smoke. He said, "I'm told I can get my broken arm set tomorrow and some new eyeglasses within a couple of days. I can charge my room and board to U.P. but I'll need cash for that other stuff, and for gasoline. It's a long story."

"Broken arm ... eyeglasses? Jesus H. Christ ..." the sound of sputtering came through from the other end. "Jenkins over in Chicago — he'd fire your ass, you know that? I ought to fire your ass. If you don't have a broken arm when you get back here, I'll break it for you. Damn it, now I got to shit, hold on a minute." There was silence on the line for a bit, then Campbell was back. "I'll phone the Rapid City freight master and arrange things. Don't you take any detours, don't wreck your car. Get yourself back here so I can chew you out proper."

"Will do," said Murphy, and he meant it.

Elements of a plan percolated through Raylene's mind throughout the two days of travel that followed her stop in Oglala, details forming before receding in favor of others until her thoughts had solidified. Even injured, Ray would retain good reflexes, so Raylene might have to incapacitate him in order to exact a fitting punishment. She intended to spot him first and not the other way around.

Nearing Manderson, she avoided the main road in case Ray's old black truck should appear, coated with prairie dust and battered from driving backroads choked with willows. She was wearing pants that Henry had outgrown, given to her by Wilma who had not known that Raylene would use them to trick Ray. He would not recognize her handed-down barn coat either.

Before advancing, she dismounted and hung her hat on her saddle horn. Using Kota as a shield from the breeze, she pulled Ray's knife and working by feel, cut away her long braid. The blade was sharp and fine, and with each motion she felt a fragment of herself fall away — the years with Annie and their grandmother, a healer and midwife, and the years of ranch work under the prairie sun. There were a few remaining memories of the earliest years under her mother's care and being at turns doted upon and instructed by men who each acted as father, identical on the outside but clearly different on the inside. Even the insult of having had her childhood braid hacked off by nuns fell away. She remained Raylene Little Moon, daughter and substitute-son of Thomas Yellow

Moon and Helen Longman, niece of Raymond Yellow Moon, grand-daughter of Helma She Walks. But with this act she became another sort of being. Not only daughter, son, niece, and grand-daughter, but also, just now, a hunter of men.

Mary's coat, Henry's pants, and her newly shorn hair were a partial disguise at best, possibly good from a distance. If she gained an extra minute while closing in on Ray, that minute might be enough for offensive maneuvers. Into a square of the paper saved from one of her pemmican meals, she folded a handful of the cut black strands. No reason, really, just because.

The nearest parcel of land led to the next and that one to the next. Working her way toward town she avoided houses for as long as possible, following dirt and gravel side roads dividing homes each set on an acre or more. After that she reached the blacktop of the business district a generous three blocks long. Steering Kota to the next street over, she peered between buildings to gauge the amount of vehicle movement on the main drag. Fairly thin. Satisfied, she rode back along the main street, studying vehicles parked or in motion for the telltale pattern of buckshot, like two dozen rusty-red eyes, in the tail-end of Ray's old Ford truck.

On a side street she located a stable. Approaching its open door, Kota whinnied and tossed his head in a signal to his fellow creatures. Raylene dismounted and called a greeting. Receiving no answer, she led Kota around the far side, where she found a pimple-faced teenager emptying a wheelbarrow of straw and horse dumplings onto a great mound of the same. The air all around was ripe with the smell of manure, the perfume of country life.

The young man looked up from his work, ignoring the bluebottle flies buzzing in circles above him. He gave her a curious look, his gaze catching briefly on the choppy hair showing beneath her hat.

"Can you put my horse up tonight?" she asked.

"Not in the barn. Four of them are spoke for and the others are full. But you can pasture here for four bits and store your gear in the tack room."

"Four bits!"

The boy shrugged. "Prices for race weekend."

Raylene assumed an innocent look. "For what?"

"Bareback racing. People come from everywhere."

"If you say so." She pulled a dollar from her pocket. "I'll pay your price for two nights but I might pull him early."

"That's fine." The young man was not a full blood, but *iyéska,* maybe half white. He admired the dollar before cramming it into his pocket and studying Kota a moment. "Good looking horse. He got a name?"

"Kota."

"You can turn him out when you're ready." The young man returned to shoveling shit.

Raylene knew how the racing circuit worked but she needed local information. She asked, "So, this racing thing you mentioned ... If I stick around, where would I find it? At the rodeo grounds?"

The stable hand snorted as he turned back to her. "Rodeo grounds? It'll be in a pasture. They might put up some ramps for watching, but most people just stand."

"On someone's ranch?"

He seemed to warm up a bit, as if he'd been taken for an expert on the subject. "The Two Medicine, out the east side. There'll be traffic going that way. Wagons and such, and people who follow the teams."

"You sure know what's going on around here," said Raylene, shading her voice with admiration. "I suppose the ones who are going to race, they camp near the track?"

"Most of them. There's places all over glad to make room for the teams. Grass is free, but a team might pay for alfalfa or like that."

Raylene looked around as if contemplating a new subject. "I guess the riders wouldn't want to get too far from their stock."

"They'll come into town for beer and steaks, but there's always someone left behind to watch. Some of those horses are pricey."

"You might race someday. You could, right?"

"Haw! I ride fine, grew up riding. But racing, that takes dough, you know?"

Raylene nodded as if his observations were sage indeed. "When do things get crowded around here?"

"Friday night. The racing is all day Saturday."

Raylene nodded, her intuition confirmed. "If you'll keep an eye on Kota when you're around, I'll do right by you."

The young man perked up. "There's a grain bin inside if you want to give him a scoop."

Raylene said thanks and led Kota to the pasture gate beyond the closest corral. A handful of other horses turned to watch them. In the barn, the occupied stalls had tack hanging alongside their gates. In the tack room, she hung her gear over an empty sawhorse then with her saddle bags over one shoulder, she carried a palm full of oats back to where Kota stood by the fence. As he lipped the treat, she patted his neck and spoke to him low, promising to return.

Heading for the traveler's hotel on the main street, she hoped she wasn't too late for supper. No matter what the dining room served, it would be a nice change from pemmican.

October 5, 1936

Dear Catherine,

I apologize for the tardiness of this letter. You will see that I am sending this letter from a hotel in Rapid City, this time practicing the ambidexterity of my youth. Thus, the wobbly printing.

I have been here for three days and am now readying for my return south. Such a strange week this has been, though I must commend the weather, which benefited my travel by auto. The nights up north are cold, no doubt about it, but the colors of grassy plains, rivers, undulating hills dotted with trees — all are magnificent. Golds and browns and yellows, some places still green, the sky the bluest blue. A poet could do justice to this time of year.

My first bit of business was in a small Nebraska town I suspect you would not know, keeping as you did to the city. It's quite small, north of K.C. on the U.P. freight line, where I found the county Sheriff cooperative. We discussed a rail rider who had met an untimely end along the tracks. That death is one I found suspicious for reason of a knife found with the body. I now wonder what I made of that case that I should not have, or vice versa. The detective Holmes would have solved it, I'm sure.

As for locating jewelry for my boss, that too proved a disappointment. I hesitate to call that assignment a failure as I may have come to it too late to identify a culprit disposing of the goods. It's only because I take such pride in tallying cases I solve that I find myself wounded by this one.

Such curious people associated with the missing jewelry, or I thought they were, linked to one of the deaths I mentioned in my last letter. The reservation world they inhabit is unlike our city life with its busy streets and everything a person could want for home and hearth. And conveniences such as merchandise stores of all kinds and repair shops.

If an item can't be found in our city, it can be purchased by mail from Sears Roebuck, delivered to the door. I'm not sure about the latter, but the former is not how things work in very rural places. Homes look decidedly plain without much adornment, businesses too.

I only saw the inside of one business and it contained none of the finery to which we are accustomed. On the Pine Ridge, as it's called, people knit together in rough ways, which must make for deep connections, but I can only guess at their daily diversions. I thought I had seen a bit of middle America but I had not before seen the true land of these people.

Thinking you might never have seen the regalia of the Plains Indians, I enclose a postcard I had thought to use for correspondence before deciding it would make for the meanest note of a few lines only.

~~One individual I found rather~~

A part of me wants to return to this place, but I don't know when there would ever be a reason.

I'll leave off for now, wishing you a colorful fall season in the high country.

Yours always,
John

Posting the letter to his wife, Murphy thought once more about the balance sheet he had mentally constructed on his drive north from the Pine Ridge. At the bottom of each column where the totals normally went, he pictured not credits and debits in balance, but the name Raylene Little Moon. On both sides. He could wish to someday search her out again.

Thirteen

Raylene woke early in her bed in the traveler's hotel in Manderson, the sound of gusty wind pushing against the outside walls. She had never been shy about sleeping rough, but there was something to be said for a proper mattress stuffed with cotton or straw. This one was as good as those at the H-bar-H. She had slept hard without the dreams that had followed her the last two weeks — dreams of her father grappling with Ray, a knife in his own hand and a knife in Ray's. And dreams of Annie dissolving into the sky without a look back.

Rising, she washed at the basin on the dresser then went down the hall to use the communal bathroom. Of the four rentable rooms, only two were currently occupied. This, she had gleaned from the owner who had been waitressing tables last night. The relative quiet of the place felt like a bit of luck, but she could not count on luck to help her determine where the Dark Cloud team would camp with their gear and steed for the weekend. The stable hand had said to expect teams arriving tomorrow. That gave her twenty-four hours to scout the ranches around town.

Carrying her saddle bags and hat, she descended the stairs to the main room and glanced around. No Uncle Ray at the desk or in the restaurant. Good. She did not want a public confrontation but to face him on her own terms. Claiming the table by one of two windows at the front, she studied the half block immediately south. Pedestrians coming into view were buffeted by wind, their hats pulled low.

After a meal of eggs, biscuits, and coffee, she asked the owner-waitress to fill her canteens and wrap two bacon sandwiches to carry out. When the woman returned with her items, Raylene said, "The nephew of a friend rides a horse called Dark Cloud. I haven't seen him in a long time. I thought I could look him up tonight or tomorrow."

"The horse sounds familiar," mused the woman.

"Maybe you've seen him race."

The woman held Raylene's gaze. "You mean instead of serving meals and running my hotel business?"

Raylene smiled wryly. "I guess not. I'd like to figure out where his team will camp."

"There aren't enough rooms for all the fans to stay in town, let alone the teams. You're lucky to have gotten here early when I had a vacancy.

"Last year there was a lot of camping on the Dahlburg where they were racing, but this spring the owner took sick and moved with his wife to Rapid City for special doctoring. Far as I know, everything's on the Two Medicine."

Raylene shrugged. "I suppose I'll find them, and you'll be here working."

"Right," said the woman as she cleared Raylene's empty plate. She stood there a moment with it balanced in her hand. "'Course, I might not mind working inside 'cause they're talking about snow."

"I guess this wind is bringing it."

"Supposed to rain then get cold. Might make the racing tricky."

"Will they call it off?"

"Only if it's dangerous for the horses."

Raylene nodded. "I suppose you see a lot of the riders for supper."

"They're outnumbered by the fans. There's a restaurant on the north end with no sign on it. Either place, some will have to take their foil plates outside, but some just want drinks. The bars, *they* do a hell of a business." She shrugged.

Raylene scooped a handful of brown sugar lumps from the bowl on the table and after settling her bill, went out to walk through the morning glow along the back of the hotel where the wind came in fits and starts. None of the doors on the backs of buildings displayed signs identifying their businesses. Back doors, though, they could come in handy.

At the stable's pasture gate, she whistled for Kota and delivered the sugar treats, saving one each for a roan and a bay who ambled over. The pasture looked healthy.

"We're doing a different kind of work today," she told Kota. "Reconnaissance."

Kota tossed his head and nuzzled her hand.

"I will take that as agreement."

She found her gear where she'd left it, and carried it out, passing the same stable worker from the previous day.

"Hey," he said. "Everything look okay?"

"Looks fine."

"You gonna pasture him again tonight?"

"I think not." She had decided that her piebald stood out too much among the others. Uncle Ray would notice him while scouting the local horseflesh, as was his practice. "You keep the difference."

The teen's eyes widened. The four bits she was leaving on the table was probably a day's pay, but just like magic it was now his. Raylene counted the cash as insurance against her needing something from an appreciative teenager, if it came to that. In fact, she would test him now. "Do me a favor," she said. "I'm keeping watch for someone who might come through this way. He owes me money but if he notices I'm here, he'll take off." The kid gave a nod so Raylene continued. "I'd be obliged if you wouldn't mention my piebald."

"There's not many around."

"Exactly."

The kid blinked at her as if in thought. "Okay," he said. "I know how to keep quiet."

Raylene gave him a smile. "And I will remember that you did. Say, do you have another hat, one you could wear if you sell me the one you're wearing?"

The young man looked at her like she had two heads. "Sell? What for?"

"I have my reasons. Would two dollars do it?"

He lifted the stained brown hat from his head and looked it over as if trying to discern the attraction it might hold for a stranger, a woman, no less. One with chopped hair. "Yours is good. What do you want my old one for?"

She knew then that she had made a mistake in giving him an extra reason to wonder about her motives. Even without her name he knew her horse and that she had asked him to keep that knowledge to himself. That would be enough to attract gossip in local circles. Hoping to sound like her deception concerned the man who owed her money, she said, "Never mind, I'll catch up to him, even if he sees me coming."

She carried her tack to the pasture gate and opened it for Kota to amble through. After saddling up, she stopped back by the barn and spoke again to the young man as he prepared to turn the stabled horses into the nearest corral. "We have an agreement, right?" she asked. "Just until Monday."

The young man shrugged.

"You gave me your word, Charlie Ox." When his eyes grew wide at hearing his name, she was glad for the friendly and informative restaurant owner who had provided it. Mounting up, she turned Kota toward the sunlit horizon. Tomorrow the town would fill with strangers. When that happened, she would need to be ready to find her uncle.

Assuming a casual posture, Raylene rode Kota slowly around the perimeters of the area's four most sizeable ranches, noting fences and their closing mechanisms. Three seemed to each encompass a hundred fenced acres. The fourth was closer to three hundred, giving way onto open grazing. One appeared to sport a short grass track inside a nearly flat pasture. A carved wooden sign near that ranch's gravel driveway identified it as the Two Medicine.

The Two Medicine lay roughly two miles east of the heart of Manderson and south of an access road, which ended at the ranch. From beyond the ranch's boundary, Raylene made out a cluster of buildings. Two vehicles sat parked near the ranch house. Closer to the mowed pasture, a handful of people were putting up a big canvas tent, for wagering, perhaps, or concessions of some kind. Nearby, a couple of other men looked to be assembling a small grandstand. Tunneling into memory. she recalled watching her first bareback relay race where each rider reined to a stop while sliding from his mount to leap bareback onto another in order to speed away. One rider, three mounts, three laps per race.

One of the vehicles parked by the ranch house began to move down the long ranch road, its progress marked by a rising cloud of gravel dust that blew haphazardly into the air. On the Dahlburg ranch across the road stood a shed holding hay bales, but there was no noticeable action around the place. Just like the restaurant owner had said.

Now she broke from riding for a meal of bacon sandwiches, Kota grazing in the grassy plot where she stood. Afterwards, they rode to the west side of town where two sizeable ranches flanked dozens of small parcels with homes perched upon them, the "neighborhoods" of town. Her circuit complete, she doubled back to a lot holding a small house, a barn, and a chicken coop. An hour prior, she had noted an old woman working behind the house in a garden patch, dashing a hoe into the broken soil. The set of the woman's shoulders gave her the determined aspect of Raylene's departed grand-mother. Or Wilma, sandpapered by the vagaries of physical labor while remaining largely unbowed. Proud. Wise. A lifetime spent in one place.

At the front of the house, Raylene dismounted. Removing her hat, she stepped up to knock firmly on the door's frame, retreating afterward to a respectful distance. Before long, a native woman came to the opening, wiping her hands on a towel hanging at the waist of her skirt. Wisps of gray hair clung to a face damp with perspiration. "Are you in need?" the woman asked.

Raylene averted her eyes. "Elder sister, I am in town on personal business but the stable is full so I am wondering if you would have room for my horse in your barn."

The woman considered Kota waiting calmly behind Raylene before saying, "Not many people would leave a handsome animal with a stranger. Is he not yours?"

"He is mine. I need to do my business on foot." Raylene glanced past the house toward the barn and then at the woman. "I was hoping to pay for some hay, if you have any, and a night or two of shelter."

Raylene read her own words being turned this way and that behind the woman's eyes. The woman pushed a damp hair from her cheek. "I recognize your horse. You rode past the back of my property earlier. I thought you were scouting my chickens."

Raylene knew she had not been invisible. She said, "I was looking for shelter for my horse, perhaps also for myself."

"Is that not what the hotel in town is for?"

"The hotel would be fine, but the stable is full."

The woman glanced up at the sky and back at Raylene. "You are telling me that somehow the stable's pasture is full as well."

Stuck for another falsehood to offer, Raylene kept silent as the woman spoke again. "There are reasons for a person to avoid our main street but none that I can think of would include lack of good pasture. Child, what has happened?"

Child, what has happened? At hearing the same phrase her own grandmother had used, Raylene became six again arriving with her shin torn and blood on her hands, or carrying the still-warm body of their dead dog, Black Boy. Or vomiting up the remains of mushrooms she had plucked from a rotting log on the bank of White Clay Creek. This was a compassionate question underpinned with the expectation of an honest reply.

The question cleaved Raylene and her concern over confronting Ray. "I am expecting to find the person who killed my father."

The woman narrowed dark eyes at Raylene, then her look softened. She nodded almost imperceptibly as if thinking certain thoughts that she would not speak aloud. "And you would avoid this person — no, to do that you would leave town. You mean to watch this person, or perhaps confront this person." The woman seemed to be contemplating the implications. "The killer is not a stranger."

Raylene turned her hat in her hands as she nodded.

"So, it is someone you know, who knows you."

"Yes."

Nodding as if to herself, the woman said, "You are not to bring your troubles here, whatever they are."

"I will not."

"Then there is one empty stall and a bit of hay left from my nag that died in the spring. The other stall is stacked with wood. I could use some of that for my stove."

"I'll bring some in before I walk back to town."

The woman hesitated, giving Raylene pause. "That old truck parked round the side," she said. "I don't suppose I need it until the racing crowds let up. If it starts for you, you might find it useful."

A nondescript vehicle would come in handy as a type of blind from which to watch the main road. Gratitude for such generosity welled up inside Raylene. "I will treat it with care," she promised.

The woman nodded.

"He is Kota," said Raylene, gesturing at her pony.

"And you?"

"I am Raylene, from Oglala."

"And I am Edda."

As Raylene turned to fetch her pony, the woman stopped her with another question. "What if you don't return with my truck, Raylene from Oglala?"

"Then someone will find it in town and you will have it back, plus a fine cutting horse who likes a lump of sugar now and then."

"And you?"

"If I don't return your truck, I will have no need for a horse."

Again, the silence grew between them, broken only by the wind playing hard then soft. Then, "What is your plan for this evening?"

Raylene had thought to settle Kota for the night and walk back to the main street, holing up somewhere so that when morning broke, she could watch new arrivals. Now that she had the use of a vehicle to ease her approach into town, she could keep the woman company until it was time for sleep.

"Perhaps," she said, "I will bunk in your barn and start for town in the morning."

The smallest twitch of the woman's mouth suggested satisfaction. "In that case, you can join me for a plate of cold venison and warm flat bread."

Raylene turned to beckon Kota. He had earned a thorough currying and the last of the oats from the saddlebags he had carried on his back that day. She would learn more about her host over a shared meal and divulge a few more details about her own circumstances. How she was not inclined to hunt people but meant to catch her father's killer unawares. She would not share the type of punishment she imagined for him because Edda's disapproval might reduce her own resolve. And though with a sorrowful air they colored her every thought about future hours and future days, some plans were meant to be left unspoken.

Fourteen

The next morning, Raylene parked just off Manderson's main road under a patch of poplar trees, not far from a used-equipment business with two barking dogs inside a wire fence. Her view was the leading edge of downtown.

The main road curved such that neither end offered an unrestricted view of the entire run of businesses, so she was posted at its south end, where teams and fans would arrive if coming from the direction where Ray was last sighted. The odds of spotting him arriving were fifty-fifty, but a lone watcher could not do better. She had angled the old Dodge to catch a glimpse of each passing driver and whether any truck sported a shot-up tailgate. With her bedroll wedged behind her and her hat pulled low, she reclined against the driver's door as if sleeping off a drunk when in fact she was actually scanning northbound arrivals.

Squirming to change position brought a pinch from the sheath at her belt, and this incited thoughts about the utility of knives and how they were useful in many pursuits. Removing the entrails of fish, for instance. First, the firm thrust through the resistance of belly flesh before the slice upward to the throat. Or for the shaving of a branch on which to string one's catch. For the skinning of big game and the scraping of a hide for tanning. For the slicing of a hide into strings for braiding lariats. For butchering lambs or steer or even rabbits. For the beheading of cattails for their golden pollen to mix with flour. For the lancing of a boil and a hundred other tasks. What would people accomplish without such a tool? Fewer killings, perhaps, but many types of work would be near-impossible.

As the sky filled with leaden clouds that turned the day gray, intermittent raindrops fell against the truck's windshield, blown quickly to mist by the wind, now steady. During a storm in open country, the sky could sometimes be mistaken for land. Raylene's grandmother used to say, "The wind brings our dreams."

Ten hours later, Raylene knew she had been dead wrong, either wrong about her uncle Ray and his interest in the final racing event of the season, or wrong about how or when he would arrive in town. She had watched a stream of variously shaped vehicles roll by. Automobiles with bedrolls tied on top, and a hundred arrivals on horseback and in horse-drawn wagons. Some trucks pulled horse vans or open trailers, some seemed to overflow with passengers surrounded by cartons and bundles. One came loaded with firewood, but none of them looked like Ray's old truck.

The owner of the restaurant had not overstated the crowd. If half these people sought food or drink, Manderson's establishments would see customers standing shoulder to shoulder. Watching the crowd, a casual observer might think the hardest times had run their course, but in fact hard times had gripped the reservation for longer than most other parts of the country. For many of these people, the sojourn to Manderson would constitute their only days off from field work this year, never mind that for some, travel to and from Manderson would entail a half-day's drive or more each direction. But meeting up with friends and family took priority.

Raylene walked to the edge of the main road. She had not napped, she had emptied her bladder behind a tree only when a break in the traffic presented itself, and she had watched the road and its travelers for so long her eyes felt gritted with sand and her back unnaturally stiff, but somehow, she had missed the one race fan she sought or else that one fan had beaten her to Manderson.

The business district was now chaos, vehicles parked in any spot where horses weren't tied. Waves of people crowded every wooden walkway. There were greetings and calls and whistles from people in bunches and knots. In a single day the town's population had at least quadrupled.

Standing on the edge of the road, peering toward town, Raylene stilled her mind to detect Ray among the flood of racers and race fans. Yes. Faintly she could feel his stoical, watchful energy even if she could not see him. To pinpoint him would now require footwork and yet more patience. She moved to join the crowds milling in the gathering gloom of Manderson's business district, stepping into and out of the few lanterns illuminating the fronts of stores still open at day's end. First, she watched the legs and boots ahead of her as they cut left and right, but in due course she decided to risk scanning faces and hats for the person she sought while leaving to luck whether he spotted her first.

The market's closing time was near, so she stood off to one side watching shoppers entering and exiting. After a quarter hour or so she concluded that Ray was not among them. Next, she strolled the sidewalk with the masses, sweeping her gaze across approaching figures and those crisscrossing the street. At the next business, a saddle and leather shop, she glanced through the plate glass window at customers fingering the goods in the golden light of its oil lamps. Still no Ray.

The town's energy seemed fueled by people satisfied with this day and this hour — Lakota, Blackfoot, Omaha, Crow. Old and young, men, women, and children, in ranch wear or snap-front western shirts. Raylene continued surveying businesses and crowds up the west side of the street until she reached the service station, where the aromas of fuel and motor oil grew obvious, but nowhere did she sight Ray or his truck.

Glancing up the road and opposite, she considered a feed and grain store in front of which were parked a half-dozen wagons, their horses waiting for release from their harnesses. None were race horses, just solid, muscular beasts more valuable to a working family than any sleek steed could ever be. She crossed over and started down the other side, peering through the falling dark. The wind had shrunk to a mild breeze but plumes of breath now rose from people she passed who were no longer distinct, but shadowy shapes.

In the doorway of a darkened tool shop, two men dispensed paper cups of keg beer, pocketing the money thrust at them. From the gap between a dry goods place and the abandoned storefront next to it came the clicks and shouts of a dice game. Raylene next moved to an unmarked building with a sluggish river of people flowing out while others slid in. There, she watched the people who exited the place toting small packages that she assumed were food. Quite a number of the men coming out stepped to the very next business. The first was a likely restaurant and the second a saloon, both of them places for lingering awhile. If she meant to find Ray, she would have to venture inside them.

This string of buildings had back doors opening onto the street that led to the stable where she had pastured Kota. She took a narrow passageway to the rear of the buildings and there, skirting clots of men wreathed in smoke, headed for the unmarked restaurant's back door, which stood ajar.

Slipping inside, she found herself within a deluge of conversation and body heat. It seemed as if a hundred people crowded the place, some sitting, others waiting for tables as they stood shoulder to shoulder along the walls. The air was a writhing, smoking, fried-food miasma that laden waitresses pushed through to reach the twelve or so tables. From her place at the perimeter, Raylene looked for Ray's head above the others in the crowd. She studied the gathering before giving up and pushing out the back door into the chill.

Outside, she paused to let her senses clear, then it was on to the saloon next door, accessed again through the back. Inside, another crush of clamoring revelers, virtually all men, most of them boisterous. Delivering pitchers of beer and glasses of hooch, three young women dressed in white western shirts over red skirts pushed through the crowd between tables set so close that the servers' hips and thighs brushed against the arms and backs of seated customers. One server had a grimace-like smile pasted on her face. The other two looked relatively comfortable with so many eyes on them, accustomed, perhaps, to the whipsaw of leering grins and looks of disregard. Every so often a shout would go up as one of the drinkers reached out to stroke a red skirt sliding past and got his hand slapped.

From the far corner came the crack of balls colliding on a pool table. With each play, a chorus of murmurs and half-shouts of derision and glee rose from those gathered three deep. Raylene assumed a manly posture, her vision adjusting to the haze of blue air as she studied the room from beneath the brim of her hat.

One of the red-and-white servers with a tray of drinks slid past the line of those leaning against the wall. Raylene gave her boots a glance until the woman had passed her. When she glanced up again, her eyes went to the crowd bunched around the pool table. Her pulse ticked up as she noted the familiar head of disheveled hair above a black vest that had seen better days. It was worn by the one person she did not want to encounter and whom she did not want finding her while she was bent on her own pursuit. Lyle Stoneman.

When he turned as if to menace a man trying to push in closer, Raylene tilted her head down and away. When enough moments had passed to make it safe again, she glanced Stoney's way. He had turned back to the action of cue ball and side pockets. When the red-and-white server started taking orders along the line of wall-standers, Raylene pulled five dollars from her leather pouch and held it in her open palm.

Catching a glimpse of the money, the server glanced up under the brim of Raylene's hat, her look of concentration turning to curiosity then suspicion. Raylene leaned in to describe the man in the black vest and what she hoped to purchase with her cash. Transaction completed, Raylene turned for the back door and the next saloon. If all worked well, Stoney would remain occupied with getting very drunk for the remainder of the night, courtesy of "an admirer."

By Raylene's recollection, the next block held a trading post with displays of baskets and blankets, worked metal and other items for just this sort of occasion. In winter, the store would offer pelts of bobcat and coyote, beaver, and the occasional wolf, attracting ranchers and ranch hands who worked just beyond the reservation's borders.

One door down sat another saloon, whose streetside sign read S-BAR-S with the S letters painted in the likeness of prairie rattlers, and beyond that, a used-goods shop. In this part of the back street, voices carried to her on the slight breeze, their owners tucked into the shadows, unseen but for the flare of matches and the red eyes of fresh-lit cigarettes.

As Raylene stepped past the padlocked back door of the trading post, the sound of laughter came from the dark on her left, followed by indistinct conversation. She advanced until a low-throated warning growl stopped her. Dead ahead, a mongrel with upright, silvery hackles. When she stopped moving, it quieted. Now what? Raylene took a step forward, which incited more growls, steaming breath, and the gleam of bared teeth. Of all the strays and pets that on this night roamed the fields and streets of town, this one had chosen her. She wondered if its appearance was an omen. If so, it was not a good one.

She shook off the thought. The creature was rabid or angry or hungry. There was nothing to be done about the first two, so moving slowly, she pulled from her coat pocket the paper packet containing her last slice of venison. After waving it in the air to disperse its signature, she flung it to one side. It landed with a crinkly sound as the mutt, which had followed the motion with its head, leaped after it.

Outside the back door of the S-BAR-S, she stood and again cleared her thoughts so that Ray's presence could spark there. When she was young, they had communed with foreheads together, most often before some contest involving galloping on horseback while aiming stuffed leather packets into baskets or through bent willow hoops. He would say, "You must outthink your opponents in order to outmaneuver them. Use the strength of your mind." Raylene felt Ray's words as if he were coaching her this instant. The problem was, at this moment he was the opponent she needed to outmaneuver.

Stepping inside, the saloon's odors and heat assaulted her senses. Hot bodies and sweat, spilled beer, and cigarette smoke. Someone in the crowd had lit up special herbs. Just inside the back door, a table held a game that looked like five-card draw. At another, players bent to rolling dice. Each table held six men with a dozen or more observers gathered close.

The saloon held a shifting mass of drinkers. Raylene watched its swirls and eddies until she realized that one figure in the throng at the bar stood like a stone in the river.

Ray.

The sight of him nearly shattered her, her legs suddenly heavy, her ribs and throat becoming nothing but bones holding a body reduced to air. His silver earring glowed against his copper skin and he seemed to be listening to the bartender's chatter. Or maybe not. Perhaps he was reading the change her entrance had made in the crowd. A part of her had imagined that Ray would elude her entirely, so what did it mean that she had found him standing among fifty or sixty merrymakers as if he had not recently killed a man, his brother, her father. As if he could go about his business without interruption or anyone recognizing the killer among them. Not that these people would know about Ray's deed, not yet. The news would eventually circulate among Manderson's residents, but the majority in this saloon were not locals. Ray could have chosen any place to be. There were many places less crowded. It was almost as if he meant to be noticed, meant to be found. By her. She studied his posture a moment longer. His stance and stillness were that of a person sensing her arrival and nearness, which meant that now she would have to finish what she had started, or more accurately, what *he* had started. She would finish because if she did not, he would know it.

He glanced toward the door then turned to push through the crowd. Raylene nearly fell over the men in front of her as she willed her feet to move. Focusing on Ray's blue denim shirt and the back of his head, she wielded her hands as wedges to open a path through the crowd.

Someone grabbed her arm, growling "Watch where you're stomping."

"Sorry," she said, trying to pull away. Ray's earring flashed as he reached the door, then he disappeared. She was only halfway to him.

The grip on her arm tightened. "You hear me?"

She was forced to turn toward her accuser. "It was not on purpose!"

Twisting away, she pushed forward again, squirming through the barricade of drinkers filling every inch of space. After what seemed an eternity, she reached the door and pushed out onto the walkway, glancing left and right. A small break in the clouds let the half-moon cast highlights on windshields and the hats of people coming toward her. Ray usually stood taller than a crowd, but not tonight. She started through the stream of people on the walkway, conversations spiking with peals of laughter. Vehicles moved along the road while up ahead, a faded white horse van pulled away from the curb. She stepped into the street, narrowly avoiding a rider on horseback, and dashed after the receding van. Was Ray driving the truck pulling it? The van blocked her view of the vehicle in front. She swerved into the oncoming lane for a better angle, making out just one detail: splashes of color that the night painted gray. The rig gained ground and faded into the night.

She slowed to a walk and stepped out of the path of an automobile filled with revelers who whooped with joy as they rolled past. She had lost him. Now, without a doubt, she would have to outthink him.

Raylene returned to Edda's house in the dark. She had located Ray, then lost him, but what had she thought, that she would follow him unseen to his lodgings and thereby know exactly where to catch him unawares? This reckoning would not be that easy.

In the barn she greeted Kota, who stomped and whinnied as she approached. After blowing gently into his nostrils, she stroked his face. He looked none the worse for having been left all day, but restless, perhaps reading her mood. Now that she knew for certain that Ray was in Manderson, she knew he had indeed come for the racing.

She wanted this duty of hers done. He would call her obligation an honoring of tradition, a rightful continuation of their culture. He would call it noble. She would have gladly followed Ray across various states for months, never arriving in a place where she would be duty-bound to accost him. A part of her felt that peace should prevail in the face of his dishonorable deed, but another part recognized the need to hold him accountable for destroying the last of what little family they possessed. He had punctured her equilibrium, leaving her paddling through each day without making shore. She wanted dry land, she wanted her family back, each of them alive and busy, but barring that, she wanted these days of following and wondering and hurting over with. Damn him. She wanted peace.

In the stall where she had slept the previous night, Raylene found a bale of hay smelling of ripened grasses and northern winds. A gift from Edda. Using Ray's knife, she cut the bale open and pitched some of it into her sleeping place plus a flake's worth into Kota's stall. He stepped right up to chew a mouthful, blades of green hanging from his lips before falling free. Then he looked at Raylene as if asking her thoughts.

"I know," she told him. "You have been stuck here all day." She glanced around to avoid his gaze, those long eyelashes. "It's dry and warm, you ought to be glad. I am."

Kota, who had worked so diligently, answering every request she made of him through every season and carrying her to every place of her choosing — he deserved release from the long hours of waiting, for someone to grant him what he did best. She pushed the stall door open wide and led him from the barn. The half-moon flashed briefly from behind heavy clouds as she grabbed a fistful of mane and leaped upon his back. He trembled with excitement as she walked him to the end of Edda's property where they stepped out onto a dirt road leading west. A ride in the dark on a hard-packed road was at least as safe as galloping across an open prairie, perhaps more so. They would have to trust. After a short walk and a longer trot, she gripped his ribs with her thighs, his mane with both hands, and gave him his head. They were off.

Kota was built for quick turns and bursts of speed, for the cutting of cattle from a herd or a chase through scrub land, but in seconds his gallop was flat out as if to gain the great beyond, hooves pounding out a rhythm to power the ache from her heart. She plastered her sternum to his back and neck so that they rode as one, steaming into the night, the wind whipping his mane into her face. Together they were thunder and lightning and the earth spinning to meet the stars. When he descended a dry wash, she held fast until he powered up the other side. She thought her heart would break from cherishing this creature.

With frozen mist stinging her face, they turned north. When at last he relented and slowed to a trot, she hoisted herself upright. The moon now lit a break in the clouds that could have been a doorway to the other side of the sky. Was Annie there waiting for her? She would see the other side someday, but not just yet. If she could help it, she would not cross over any time soon.

The moon's position high overhead meant Sunday had arrived. Kota was blowing great steamy breaths. Raylene turned him back the way they'd come, knowing he would return them both to the protection of the barn and its sweet-smelling hay. Tomorrow's races would bring her best chance for finding Ray and avenging Thomas's death. Afterwards, she would saddle Kota and ride away. They might not look back.

Frozen crystals fell off and on overnight so that by mid-morning, vehicles threw no dust as they rolled toward the Two Medicine. An open fence to the right allowed parking inside a mowed field, one half designated for horse-drawn wagons, the balance for motorized vehicles. Single horses were tied well off the road and closer to the ranch entrance where people milled about.

Raylene parked Edda's truck among the other vehicles already present and set out with her saddlebags, which could double as a shield should she need one. She hoped it wouldn't come to that.

The racing teams would have spent the morning applying wraps to their horses' legs and walking the animals about to keep them limber. A lengthy warm-up demonstrated each team's readiness, enticing gamblers to wager on their favorites. Ray might be among them.

Having read the signs of more wet weather to come, Raylene wore two shirts and had stuffed her riding gloves into her coat pockets. The wind had relented once more, but the wet air chilled lungs and dampened the sounds of the crowd. The horses would benefit from cool weather if the grass track did not turn to mush. Riders, however, would have to hold their seats on damp mounts.

Raylene fell into line behind a group of white men wearing ranch clothing, their necks and ears glowing pink atop their tans. When she reached a ticket seller at the main gate, he grinned as if energized by the weather or the size of the crowd. "You have lost your horse," he said, taking her fee.

She touched a hand to the saddlebag draped across her chest. "I hope not. Have you seen the Dark Cloud team?"

"They'll be on the track by now, or just beyond. The contests are posted in that tent over there."

Raylene nodded her thanks as the river of those arriving carried her toward the track. She quartered away, toward the fence line bordering the field. Voices rose and fell around her in the breeze that had freshened once more.

Minutes later, she caught sight of Wilma's nephew Leonard on the far side, leading a black stallion whose one white sock glowed in the gloom of day. The young man was no taller or broader than other riders, but his hat set him apart — black beaver skin of a western cut, with two eagle feathers stitched to a red-beaded band. When he raced, he set his hat aside; all of them did, but she had known him for years and never seen him elsewhere without that hat.

She turned toward the crowd, her own hat pulled low. If Ray meant to watch the Dark Cloud team, would he buck these thick crowds to do so? She thought it unlikely. Her uncle would be more apt to find a quiet place from which to watch. No standing flattened against the fence among shouting, hooting fans.

As the first race was announced through a megaphone, the sky let loose a flurry of half-rain, half-snow that melted as it touched ground. As the first race's participants took their places, the crowd grew agitated, like water soon to boil.

Finding a quieter spot where the betting tent's canvas wall blocked a little sound, she repositioned her saddlebags and closed her eyes to deaden distractions. If Ray was here — he *must* be here — where would he be in this mess of humanity? Perhaps at the far end of the field, watching from a place removed from the crowd. If he was not in his own shot-up truck, might he be in one of the trucks or horse vans parked on ranch property? Last night she had not seen him enter that unidentified rig, the one downtown. But he might have. He might even be in the company of someone else. If so, she would be obliged to wait for a chance to accost him in a place where others were not present. Her business with him was no one's but her own.

Stepping forward and opening her eyes, she almost collided with Charlie Ox, who stood directly in her path, bundled against the chill. His hat held a layer of the frosty crystals that continued to fall.

He said, "I wondered if I'd find you here, if you might need some help."

She tried for a neutral expression. "What sort of help?"

"You wanted my hat, which I figure means someone will be unhappy about you collecting your money. I could stand by in case there's trouble."

"There will be unhappiness, but I will see the matter resolved."

"Be a shame if you get hurt trying to get what's yours."

Raylene wondered what this young man knew about being hurt. Given that he wasn't a hundred-percent red or white, he would not have reached adolescence without some fistfights. Like everyone else he would regularly be pinched for money, scraping by and probably borrowing a few coins or a dollar now and then and arguing about who owed what. But what did he know about facing someone practiced with knives, someone who had exited bar brawls with little more than scratches and a black eye, someone who had killed his own brother. The kid meant well, but he either had some inflated notion about helping a woman out of a scrap or he fancied she would appreciate his concern and show it some way. She needed to deflect him without malice. "Now that you mention it," she said, "I do need help with something."

Charlie answered a little faster than someone with good sense might. "Anything."

From her pocket she pulled five dollars of her ranch pay. "I have heard mentioned the team that rides Dark Cloud, which gives me the idea to place a bet. But I haven't done that before and I would rather not spend time at it. I need to keep watch. You understand."

His nod was tentative.

"So, would you place a bet or two for me?"

The teen stood a little taller. "Sure will. On just that team?"

"I think a dollar or two on Dark Cloud."

The young man paused, his eyes on the money in Raylene's hand. The decision seemed to weigh on him — handle the money, or wait for the action Raylene seemed to expect.

To help him make up his mind, Raylene said, "Bet on Dark Cloud plus whichever others you like the looks of. I can check back with you to see how it's going."

After a pause, he said, "Okay. That's more than I thought you'd have."

"It's the last of it. If we win it will make up for what I might not get back from ..." She shrugged.

Charlie wiped his coat sleeve across his mouth then pointed at her saddlebags. "You could have left those where you tied your piebald. No one would take them."

Raylene brightened her expression. "So right." She shrugged to suggest she'd been caught out being silly. "Old habit." She held the cash out to the teen. He accepted it with a kind of reverence before dipping his head as if embarrassed to say, "I guess I should know your name."

Raylene was caught off guard. "Well ... call me Ray." She watched him walk away. As he disappeared into the crowd, she turned quickly and set out for the far perimeter and the vehicles parked at a distance.

An hour later, Raylene had scanned each horse rig on the track side of the Two Medicine, falling in behind this group or that, this couple or that, as they wandered one way or another, keeping a low profile as best she could. Every so often there came the rumble of the crowd near the track, its volume rising and falling with horses turning toward home and riders leaping aboard their mounts. Though icy moisture fell in waves, she knew this wasn't the weather of winter, just that in-between time that reminded people that they were not in charge.

The Two Medicine's ranch house was like many in this country, ordinary and serviceable. This one was larger than some, but with the same chipped, peeling look as any other. Fifty yards or so beyond the house sat a barn with doors ajar. Further out were the black shapeless forms of grazing beasts. The outfit would own a van or two for moving their own stock, but Raylene's gaze stopped on two rigs hitched as if having been used recently. Neither had a view of the track; they could belong to race teams, or not.

She moved in that direction, first skirting the windbreak north of the house, then moving behind a stand of poplars on the west side. Soon she could make out a paddock behind the barn where a handful of horses stood with rumps to the wind, their tails dripping water. She stopped beneath the last tree in the row, sheltered for a moment by leaves that clung to its lower branches.

As she contemplated whether to backtrack, there was movement at the barn door and two men appeared. She made herself smaller to watch the men progress slowly toward the house, the nearest one carrying a length of something coiled, the other, an object with a metal sheen.

Before long, the closest one lifted a hand as he turned for the house. The second man, newly revealed, had a familiar walk. Before he passed behind the house there came a silver flash of earring. Her pulse quickened. Raymond Yellow Moon had reappeared.

She spun and hurried back toward the racing field and the ranch's entrance. If Ray reached his vehicle first, she might lose him again. Nearing the area thickest with race fever, she swerved toward the tent, which could shield her from the ranch's front yard and the spot where the driveway widened just inside the gate. She calmed her breath and waited.

Before long, roughly eighty yards distant, a figure appeared at the far side the house. The same rolling gait, same posture, same form. He seemed to be headed toward the ranch entrance, but there were vehicles using the circular drive and people moving about so that she kept losing sight of him. Nearby voices spiked in debate — "He doesn't kick enough" — "...all my bets" — "...why's that?" — until they melded with her calculations of whether Ray might cross through the parked vehicles and end up on her side of the property.

When next she glimpsed him, he seemed immune to the sound of the crowd as it roared to life with the start of another race. Eyes straight ahead, carrying that metal object, he —

A voice broke her concentration as a hand tugged her coat sleeve. "Hey, wait 'til you hear this!" said Charlie Ox.

Trying to keep Ray in sight, Raylene shook her elbow free. "Not now."

"One race we won, then the next we lost. After that I put money on Dark Horse." He pulled again at her sleeve until she glanced toward his grinning face. "Don't you want to hear?" he continued, waving paper bills in her direction. "You won a little. Not much, but more than you bet. I told you I could do it."

"That's fine," she said, turning her attention back to the ranch entrance where her view was blocked by a group of people loading a truck. She craned her neck. *Where was he?*

Charlie inched closer. "I could bet the last race too, with all the early winners in it. Do you want me to?"

"Sure, okay, do that," said Raylene, nudging him out of her way. Why hadn't Ray appeared? There were too many people and vehicles in the way now. She broke away from Charlie, heading for the ranch's circular entrance as Charlie's voice reached her. "You're a winner!"

Raylene loped across the flattened grass and dodged between parked vehicles to reach the far side of the ranch entrance. No rig had pulled away, she was certain, and she need not check the roadside ditch. No lame-legged man would walk there, even to avoid observation.

Arriving beyond the farthest obstructions she noticed a wire gate in the fence that led onto the half-abandoned Dahlburg ranch. Beyond the gate, angling north across a grassy field was Ray, on a route that would bisect the ranch's long driveway and carry him across it toward trees the tops of which rose beyond a slight rise.

On her ride around the Dahlburg's perimeter, she had not noted any outbuildings on the northwest side of the acreage, only that little stream cutting through the property in the direction of the wooded grove. Ray had to be hobbling toward the trees in order to reach the seclusion of his own camp. Raylene stood watching until he disappeared. She knew now where to find him come nightfall, and his seclusion would benefit her plan.

Back near the race tent, the crowd stood thickly behind the fence marking the field of play. For a minute, the air seemed to clear, a break in the swirling white. Then another minute, and another. The five teams racing in the final event were called to the starting line and as if to form its myriad wills into a single organism, the crowd drew a breath.

With a wave of a blue scarf, the shouting started. A moment later, five racers thundered toward the crowd, passing in a blur of steaming horseflesh and flashes of color. Hooves churning wet grass, a snippet of black, a red bandana round a throat. What at first was a close pack began to separate at the turn.

At the perimeter of the pulsing crowd, Raylene remained watchful even though Ray could not have returned to the track with any speed. A rising clamor signaled the racers rounding the far side to head back toward the crowd. The collective crowd shouted then gasped. Two of the horses had become tangled on the change of riders. One was off in a flash but the other danced a bit until a muddy rider appeared on its back. It too flew from sight. The crowd seemed to exhale with relief.

Glancing around, Raylene caught the eye of a nearby man.

"You watch from behind the crowd," he said. His smile was subtle as he tipped his black western hat in her direction. "Is your favorite not in the final?"

"If I favor one team, it is only that I know people who care about them." She did not explain that a relative of hers cared most about the horse and a friend most about its winningest rider.

"You carry other people's hopes."

She nodded. "A win is good, but beneath it all is the wish that they come to no harm."

The spectators boomed again as the man made a gesture to encompass them. "Most here want a winner above all else."

"Winning is good but there is also —"

"Raylene!" came a cry from behind them.

She turned, ready to greet Charlie, but it was Lyle Stoneman staggering forward, one fist cocking back in slow motion.

As Raylene put a hand out, her companion stepped forward, saying, "Hey now!"

"You bitch!" cried Stoney. His eyes were red and spittle flew from his mouth. "I'll teach you to cross me."

"You are drunk," said Raylene.

The fair-haired man spoke. "Is this your man? Do you want me to turn him away?"

"He is not my man," said Raylene, "just angry over things beyond his control."

"Don't you say anything about me. You don't get to talk about me," said Stoney, slurring his words.

The man lowered his voice so that only Raylene could hear. "I carry a badge. I can take him away." When Raylene gave him a questioning look, he added, "From Rapid City, hired for the crowd."

She said, "It is best I face the troubles I have played a part in. Perhaps if you walk away, he will not have to fight."

The lawman hesitated before speaking louder. "I will be watching. If he assaults you, he will answer to me." He turned away and let the crowd swallow him.

Raylene held Stoney's unsteady gaze.

"You," he said, "made a fool of me."

She sighed. "Joseph could not know what I told you in confidence. If he knows, then *you* told him."

Stoney shook his head as if to clear his thoughts, his fist still in a knot. "Not Joseph. That girl last night."

Raylene reeled her thoughts back from Joseph's house in Oglala to the previous night when she had paid the saloon girl to ply Stoney with drinks. Drinks were nothing to fight over. She had only provided funds to keep him out of her way.

"That girl," said Stoney. "I went around back with her and then we ... well, when we came back, she joked in front of others ..." Here, he seemed on the verge of tears.

So that was it. Raylene had known Stoney for most of her years. Even as a child, she had known how different he was, could see in him what he refused to acknowledge. She knew why he called others *wínkte*. Because he himself was. In a

212

previous time, a tribe would have accepted a *wínkte* man as special for being different than most men, but that time was past. Raylene had only asked the drinks girl to offer him booze, but he must have made advances that she accepted. Now he blamed Raylene for his embarrassment.

To better explain, she took a step toward him, but he lurched forward at the same time, his fist coming up in a blow that swept across her jaw and knocked her backwards. He fell forward to his knees as she landed with a thud at the back of the crowd. The closest fans turned in mid-cheer, looks of surprise on their faces. Before any could respond, the Rapid City lawman was at Raylene's side, offering her a hand to right herself. Upon rising to her feet, she felt her painful jaw and touched a finger to the blood seeping from one nostril.

"That does it," said the lawman. "I'll take him away." He held out a white cloth to her.

She recalled Stoney and Joseph with Henry following them around like a dog in need of a pack. She said, "It's not a crime, being angry. That's just him."

"But he hit you, unprovoked."

"You didn't witness my provocation." She dabbed her bloody nose with the lawman's handkerchief. "But it was there. He'll be fine after some sleep."

As a person might guess, the lawman man could only see what was before him, and what was readily visible cast a cloud over Stoney. He said, "We'd better move him before he gets trampled." He stepped to Stoney and took him by the shoulders. Stoney tried to shake him off, but Raylene joined the lawman in tugging Stoney to his feet and drag-walking him to an empty folding chair beside the betting tent. "Coffee?" said the lawman.

"Not at a horse race," said Raylene.

The man glanced around. "Maybe up at the house? I guess

I could check. Say, where's this one from?"

"Oglala."

"I guess if he can walk by the time they fold this tent, I can drop him on my way back."

Raylene gave him a grateful look. "The owner of the town market would see that he gets home."

"Or, if I arrest him, he can sleep it off in jail."

"I wish you would not."

They stood looking at each other until the lawman said, "I'll go ask at the house for coffee."

"Thanks also for the handkerchief."

"You might keep it for ice."

When the man had gone, Raylene gave Stoney's shoulder a pat and started off in the other direction. "Hey," he called after her. "I got somethin' to say."

Raylene was beyond listening to him and had no wish to stick around and encounter Charlie Ox again. Stoney began a recitation of resentments, but Raylene kept walking until the sound of his voice dissolved in the wind.

Fifteen

Raylene had not eaten since sharing hot cereal with Edda. Thinking she would seek a bite to eat before what could be a long night ahead, she drove Edda's truck the two miles back to Manderson's business zone among a slow trickle of vehicles. After refueling, she parked near the town's hotel and in the truck's mottled mirror checked that she had adequately cleaned the blood from her nose and chin.

Once she stood inside, with aromas of savory fixings swirling round her and the lady owner eyeing her, she didn't have it in her to order a full meal. Instead, she settled for coffee, strong and black, and a buttermilk biscuit with honey.

Passing by with an armful of empty plates, the same proprietor she had spoken with yesterday said, "No offense, but you look a little rough. Step in with the horses, did you?"

Raylene ran a hand across her swollen jaw. "A gift from an admirer."

"Some gift. Did you find whoever-you-said ... the team, or was it the rider?"

"I saw him at a distance. He looked fine."

"And how did he do?"

"I don't exactly know."

This drew a puzzled look.

"I was there," added Raylene. "Just distracted."

The owner gave a shake of her head as she turned toward the kitchen.

While sipping coffee, Raylene pondered whether to

retrieve her cow pony from Edda's barn. Having him with her would provide comfort, but also concern about secreting him on the outskirts of woods skulked after dark by coyotes and big cats, perhaps a wolf or two. No, he was safe where he was and she would soon make it back to him. She *must* make it back to him.

By the time Raylene left the restaurant, other customers were waiting for tables, and the main road had come alive with a variety of vehicles, horse-drawn wagons, and lone riders. A good many of them slowed for parking. As she pulled away, another driver took the spot she left open.

Overhead, waning rays of light from between broken clouds shone upon the road and its verge of grasses which had baked through the summer months. The hour for predators was coming.

John H. Murphy
Chestnut Avenue
Kansas City, Missouri

October 6, 1936

Miss Raylene Little Moon
c/o Postmaster
Pine Ridge Reservation
Oglala, South Dakota

Dear Miss Little Moon,

Please forgive my poor onehanded typing which will make for errors since I dont even type on my best days. I know not when or if this will reach you but have decided to break with procedure to express in confidence that which I spent three days thinking about while on my drivehome.

The jewelry I searched for rightfully belonged to another but was given by my U P boss Pherson Campbell to your sister. He provided me with that photograph but not the location where it was taken. I can attest that he was not in KC at the time of Annie s death, but soon returned by rail from business in Chicago. I did not think to refuse the assignment to locate that jewelry, nor do I regret my efforts as I feel somehow changed by the whole affair.

After I met you in the Conboie parlor, Annies

landlady described a man claiming to be her father, whom she said took a valise

After meeting you I read a police report containing what appeared to be standard language and specifying no suspicions regarding your sisters manner of death. There was a mention of possible pregnancy, unconfirmed. In my memory that report now seems pitifully thin. There may have been more not yet in the file or for some reason kept elsewhere Or the paperwork was yet to be completed. I might be wrong, but that is now my impression.

Again I offer my condolences, which as I type this seem inadequate.

~~If you ever need assista~~

Sincerely,
John H. Murphy

Back on the road leading to the ranches, Raylene met only sporadic traffic. The day's racing activity on the Two Medicine would be winding down. After pulling to one side and shutting down the truck, she settled in to watch the roughly 50-yard section of the Dahlburg's dirt driveway visible from her vantage. The driveway rose slightly to disappear over the rise that led to the woods. The truck's engine clicked in time to a symphony of crickets not yet gone to ground. Now that she was this close to Ray's camp, her stomach felt empty, her whole being empty. She took a sugar cube from her pocket and tucked it in her cheek, and waited.

As dusk fell, she exited the truck with her saddlebags and crossed to the ranch gate where she unhooked its looped metal latch, closing it securely after her. Inside the wire, she followed the narrow stream where it cut through the first rise, visible for another hundred yards, exposed to anyone watching from the stretch of poplars and cottonwoods whose golden foliage fluttered in the breeze. The closer she drew to the trees, the more obvious it became that somewhere within the woods, or at its distant perimeter, a small campfire glowed orange.

Reaching the leading edge of the trees, she stepped into shadows as black as a starless night and onto leaf litter softened by time and moisture. As she worked her way through the trees and thick undergrowth, rattling leaves overhead obscured the sound of her steps. An angle leftward brought her closer to the stream's gurgle. She kept the flicker of orange to her right as she listened for voices. Murmurs reached her first, then a whiff of smoke and a hoot of laughter. At the sound of a young woman's giggle, Raylene knew that this was not her uncle's camp. Ray would not countenance a giggler. She need not look closer.

She moved on, a shadow among shadows. Once she was

parallel to the fire's glow, she glanced in its direction and caught a glimpse of silhouettes plus what appeared to be the glow of skin lit by dancing firelight. Now she heard a man's laugh. Night had not yet fallen, but darkness was not needed for the attraction of flesh to flesh. She moved forward to a grassy break in the trees. Crossing it, she glanced right to note the distant ranch house, a sturdy rectangle of a building with curtained windows.

Back within the trees again, she moved toward a second fiery glow. In Sioux City, the sun's dancing fire behind her eyelids had revealed racing horses. Fire, it seemed now, would lead to her uncle.

The second camp was also set on the driveway side of the woods, close enough for fetching water from the stream and kindling from beneath trees. Drawing closer to this encampment, she made out strings of conversation, unintelligible at first, then, "*Te dije que no apostaras tanto.*" Something about betting. "*Dáme esa botella,*" a reference to a bottle. Moments later there came, "*Ella no te estaba mirando sino a mi´.*"

Having worked throughout the years alongside a caballero or two, Raylene knew a few words and phrases. There was Raul, who said things like, "*Sexo contigo me mata,*" which was followed by something he did with his hands that tore her attention from the clean-smelling hay or the storm raging outside or any other thing he uttered. He never provided a proper translation and she knew better than to ask the other cowhands because it wouldn't take a detective to know who she had heard it from.

She would not find her uncle in this second camp because he scorned Mexicans, who worked for less pay than Indians and Negroes, who themselves earned less than whites. Perhaps such was the truth on worksites where he'd been, like the Fort Peck Dam, built by hundreds of workers, or maybe a thousand, but in ranching, seasoned cowhands made roughly the same wages no matter their tribe.

Maintaining her cover behind the trees, she moved forward, circling right a bit before the woods petered out. Half-hidden, she glanced back toward the last encampment. In the damp grass near it sat a vehicle, and at the fire, three unfamiliar figures.

Out past the end of the woods were silhouettes of the ranch's graveyard of old equipment. Worn out hay rakes and tractors, cast-off gate grills and stacks of tires, two- or three-decades' worth. From where she stood gazing at the graveyard's narrow end, some of the shapes resembled huge, square elephants, and now there came a different fire's glow from among the derelict machines.

The shadowy graveyard was quiet and secluded. Her uncle's kind of place.

Raylene checked the contents of her saddlebags. Her plan was simplicity itself, comprised primarily of two special ingredients plus stealth and resolve. Otherwise, she would be no match for him.

This last week had brought reports of an injured Ray. He would have been healthy when he faced Thomas across the saloon's polished wood bar, the two of them likely arguing first in low voices before growing louder, eyes glinting blackly as one brother circled round to meet the other. Had Thomas made the first move, or Raymond? Each knew the other's strengths and weaknesses and how to strike a deadly blow. In childhood they had played at warring with white soldiers or pretended to be marauding bandits, had played at counting coup, racing in to touch each other without deadly force. But Ray's fight with Thomas had been all too real. After the first exchanges of blame or the refuting of accusations — whatever it was that had divided them — once blades were drawn, words would have fallen away.

To calm herself, Raylene took a series of deep breaths. Ray had counseled deep breathing to quell flighty thoughts and fear beyond that which honed the senses.

Backtracking deeper into the woods, she struck out for its upper end, which thinned and quit thirty yards or so from the closest hunk of discarded farm equipment. The growing darkness would obscure her some, but it would also dim the details of distant objects. And people. She had not yet found Ray's camp, which meant it must be up ahead.

Mindful of the uneven ground underfoot, she studied the leading end of the equipment graveyard for any sign of a person, or people. Ray might still have a companion with him, but she doubted he would keep company with more than one person. Certainly not Wilma's nephew and his team, who had no reason to spend time in seclusion, camping alongside derelict vehicles and farm machines when they could enjoy the companionship of other racers or the attentions of ranch owners and racing fans. Which meant that if another person had made camp with Ray, it was not Leonard and his bunch.

With her second step out of the trees, she froze as a great owl, wings as wide as she was tall, glided close enough to silently ripple the air around her. The hour for predators had indeed arrived.

Minutes later she reached the first of the dead, as she thought of them now, mechanical beasts set aside until such time they could again fulfill a need. Now the air smelled heavy with decaying metal and rubber. She ran a hand along the rusting surface of the nearest tractor, whose pocked and scabby body suggested it had not known paint in long time. In coming storms, its rust would run in rivulets like blood. Given enough time, the whole of it would be reclaimed by the earth.

Crickets started up again while Raylene lingered, but quit when she moved on. She picked her way, now faintly lit by starlight, past assorted abandoned vehicles until she could again make out a glow of light sliced and reflected by the shapes around her. She advanced with the stream to her left until in the gloaming she could read the lettering on one of the huge, square-backed vehicles. "Glacier," "ark," and "Tou." A retired tour coach, then, brought here for parts, maybe, or some future project.

By her estimation, the source of yellow light lay just ahead. She drew Ray's hunting knife and held it at the ready as she advanced to crouch at the front of the Glacier coach to peer at a flickering orange glow beneath the next coach over. Someone's fire. Since no resident of the prairie would leave a fire burning unattended for long, someone who belonged to that fire would be found nearby.

Raylene dropped prone to the ground to peer beneath the coaches, catching a glimpse of thin metal legs near the fire. She stood again and was debating how to advance when the crickets near the stream suddenly fell silent again. Frozen in place, with senses on alert, she squinted until she caught the movement of an upright shape beyond the graveyard's black outlines. A shape the right height with a glint of silver at its head.

Withdrawing, she crouched again behind the Glacier coach, knife readied for the sound of advancing footfall. Breath held, she waited, listening for Ray's slight drag of foot from his Fort Peck injury. Seconds stretched to breaking until she took another breath. Had he glimpsed her hair or the toe of her boot, he would be upon her by now, but he did not come, which was good because he could be armed with any of the many knives he had made in his lifetime. If so, he — a CLANG of metal resounded in the night, followed by an indistinguishable curse.

Raylene ventured a look around the front of her barricade. The glow of a fire beneath the next coach persisted, and now she detected a dark shape moving about high up inside that coach. The silhouette folded out of view, perhaps to rest on a seat bench, at about the time the first notes of coffee reached her.

Many times, she had lain in her childhood bed alongside Annie, the aroma of coffee in the air while her mother and father, or mother and uncle, conversed through the night. Occasionally she and Annie defied the call of sleep in order to rise and plead for a mug of sweetened coffee to share. Success came only after satisfying the adults with imitations of antelope or other animals or birds of the field. They had, in effect, performed for the bittersweet treat.

Now she was certain that this was Ray's camp. Other racing camps partied with alcohol, but this one ran on coffee. Raylene sheathed her knife. Settling her saddlebags on the ground, she opened one side and from it pulled three of the medicaments she carried. One was an emetic purchased from the doctor's woman near the Omaha reservation. Another was belladonna powder that could kill a person if used in quantity. The third was laudanum in a brown, stoppered bottle. She tucked the powder and the bottle into her coat pocket.

Raylene sheathed Ray's knife and removed her boots. In a half-crouch, she dashed across the divide to creep past the front of Ray's coach. There, she found that the vehicle was door-less and the steps inside, unoccupied. Two much-weathered coach benches sat upright near the fire. A third lay on its back.

The campfire was banked low, its coppery flames licking skyward. On a heap of stones set in the flames sat an aluminum coffee pot, bubbling away. It seemed placed there just for her purpose.

With a stick of kindling, she lifted the pot from its place, flipped it open, and poured in a third of the laudanum plus a pinch of the belladonna powder. Returning everything to its place, she stole out of the circle of warmth to a spot out of sight at the coach's front bumper.

Time slowed and the sky held its breath as she waited for her plan to succeed or fail. Failure would force her to accost Ray during the night while he slept. Of course, he might be asleep in his coach at that very moment, forgetting his coffee as it boiled away. Or, if he detected the coffee's odd odor, take only a sip and suffer some lethargy but nothing more. She needed him to follow his habit of drinking heartily.

She had thought this through. Kill her uncle outright would result in her never learning his reason for killing Thomas, which she wanted to hear. She also wanted to know what he knew about Annie's death. He was due a reckoning, but she wanted information before completing her plan.

A creaking sound vibrated through the coach wall, followed by footfall on the steps. The clank of the pot, and then silence. *Patience,* she told herself. Patience was a warrior's virtue, followed by a quick strike when the time was right. She had not imagined being tested against someone who embodied more warrior ways than anyone else she knew. She did not think herself a warrior, but patience was one of her virtues.

From a distance came the calls of coyotes on the prowl. Then a twig snapped nearby. Raylene leaped to her feet and jumped backwards as a black shape appeared at the front corner of the coach, arms stretched wide, hands like bats taking flight. "Poison!" croaked Ray.

He staggered forward as if to fall upon her. Raylene backed away but still he kept coming, dragging one foot. She was at the coach's far end with nowhere to go but into the open —

never turn your back on an opponent — when her coat snagged on the jagged back bumper. She yanked it free. As if energized, he advanced upon her.

She turned now and struck for the outer glow of Ray's fire as he stumbled after her, stopping suddenly as if seeing the fire for the first time. Instantly, he changed course, weaving a line toward the flames until Raylene dashed forward to stop him at the fire's ring of stones.

With a gut-wrenching groan, he bent forward and vomited into the ruby coals. "You poisoned me," he said.

"They're medicine, sometimes."

Ray wiped his mouth on his sleeve. His glassy eyes were beginning to roll back in his head. Hands on his knees, he retched into the fire then turned awkwardly from his bent position and displayed a face masked by fear and wonder. His features contorted even further as he lifted a hand to grasp her coat sleeve. His head rolled one way then the next before he finally fixed his eyes on her. After a moment he coughed and licked his lips. Then he said, "Helen."

Raylene paused. He had not mentioned her *iná*, her mother, in years. Was it the laudanum speaking? Thoughts about people now gone — her mother, Annie, her father — arrived like pinpricks from ghosts. She said, "You need water."

"Uhn," he grunted, his eyes following something over her shoulder.

She turned, but saw no creature on two legs or four, which eased her mind a little. "I'll help you."

With her help, he straightened and wobbled over to one of the upturned coach seats. There, he collapsed with a groan, his lame leg outstretched. Raylene went into his coach for a container to use for water. The moon's light and a bit of fire glow cast light enough to make out wood shavings strewn about the floor and Ray's old bedroll in the spot where benches had been removed.

A tin pipe hung from the ceiling over an upturned barrel lid that sat upon bricks, a perfect arrangement for an indoor fire. There was the old canvas duffel Ray always carried, and a walking stick, half-carved with birds, feathers, and other symbols. Next to it, a two-dollar jack knife, the sort any ordinary man might carry. She touched a hand once more to the bump beneath her coat which was Ray's knife. Tonight, he would meet it again.

She located an empty pail and carried it to the stream, Ray's mutterings following her. When she returned with it half-full, Ray's head was bobbing almost imperceptibly to what by then would be fantastical imaginings. Seeing him so disarmed that he lay sprawled half off his seat softened her heart, but only a little. He had brought upon himself the difficult duty that lay ahead for her.

"I'll carry this inside for you," she said. She made a show of picking up the discarded coffee cup and rinsing it with water from the pail before carrying them both into the coach. There, in the upturned metal lid she lit a small fire that gave off modest heat but threw enough light for navigating the space. Returning to Ray's side, she said, "Come to your bed."

His answer was a drawn out "No."

"You'll rest better in your own blankets."

Blinking as if at some invisible motion picture show, he shook his head.

Raylene needed him in a location that would shield them both from prying eyes or those who might hear what came next. She took his arm. "The fire will die soon," she said. "Leave it for tomorrow and come inside where it is warmer," an exaggeration she needed him to fall for.

Finally, he let her tug him to his feet and hoist his right arm over her shoulder. Through his coat she felt the bones of his back, and this surprised her. How had he shrunk so? At the stairs leading into the coach, she gave him a hand up.

"*Khéya*," said Ray. Turtle. The name she and Annie had given their doll, which waited with her other possessions in Edda's barn. She wanted to say, "Don't you call me *Khéya*. That is a name you may no longer speak to me." But to refute him was to interrupt his reverie and perhaps his compliant state of mind.

Raylene backed down the coach's aisle, one step, another step, prompting Ray to follow her. He gripped the coach seats with one hand; the other he held against his hip. His eyes seemed focused elsewhere.

She prompted him to doff his coat to use as a pillow though he had a rolled sheepskin for that use. Now she could see his left shirt sleeve caked with dried black-looking blood. Delivered by her father, no doubt.

With Ray prone, she dipped his tin cup into the pail and splashed liquid from the stoppered bottle into it. Back at his side, she knelt, saying, "Sit so you can drink." He lay with his hair splayed out around him like the rays of a black sun until she tugged his upper body into position. She held the cup to his mouth as he drank.

"Good," he said with a sigh.

"You killed Thomas," she said. "Tell me if this is so."

His eyes were closed as he answered. "My duty to kill him."

"What about Annie?"

"Already dead."

"You knew she was?"

He fell silent against his makeshift pillow so she waited, but after some moments she went out to bring in her saddlebags from which she pulled long, thin ropes strong enough to hold a man. When she sat near him again, he spoke, startling her.

"Waiting for you," he said. "I was ..." His words trailed off as his head lolled to one side. The second dose of laudanum, this time without the belladonna, had taken over.

With the ropes she secured Ray's wrists and ankles to the legs of the bench seats nearest each side of him. Bolted to the floor, the seats would withstand the thrashing of any man. Next, she unfastened the buttons of his shirt which was stiff with old sweat. He had always kept himself clean, but now he wore a rank odor, not simply from a lack of washing, but something else, perhaps from his wounded arm that didn't seem to work.

She tamped down her instinct to heal and soothe because this was the man who had killed her father in what must have been a swift encounter because her father was also skilled with a knife. She knew she should get this over with, but instead she got up and left the coach. She crossed to the stream and stood beside it, gazing at the inky sky and the half-moon shining between clouds. Her breath rose around her in plumes, but sweat dampened the small of her back. She had hunted her uncle and poisoned him and bound him so that she could exact a retribution that he himself would expect, but her heart was in opposition. *Do it. Don't do it.* A sign would be helpful.

Fingers of night breeze moved the grasses at her feet as somewhere way off came the squeak of a rodent. The sky blinked its myriad eyes, but none of these things could she read as counsel. She changed tack. What would Annie, a citified reservation girl, say about a warrior tradition that put a knife in Raylene's hand and their uncle at Raylene's mercy? She thought on this a moment but she did not know what Annie would say. Thomas would say, "A Yellow Moon finishes the fight." And Ray, a man this very moment bound by ropes and awaiting her retribution? He would say *Finish the fight.*

She left the peerless sky and perpetual breeze for Ray's coach and knelt beside the man who, except for a nearly imperceptible scar above his left ear, was a carbon copy of her father. The same face, the same heritage, the same honoring of the old ways. Much of what she knew about horses and riding and taking pride in her native blood she had learned at the side of this man, who never apologized for his brown skin or his landless ways. Memories of Thomas and Ray and Annie and their mother had ridden with her to the town of Manderson, and followed her on foot into the crowd at the racing competition. Memories had draped themselves across the seat of Edda's truck and a few memories were this very moment tucked into her pockets.

Across the miles, she had considered various responses she might make to Ray's crime. Had he been Annie's killer, she would feel justified in killing him, but in this place at this moment, with the weight of their shared history plus her many unanswered questions, she could not deny that killing a Yellow Moon was simply beyond her. She could not kill him yet she could not leave him unpunished. In the olden days, a crime might be punished with death or by banishment from family and community. But their family had split apart long ago, traveling far from home at different times, even moving far away, as Annie and Thomas had. And as Ray had through his wanderings.

She wanted him to live with his crime and be reduced by it the way she had been reduced by it. One way she could assure that he would never forget killing Thomas was to use his own knife against him. That itself would render a proper reprisal. She returned to his coach.

Lashed to the bench seats, Ray lay prone, his shirt turned back to reveal protruding ribs. His breath gave evidence that he still lived and his eyes behind their lids rolled this way and that, following some drug-induced dream.

Raylene passed the knife blade through the tip of the flame burning in the can — a hot blade would reduce the amount of blood — and stilled all thought but that which directed her aim. A welt of blood appeared behind the blade as she split the skin of Ray's left chest with a stroke intentionally shallow and precise. Though Ray did not flinch, her own chest tightened and she imagined she could feel his nerves shriek in response to hot steel. When her vision began to swim, she blinked to clear her sight.

Stilling her heart amid all that clamor, she finished a vertical line then a shorter, horizontal one. Ray's eyes flew open and his mouth formed a silent, tooth-baring scream, which halted her hand for an instant. But she knew that the opium's iron grip made her actions unrecognizable to him within its trickery of phantasms.

She worked quickly, passing the blade often through the can-held flame. With the third letter, tears formed in the corners of Ray's eyes before trickling down onto his neck, but still he made no sound. She squeezed her own eyes shut before opening them to continue her work. His limbs jerked a little.

When she was finished, she sat back. She had altered the man known as Raymond Yellow Moon. He who had once been a type of warrior strong and true was now someone who carried upon his own body, proof of his crime against his brother. Seeping blood exaggerated the inscription now atop his heart, which he would carry for all time — the initials of her father, his brother — TYM.

Sixteen

Raylene released the bonds holding Ray. The rope had chafed his wrists, so she gave each a rub then pulled his torso upright to pour sips of plain water into his mouth before she herself drank a cupful.

With Ray lying back again, she set about cooking a yarrow and burdock tea, using dried flowers and stems from her herb kit and a tin cup of water balanced over the can fire until it steamed. When the tea was rich in color with a woody fragrance, she took it off the heat to cool. Then she ripped strips from the cleanest shirt in Ray's duffle and wet them in the tea and applied them to his wounds. Listening to him breathe, she watched for signs of a greater failure.

From Wilma's supply, Raylene carried a small draught of atropine crystals in water, a potion used for Lizzy when her heart fell to failing. If need be, she would revive Ray because though she was done with administering violence, she had more business with him. She wanted to know what had driven him to kill his only brother. To her mind, each had seemed one half of what made the other whole. With one of them dead, the other was surely incomplete. So, why kill? She could not ride away without knowing.

The rising moon cast a pale glow through the spattered, murky coach windows as Ray lay in place, twitching now and then. One window, she saw now, had in its center a round wipe mark where someone had tried to clean it for looking out. Another held only spines of broken glass.

She covered Ray with his coat and a layer of spare clothing from his duffle then allowed herself to doze, waking sometime later to the sound of his moaning. He moved his good arm a little and bucked his legs as if to test their worthiness. She moved to kneel alongside him, where she could look into his face, and he into hers. Blinking, he opened his eyes as he fumbled with one hand at the dressings laid across his wounds.

"You are in your camp on the Dahlburg ranch," said Raylene.

He licked his lips as if to make them work, so she fed him more sips of plain water until he could speak. He said, "You cut me, daughter."

The bitterness she had tasted at seeing her father's dead body came over her again. "Do not call me 'daughter.' I was a daughter to you, but no longer. I am done with you. I have marked you with a reminder of your crime against our family."

"Little Ray. I waited." Each word delivered with effort.

Little Ray was his pet name for her, unused since childhood but excavated now for some unstated purpose. That Ray dredged up names from the past could not cure what had come between him and her. Thomas waited now beyond the sky. Having been sent away without proper ceremony, his waiting might never know an end.

"Do not toy with me," she said. "I will see you stand again because it is in my nature to do so before you move to a place from which you will not return as long as an ounce of your honor remains. Also, because I mean to hear your reason for taking my family from me."

Ray blinked and shook his head as if to clear it. When his eyes fell shut again, Raylene thought he might have closed his mind to her as well, but after a moment, he spoke. "Did not kill Annie."

"I did not think you capable of that. If there is mercy in the world, I will one day learn more about her death." She thought a moment. "I thank you for seeing to her burial."

Ray seemed to shrink into himself, though he was nearly a shadow already. When he spoke again, his words were weak. "I did not."

"You must have."

"No."

Raylene tried to think what it meant that he had not arranged Annie's burial. The undertaker would not have made an effort unless someone had paid. "But Annie —"

"Hooch," said Ray. "Thomas."

He had fallen to nonsense again. Thomas did not succumb to hooch. He had clearly been killed by knife, and Ray was trying to suggest otherwise. She had looked into the pine box that held Thomas's body and beheld that he would never again observe the lands around them — the gold of fall grasses waving in the breeze, the soaring birds and singing waters, the wild places tucked among weathered sandstone cliffs. He would never again walk the land of his own birth or the land of his children. She had fingered the stitches that closed the wound in his corpse and heard about the crow feather. She had known then, felt it to her core, that Ray had knifed Thomas. To suggest it had been hooch meant either the drug had muddled him beyond her expectations, or ...

It came to her.

When she had mentioned Annie, Ray had mentioned hooch and Thomas. Maybe he meant — *please* not that. Could he mean that hooch from Thomas's saloon had killed their own Annie? Powered by blood turned icy hot, Raylene's thoughts spun webs connecting the saloon her father ran with her sister's job there and the booze her father and his connections had cooked during Prohibition but had no reason to continue making now. Except for the reason of big profits from cheap, homemade booze. Had Thomas continued selling moonshine? Now she realized Billy Horse had suggested as much. Still, something inside her wanted Ray to have gotten this wrong, wanted laudanum's effect to account for his words. She had to ask, "Do you believe Thomas's hooch killed Annie?" When no answer came from Ray, she shook him gently and asked, "How could you know?"

"She drank ... it."

Desperation rose in Raylene. The so-called natural cause cited for Annie's death by the Kansas City police might have applied to death by booze. Annie was no stranger to drink, but did that mean the cause could have been deadly hooch provided by Thomas? Raylene wanted Ray to be wrong. She said, "How can you blame Thomas?"

"I see her."

A great weight overtook Raylene such that her arms no longer functioned. Her head grew heavy upon a torso sinking through the floor toward the dirt below. The weight of the sky itself now pressed down upon her. Nothing had prepared her for the thought that Thomas could be responsible for Annie's death, but Thomas would never have knowingly provided tainted hooch to Annie. Perhaps he had simply not protected her from it. He had been absent from their lives at different points and when present, a guiding light. As a child she'd had no way to know if his absences were truly necessary. When Ray was present, they had missed Thomas less. Raylene found she could blame her father for neglect of a daughter, but a direct deed — supplying Annie with tainted hooch — the very idea made her ache all over.

Incomplete as Ray's answers seemed to be, she understood what he meant. Deception in battle was one thing, and as such was admired by others, but lying to family contradicted his insistence upon living an honorable life. His placing of blame against his own twin suggested he had seen some evidence, or — she mentally recoiled at the thought of this — he was lying to her in order to sour her against Thomas. She asked, "Do you have proof?"

He shook his head as his eyes closed. He was fading again with a need to sleep off the fog of opium. How convenient — to accuse Thomas, who could no longer defend himself. Was this a bid for compassion when he must have known that if she'd meant to kill him, she could have done so by now.

She decided she would fetch her horse while he rested. She put a hand on his shoulder. "You are certain my father's hooch killed Annie?"

"No," he said as he closed his eyes.

Raylene's stomach filled with stones. More lies, or did the opium grip him tighter? Which of his words were lies, and which the truth? Urgency drove her. Leaning in close she asked, "Did you kill Thomas?"

Once more he brought two fingers to his chest. "Yes."

"Tell me true. Was it my father's hooch that killed Annie?"

When he spoke it was with difficulty, but Raylene watched his lips. There was no mistaking the words that spun her world from its orbit.

"Not father," he said. "Thomas."

Ray's declaration knocked all things out of place — the coach's cold steel floor, the worn bench seats, her sweat-stained saddlebags smelling of Kota, the fist-sized fire set upon stones. The stones themselves, her breath, the beat of life within her, all of it came unmoored. *Not father. Thomas.*

How was she to understand this claim from a man already employing lies, half-truths, and deflections? Either Ray had killed someone named Thomas who was not their family's Thomas, or having been killed by Ray, Thomas Yellow Moon was not her father. Her conscious mind erected a roadblock of memories against that proposition. There she was, being too young for school but of an age for gathering sticks on a riverbank while Uncle and Father caught fish. One or both of the men leading her around in circles on her first pony. There were meals with parents and her grandmother and neighbors gathered round. Thomas had shown her how to whittle and to read the forked tracks of birds and the imprints of animals, and Ray how to find the center of a horse and how to calm it with soothing words and a firm but gentle touch. Thomas and Raymond had both acted as father, yet Thomas *was* Father.

Now she questioned how truthful Ray had ever been, the faults in his character presenting themselves: He had not attended her mother's death ceremony, the one they'd held on the northern Pine Ridge. For the last twelve or fifteen years, he had at times vanished without notice or farewell. During her school graduation, she had bestowed the principal with a paper tomahawk in protest of his treatment of students, but Ray had not been present to signal approval with his characteristic crease of a smile. Another question: Had he abandoned Wilma and Lizzy? Not that she knew Lizzy as his responsibility, but still. And then there was his drunken behavior during the poker game reported by that ranch worker. The litany of Ray's faults was long, as long as that of Thomas's, which were difficult to contemplate while he lay in a pauper's grave.

She could not summon hate for Ray. He was in rough shape, drugged by her own hand and perhaps recognizing that she could leave him for dead in a run-down motor coach. She had never pitied him, had held him above others, but now he had fallen to the status of an ordinary man, his own best friend and worst enemy. She decided to let his words rest in shadows until daylight shone upon them and they either held up or fell apart.

From somewhere nearby, coyotes began a chase song that stood her attention upright. Breaking from her reverie, she found that she was standing among the dead contraptions of the graveyard beneath a canopy of stars. She made her way over to the shrinking coals of Ray's campfire. After checking inside to see that he rested easily, she would backtrack to Edda's truck and return riding Kota. The coming hours would bring burdensome questions. Her uncle had better have answers.

It was well after midnight when Raylene drove past parked vehicles and horses tied along the sidewalks of Manderson's main street, her thoughts wheeling round the workings of Thomas's Kansas City saloon, named Down the Street. In defiance of federal laws, he had managed the place for eight or so years and at one point mentioned working his way toward partnership. She had seen him behind the bar and in conversation with patrons, and once watched him stop a fight by thrusting a broad shoulder and two meaty hands between two drunks. When he leaned in to growl what must have been a warning, the combatants stopped to gape at him and then each other. At the time she had thought he had handled the situation well. It helped that he retained some of his youthful muscularity and the bearing of a man not to trifle with. Out of curiosity, she watched whether women drinking there turned hungry eyes upon him, but no secret smiles caught her notice.

Annie had also fled to Kansas City, where the family had lived during spring and summer of 1915, returning to visit the Pine Ridge only twice after settling in proximity to Thomas and his evolving booze trade. She had worked her way up from sweeping the saloon floor to pouring drinks and ringing up purchases. With her penchant for people and her perennially sunny disposition, Annie was a customer favorite.

By the time Raylene arrived at Edda's property on the west side, the moon's ascent suggested that the time might be 2:00 a.m. or so, but instead of the house being dark, Edda's front curtains were open to the glow from a lantern within. After steering the truck into place alongside the house and killing its engine, she went to the front of the house. A figure appeared in the window, stretching as if just risen from the rocking chair positioned nearby.

Edda greeted Raylene from the doorway. "You are safe. I tended your horse but he will be glad for your return."

Raylene stood at the bottom of the steps. "Thank you for your good care, and for the use of your truck."

"Did you find the person you sought?"

"I did." Though the woman was but a silhouette, Raylene felt the heat of her gaze.

"And you are still standing."

"Yes."

"That is good. Will you sleep again in the stable?"

"I need to go back to finish what I started."

Edda paused. "Which might bring you more trouble."

Raylene had given only cursory thought to whether Ray would present more danger to her if nursed back to health. Currently, he was weak but he would in time emerge from his opium fog. His wounded arm notwithstanding, he might with rest and decent food return to his previous vitality. If he decided that she had wronged him, he might scheme against her too. Perhaps she would keep his knife for a time, and remain watchful.

"I have no wish for it," she told Edda, "but trouble seems to have followed me. Shall I bring you more stove wood before I saddle my horse?"

"I have plenty for now. Will you not rest awhile?"

"I cannot."

"Then I will wrap some food for you."

Raylene hesitated. She had appeared as a stranger in need of shelter and sustenance and this woman had provided both. She was reluctant to accept more assistance, yet she needed something to eat and something to feed Ray until she could provision them both in town. On this day, Sunday, most businesses, perhaps all but the hotel, would be closed, and that establishment would be filled to capacity with travelers who had not yet headed for home. She agreed to accept a parcel of traveling foods plus two biscuits to eat as she traveled on horseback.

Handing the parcel to Raylene, Edda reached with a callused finger to touch Raylene's cheek. "The spirits hear us. I will ask them for your safe passage."

Raylene swallowed hard. In the soft light from the moon, this woman seemed again to embody Raylene's grandmother, with the same measured words and knowing gaze, the same generosity prized by people of the plains. "I hope they hear you," she said, "and grant you the same."

Before long she was saddling Kota, who snorted in pleasure at her greeting and quivered with nervous energy as she ran her hands over his knees to check for adverse effects from their late-night gallop. He seemed fine though anxious to quit the dark stall from which he could only hear but not taste the vast world outside.

Her brief exchange with Edda had been truthful. She was not finished with Ray. She had never thought of him as owing her anything, but now he owed her more than riddles.

Back on Dahlburg property, she directed Kota up the ranch drive, giving a wide berth to the slumbering camps of people she had scouted hours prior. Edda's biscuits had revived her a little, but she knew that she would need some sleep before long. From the cinders of Ray's campfire rose a tendril of smoke in the still air. She led Kota to the stream to drink then tethered him in a patch of grass growing near the rear of Ray's sleeping coach. After throwing more wood on the fire, she carried the parcel of foods inside.

Standing over Ray, she spoke his name. No more "Uncle" for him. He was only Ray now.

When he didn't answer, she spoke a little louder, and when he still did not respond, she knelt beside him to check his breathing, which seemed shallow but steady. With a hot brand from the campfire, she rebuilt the coach's tiny fire and warmed the tea made from steeped herbs, applying freshly dampened cloth strips to Ray's wounds, topping him with layers of clothing. He lay there as if more dead than alive, but still had a little color to him, which meant that given time, he should rouse.

Once more outside, she checked on Kota, who munched grass as if unfazed by his new surroundings. She left him saddled in the lee of the coach as protection against the cold and took her bedroll and wooly winter chaps back inside, where she made a bed atop one of the benches and there fell into a light sleep, half-listening for any movement inside or outside the coach. Whenever she woke, she rose to look out at Kota, who napped upright on three legs, his fourth cocked like a broken hinge. At daylight, Ray roused only briefly, and that's when Raylene realized that a swift departure for either of them was unlikely. Ray was in poor shape, a night sky leaking stars.

All day Sunday and into the night, she tended to Ray and saw to the camp, collecting downed branches for firewood, exercising Kota. After snaring a rabbit, she skinned it and roasted it over the fire, but Ray would have none of it, only sips of water or horsemint tea or the sweet syrup from cans of fruit he had brought with him.

Raylene polished off the cornbread and near-ripe tomatoes that Edda had provided. Staring into the campfire, she pondered whether Ray would regain strength anytime soon, also how much credit she deserved for his poor condition.

On Monday morning, Ray opened his eyes and said, "Helen."

Raylene shook herself fully awake. Was this another of Ray's ruses? "I am not Helen. Why do you speak her name?"

"She is buried."

Raylene remembered the death and burial of her mother as if it were a book whose stitching had come loose. Some pages were missing. Random scenes remained — days and weeks of her mother gripped by rasping breaths and coughs that turned bloody. The gray of Helen's skin, which foretold the day when Thomas left to return with a box of her mother's ashes. There followed wheels turning and days with her arms around Annie's waist, both of them astride their father's stallion as it pulled the family wagon. Men from the reservation brought picks to cleave the cold ground. There was chanting as people gathered rocks from canyon clearings for placing atop the dirt-filled hole. Raylene walked in circles that grew ever larger before she found the nearly round stone she then placed atop her mother's cairn. Made of sandy red, the stone looked like the sun.

"You were not even there," she told Ray.

Prairie burials required stones to keep scavengers from digging up bones, whether whole or charred or mostly ashes, and also to mark specific places of final rest. Many people of that time had attended Helen's burial or heard the stories passed round afterwards. Many had placed stones upon her resting place.

"Your stone was red," said Ray.

She looked at him. Her mother's ashes rested in country laced with layers of red stone, a well- known fact that could easily be appropriated by someone seeking to disarm her. "I will go to town," she said, dismissing Ray's words. "I need to buy oats for Kota and enough food to last us a few days. Eating will return your strength."

"My truck has food," said Ray.

"Your truck? I watched for it in town but never saw it."

"Green one parked."

Ray sounded semi-lucid, but Raylene left the coach unwilling to believe him. After checking on Kota, she began her search. Not far away she found a worn white horse van hitched to a sturdy green truck with dual tires on the back. Small insignias attached on the engine's side grills identified it as a Ford. It did resemble the rig she had briefly followed in downtown Manderson, and now she saw that the splash marks on the van weren't splashes at all but handprints in red, yellow, and black, all softened from time and weather.

This setup was considerably newer than his old shot-up truck. Perhaps the old one had given out, but why acquire a horse van when he had not ridden since being injured while working on the Fort Peck Dam?

The truck's bed was indeed full of supplies, and...suddenly, she didn't trust this rig or what Ray was doing with it here. Why the extra canned foods and extra bedrolls — two of them — and all those lengths of cord wood covered by canvas? Tucked into a metal locker were papered parcels labeled bacon and salt beef, also cans of lard, coffee, flour, and sugar. Separately sat two cartons of canned foods, one labeled for fruits, the other for vegetables, and four heavy storage cans. She opened each can, finding two full of water, two of truck fuel. There were lengths of rope, a shovel, an ax. Wrapped in a rubber sheet were two long guns, a 12-gauge and a deer rifle, and ammunition for both, that bundle held down with cord wood. Taken as a whole, the gear stashed in Ray's truck — if it was Ray's — was of sufficient type and quantity for an extended disappearance.

Raylene glanced around to absorb the graveyard in daylight, the silent machinery, the gurgle of the nearby stream, the rustle of wind in drying grass. The place's peace did little to ease her dismay about Ray's strange circumstances. She returned to the coach, went up its steps, and along the aisle to where he lay.

"Ray!" she growled, thumping the sole of his boot with the toe of her own. He was still covered in garments which shifted as he lifted his head. When she felt he had her in focus, she said, "Why so many supplies?" It appeared that he had intended to skip out. If she hadn't spotted him at the racing meet, he might have been far away by now, back to Montana, or Canada or somewhere he'd be hard to find. "Where were you headed?"

Ray blinked at her. "Find you."

"No, I found you. Where were *you* headed?"

"Helen."

"Do not call me by her name. That won't —" Then she realized what he meant. Not that she looked like her mother, though he and others used to tell her that. But that he meant to go to   Helen. Helen was long dead, buried out among canyons carved by ancient waters. He must have planned to visit her gravesite before fleeing. "You were going to disappear until I foiled your plan."

His voice startled her with its intensity. "No!" Then it dropped back to a dry rasp. "Waiting for you."

She studied him, jolted at the thought of him getting away had she not made the racing connection. She said, "Your words do not convince me, but your actions speak clearly. My sister died and you did nothing. My father did nothing worth killing him for, but you did. Then you gathered provisions for disappearing. I am done with you. From now on you are dead to me."

After a long period of gazing at the ceiling he spoke with great effort. "You are life. Must take me."

Had he lost his mind? What sort of person would ask a favor of someone who had cut them and could still kill them? Someone crazy might. Or someone with an extraordinary need. Her intention remained that as soon as Ray could walk, or perhaps drive, she would be done with him. Forever. She knelt beside him so she could speak into his ear. "Go anywhere you want. When you leave here, you go alone."

He shook his head. "I cannot."

He did not grasp her meaning so she enunciated slowly. "I. Am. Not. Taking you."

"We go."

Raylene willed herself to remain calm. She had made the arduous journey to visit the grave holding her mother's ashes three times total, but had always traveled alone in order to sit with her memories there. If Ray had killed Thomas over their old rivalry regarding her mother, she would not now reward him for it. "I have no reason to take you there."

He ran his tongue across his lips before speaking again. "Annie's black," he said.

Annie was not black. Black was Raylene's spirit whenever her thoughts turned to a life without her Annie. Without a father or an uncle. Her heart was a stone about this. She was finished with Ray and his stories.

He worked his mouth until he added, "Her case."

Now what? Black and case. Oh, *that* old thing. Annie's old valise, a used doctor's bag they had once found in a field, afterwards taking turns with it while playing at make-believe. Their turtle doll had slept in the valise for at least a year. Along the way the case had also held lustrous quartz pebbles, discarded nubs of school pencils, the shed skin of a five-button prairie rattler, scraps of colored yarn, and at one time a child-size gold band, thin and bent. That treasure Raylene had found in the stomach of a trout she caught on an earthworm dangled in Blacktail Creek.

Annie had taken the valise when she moved away to the city and Raylene, having once seen the object stuffed in the back of Annie's closet, had figured it for a childhood keepsake that Annie couldn't part with. She had never imagined any of Annie's personal property as necessary to her own future, but this was different. This was *theirs*, like *Khéya*, theirs together, and now she wanted it something fierce. But she said to Ray, "What makes you think I would want that old thing?"

With great effort he said, "Find it, has papers."

Raylene's response was to whirl away from Ray and hustle back to his truck, where she walked all three sides of its bed, studying each item stashed beneath the tarp. No valise. Then she flung the driver's side door open. Annie's valise was not on the dashboard or the seat or beneath the wool blankets stacked there. She ran her hand along the bolts that held the seat to the floor. For good measure, she went around to the other door and did the same. Next to the passenger side seat she found an old chewed up lariat and three wooden matches, but no valise.

The thought came to her again that Ray was manipulating her. She needed to think hard about whether to believe a man who had already killed, fleeing afterwards, and who had cast aspersions on Thomas's name. She blamed him now for her conflicting thoughts about Thomas.

After last exercising Kota, she had unsaddled him and

rubbed him down. Now she untied him from the coach and led him out of the graveyard to the stream, awash in mid-day sun. There, he drank deeply and tore at the grasses near the water, moving as he grazed. She looped the reins up over his withers and followed him on foot.

Kota had been willful when she acquired him as a two-year-old. She believed his spunk to be the sign of an unquenchable heart. Using her elders' techniques, she had taught him to respond to the pressure of her legs, a light touch of the reins, and any shift of weight in the saddle. He learned quickly because she did not ask of him that which he could not give.

She trusted Kota as she had once trusted Ray, and Kota trusted her for no reason other than her constancy and affection. Should something happen to her and he be left free of people, he would likely fare fine on the plentiful grasses and water of the plains. Winter would prove harsh, but his instincts would guide him and he would find more of his own kind in the hills.

Her instincts had led her to this half-dead ranch with fallow fields and a rusting graveyard, and had led her to let Ray live, the reward for which seemed to be his claims and disparagements against Thomas. From a guilty mind, perhaps. Though she wanted to resist his demands, the idea of Annie having "papers" became fixed in her imagination. Love letters, lists, poetic scribbles ... any little thing might shed light on the portions of Annie's life that had heretofore been secret. Perhaps something from the lover who had given her jewelry that the detective came looking for. Or maybe not, but how would Raylene ever know unless she possessed the valise Ray now offered? She ought not to believe him. Why should she, yet she found she wanted to.

Standing in a breeze that had traveled myriad unseen

lands, she closed her eyes and turned her face toward the sun. As she had before, she searched for meaning in the lights behind her eyelids. This time she saw only a fiery orange storm. No Annie, no Thomas, no Ray, no insights. She turned back toward Kota.

Alert to her movements, her piebald raised his head and regarded her calmly while grinding a mouthful of yellowed grass. Under his gaze, her concerns about Ray's intentions fell to dust. She retained almost as many questions as she had formulated in Kansas City and had to admit that knowing their answers would not change her sister's death, or Thomas's. Answers to her questions would not bring back her family.

Ray's advice during the riding contests of her youth rang in her thoughts: *Outthink if you mean to outmaneuver. Use your strengths.*

That's what she would do. She would relinquish the burden of deciphering Ray's truth or lies. She would deliver him to her mother's grave in country that swallowed the ill-prepared or incautious, and in that way test his word about the valise, which he must have hidden there. With the valise she might gain some of Annie's sappy poetry or stick figure scribbles, which would suit her fine. They would be more than she had now. But, if Ray's word proved false, she would ride away and leave him to survive or not while she returned to the company of ranch cattle devoid of ulterior motives. She clicked her tongue at Kota and turned back for the graveyard. Behind her came the steady thump of his hooves.

At Ray's camp, Raylene tethered Kota once more and set about moving Ray's truck so the attached van could shelter Kota at night. Back inside the coach, she confronted Ray. "I will not carry you on my back to my mother's grave. You will have to get stronger."

That day she prodded him into sitting upright with his coat on followed by walking in the aisle with her assistance. The next day she led him out to the verge of the graveyard for breaking water. Leaning heavily against her, he blinked at the sunlight and gazed around as if the world looked brand new. A line of purple clouds sat on the western horizon. Time was running out for easy travel to the backcountry. They would need to depart sooner rather than later.

Ray perched sloppily on one of the discarded benches within range of the campfire's heat as she brought him a pail of water she had heated. "I readied this for myself," she said, "but since you are upright you will bathe first. Otherwise, you will ride in the van with Kota." She set a shard of soap and a cotton rag beside him and reached to unbutton his heavy coat. When he pushed at her hands, she said, "I will bring you fresher clothing from your duffle and leave you in peace, but the days grow short. We had better move soon."

Glancing out the coach window while rummaging through Ray's duffle, she saw that the fingers of his right hand plucked listlessly at the bottom button of his coat. Sighing, she carried two cotton shirts back out to where he sat. "I will help," she said. Ray tossed his head in protest, but she prevailed, sliding his coat from his body and working the buttons of his shirt loose. The crusted blood on his left sleeve appeared stuck to his arm, so she moistened it with warm water before peeling the shirt downward. Catching sight of his bicep, she sucked in a breath.

Streaks of black ran upward from an angry red knife wound. The wound itself looked not only deep, but swollen. "Ray," she said, her eyes on the black streaks, "your arm requires a doctor." She sent her mind out to where there might be wise women or men in Manderson who could set bones or provide basic advice, but Ray's wound looked like an open door leading to death.

Ray's eyes were devoid of emotion when he turned them on her. He and Thomas had each tried to kill the other. One had prevailed, but the dead man might have succeeded in killing his killer.

The town of Manderson sat in the center of the Pine Ridge, about two days' drive to Rapid City on South Dakota's western border and perhaps a third day if driving east to Sioux City. Raylene ought to tell him that she could live without a memento from Annie's life. She ought to drag him off to medical care and leave him in the hands of doctors and nurses. But which doctors and nurses? A smallish town along the northern railroad line, Farmingdale for instance, would have a country doctor who could dispense sulfa, but only if she could get Ray there in time. For all she knew, he might need a proper hospital with equipment for transfusions and such.

When Raylene proposed that they make haste for Rapid City, Ray replied, "I go to Helen."

He had already surprised her with his resilience, but a body that looked to harbor gangrene could only take so much. She offered again, saying, "Taking time to visit her grave could mean the death of you." When he shook his head, she added, "I did not choose to kill you and I will not deliver you to a place that will. We can visit after you receive treatment."

He held up a hand to silence her.

Raylene blew out a breath. Ray was still her elder. Her elders had raised her to make her own way in the world, which meant making choices. And mistakes. She could pack her gear and ride away on Kota. She could even load Kota into the van and drive away with Ray's rig. He had no strength to stop her. She had already lost her ranch job in order to finish what *he* had started — or else what Thomas had started, she wasn't any longer certain which of those. And none of Ray's answers thus far seemed answers at all, only signposts pointing to more questions. Her mother's grave lay in sacred country known to be deadly. He could have easily hidden Annie's valise there. She would not find it without him. The uncle she had recently cut was holding hostage Annie's last possession. Was she to forego that little piece of Annie?

"Wash as best you can," she told him. "We will start tonight for my mother's grave."

"*Makhósica.*"

"Yes. We go to the bad lands."

Seventeen

By sundown, Raylene had struck camp and loaded Ray's truck plus Kota. Ray, she bundled into the passenger seat with a lap full of blankets. Taking one last look around the campsite to check for forgotten items, she paused. By rights, she ought to now be halfway across the adjacent Rosebud reservation, perhaps already starting another ranching job. Instead, she was about to drive a sick man into unforgiving country.

Her stomach roiled as if she were back beside the Glacier Tour coach, trying to choose between one poison and another. In sparing Ray, she had imagined more years for an aging body that carried the memory of its twin on its skin. But now she had agreed to drive him to a place far from help. If he died there, his death would fall at least in part on her head.

Raylene drove Ray's rig with caution, gaining a feeling for its bulk and the way it handled. At the intersection where the ranch road cut south toward Manderson, she turned north. Soon the houses on the outskirts of town were distant forms in her side mirror. The cone-shape light of the truck's headlamps sliced the dark.

An hour later, under clouds obliterating a portion of starlight, she turned onto a narrow dirt road headed west. All the roads from that point would be dirt, but at least they would be passable, for now. She offered Ray some laudanum, and surprisingly, he accepted a few drops in water. In his weakened state, a sip's worth would provide a few hours' respite from their jouncing, rutted ride.

Eventually, the road began to rise out of the grasslands, giving way to thinning grasses and upwelling knobs covered in dirt and scrub. In a flattish area near where they would need to cross Medicine Creek, she pulled the rig off the beaten dirt road. She had brought them as far as she safely could in the dark. Should they travel further tonight, she might mistake a turn, getting them lost in a maze of canyons. Ray might be willing to risk his own life for this journey, but she would not risk hers.

To one side in a flattish spot, Raylene established camp and roused Ray, who refused her offer of food but accepted water before stretching out in the cab of the truck, sandwiched within blankets. She built a small fire over which she fried some of the salted beef. The food tasted fine but she could wish for biscuits with the nutty flavor of cattail pollen and stick-to-your-ribs satisfaction. Gauging that most prairie rattlers had probably gone to ground she spent the night fully dressed inside her bedroll by the fire.

In the morning, Ray again accepted water and Raylene opted for a mug of sweetened coffee. After feeding and watering Kota and letting him stretch his legs, she started the truck and told Ray to hang on. The road grew rougher from there, the truck laboring to pull the van and its thousand pounds of horseflesh. Though Kota could have carried her through powdery basins, over rises, and across washouts more efficiently, Raylene marshalled her patience and repeated to herself that she would deliver Ray to the object of his ... longing, or curiosity, or whatever was weighing upon him, and in doing so, retrieve the object of her desire — Annie's valise. As the truck's engine heaved, she kept a firm grip on the juddering wheel.

After two more hours, red and tan sandstone formations

crowded nearer to the road, and with them, sensations Raylene had only felt during previous visits. A kind of whispering inside her which registered as wordless songs. The first time this had happened, she imagined hearing the breeze echoing between canyons, but the sensations, resembling vibrations, grew stronger as she advanced among the walls and canyons. She had concluded that the formations themselves sang songs of the immutable forces that had shaped them. Of water, perhaps, or other kinds of life. She could no more describe this to another person than she could replicate the sensation when she was elsewhere. When among the canyons, she accepted the whispering songs as gifts.

Slumped against the opposite door, Ray began to make low noises.

Raylene brought the truck to a halt. "Ray?"

His eyes remained closed while his head ticked left and right.

"What is it?"

There was no reply from the moaning man-shaped shadow so she drove on, crossing over the White River then turning south and west. All around were the dry beds of waterways and stone walls with faces blackened by shadows. As the road descended again, the walls grew higher, tapering here, sloping there, until there appeared a large clearing.

Within the clearing, blackened circles of stones held the charred remains of fires. A pinkish glow cast by the setting sun rimmed the walls. This was a gathering place, a resting place, at one time a refuge; also, the location where after visiting her mother's grave Raylene had camped with the silent songs singing her to sleep. From the clearing, openings in the walls radiated outward. One was a slot so narrow that only anyone or anything on foot could pass through it.

She pulled forward slowly and brought the rig to a halt.

"Ray," she said, tapping the blankets piled atop him. "It's time."

He roused, looking around as if surprised to find himself among the sandstone walls, and finally peered out his window at the slant of clouded light and deeper shadow.

"I'll turn Kota out and start some coffee."

Leaving Ray in the truck, she unloaded Kota from the van. Her piebald had carried Raylene to this place before, so he knew its odors of dirt and scant grass and stone-flavored breezes. She selected a ring of stones that faced the slot canyon and started a fire and set a pot of coffee to boiling. Then she fetched Ray. "Let's do this before the weather turns," she said.

Shivers ran through his body as she maneuvered him across the clearing and onto a folded blanket near the fire's heat, wrapping two more blankets around him. Before she straightened, he pointed at the pouch which had come free from the neckline of her coat.

"Totem," he mumbled.

Raylene fingered the suede. "It holds my mother's ring."

Ray lifted his chin a little. "I made."

"You made her ring? You have always had a way with silver."

"I gave it."

Gave it to her? Perhaps he had made it so her father could give it to her mother. They were brothers, after all.

Once the coffee had boiled, she poured him a cup and put it into his hands. Hunger gnawed at her; they had not stopped for a mid-day meal and now there was just enough time to travel through the slot canyon and back before making camp.

"Kota will carry you to my mother's grave and I will lead him," said Raylene.

Ray raised his hands to the fire. "No."

Raylene's own heat rose at the thought that she had brought Ray this far only for him to change his mind. Or did he mean that she should stay with him and skip her mother's grave? She would not. "You insisted," she said, her voice rising, "and you must show me where you hid Annie's valise."

"More fire."

They were close to what he had claimed to want — her mother's grave. To reach it required perhaps fifteen minutes of travel. The temperature had dropped, but still, on horseback, fifteen minutes was nothing. "Ray," she said, trying to keep her voice calm. "You insisted." When he did not answer, she asked, "Is Annie's valise near my mother's grave?"

His mouth was a line as he hunched deeper beneath his blankets. "You will find."

Raylene snapped her mouth closed. Damn him anyway. She stomped back to the truck and brought a bedroll for him to recline against and two more armloads of wood. Half the wood went into the fire and the other half she stacked beside him. Soon the heat was solid, the flames clawing upward as if alive. Ray had not touched the coffee, so she poured a cup of water from their supply and set it next to him. She would retrieve what she had come for.

After saddling Kota, she turned up her collar and left Ray staring into the fire, a faraway look in his eyes, his lips moving as if in conversation with himself.

The shadows of the slot canyon fell like a shroud around rider and horse. From the open sky, stars blinked among thick, broken clouds. Here and there fell snowflakes adrift in lazy patterns. The wordless songs were louder here, accompanied by Kota's hoofbeats. In places, she could reach out and touch the walls on either side.

The first time Kota had carried her this way, she had led him on foot through the channel whose shade in summer provided relief from the beating sun. Since then, he had willingly carried her through the same tapering passageway whenever she came to sit beside her mother's grave.

At the far end, the slot ended in an irregular clearing with many outlets. The dying light held better here, turning the tan walls gray while revealing the cairn marking the place where her mother's ashes slept in the earth. The round red stone Raylene had selected as a child still topped the stack and wordless songs were all around.

She dismounted and approached her mother's resting place against a sloping wall. Standing silent before it, she replayed in her mind not her mother's end, but earlier times, some of which were Annie's oft-told memories. Her mother's facility with leather and beads. The way her hair tumbled into a single gleaming sheet when she dried it before the cookfire. Her habit of humming to herself as she mended clothing that could be made to last another season.

A memory came to her unbidden — Ray bringing two rabbits and staying to dinner. Potatoes steaming in their jackets, and afterwards, she and Annie being sent to their pallet and covered with blankets and told to shush. The crackle of flames and two quiet voices like a lullaby ... and ... try as she might, she couldn't place Thomas in that scene because he had gone to search a bigger town for work. That's what she'd been told.

The thought of Annie brought the valise back to mind. Raylene studied the clearing for another stack of stones that might conceal Annie's two-handled bag. There were loose stones scattered like stars across the ground, but none were piled as if to conceal a treasure. She circled the clearing on foot, kicking at stones and growing hot at the thought that Ray had tricked her.

Then Kota whinnied low. Raylene turned to look but saw

no threat that would cause him concern. Perhaps a fox had glanced through an opening, or a chipmunk had dashed for cover and he had spied it. She crossed to him and stroked his neck. He was not easily spooked.

A single snowflake kissed Raylene's face. She looked up. From the broken clouds above came a flurry of dancing white. She blew in Kota's nostrils to calm him, then mounted, saying, "Ray has tricked me for the last time."

They accomplished the ride back through the slot canyon at a fast walk. Anything quicker was out of the question. Anger colored her thoughts — *tired of your lies ... dishonor ... how you played me ...*

Kota stumbled once, tipping toward an outthrust wall against which Raylene scraped her knee. With a grunt, she tucked in closer and urged Kota onward. *Damn that Ray ... never again.*

Her thoughts scattered as the odor of smoke reached her. The closer they drew to the canyon's entrance, the thicker and punker the smell. A wall of heat met them at the clearing.

Kota reared. Raylene held fast and slapped his neck to remind him that he wasn't alone.

Ray's campfire had become a roaring monster, crackling and popping and flinging embers in every direction, its smoke pushing toward them. Raylene slid from Kota and gave him a smack to send him away. What was Ray thinking? No one needed this much fire. Coughing while circling left, she called, "Ray!" In the fire, a wool blanket surrounded by flames merely smoldered.

"Ray!" she called, dashing for the far side where she had left him. All but one hunk of wood was gone. The ground held blankets, but no Ray. Dread flashed through her and thoughts slowed to a crawl as she registered the human form melting within the flames. She circled the pit while at the same time watching herself go through the motions. A part of her looked for a way into the flames so she could pull Ray back from death. Her mind instructed her limbs, but her body would not respond as the flames continued to consume that which should not fuel them — the prone figure of a man. Raymond Yellow Moon.

Falling to her knees, she pleaded with the fire, Ray, and the universe, none of whom would answer. "Don't do this ... I would not have ..."

Soot blackened Raylene's clothing as Ray disappeared before her eyes, muscles and tendons and what little fat he possessed reduced to popping sounds and a sickening stench, thick in her nostrils. Gentle snowflakes fell into the dying light as smoke scraped upward to join the night breeze. The snow, the smoke, this clearing, the stone circle — none of it would ever be the same.

The pyre's flames became dancers in the final hours of ceremony, slower and slower, smaller and smaller, until at some point the wood turned to coals and Ray had turned into charred bones. Given time, everything, it seemed, became something else. Everything.

As the night's cold settled on her shoulders, she glanced at the entrance to the slot canyon. Long ago Ray had lost out to Thomas, but now Thomas was buried in Kansas City and Ray had taken his last breath in proximity to her mother. Above the clearing, the night wind was cleaving clouds into scattered islands and continents, not unlike her family's drift between Oglala, Kansas City, places west, and this *makhósica*. Out of the blue she felt a hunger for Raul, for the biscuit-y smell of him and the way he progressed through each day. In the dead of night or the hour just before dawn, he made her feel as if he knew her the way no one else did. She could almost summon the taste of his peppermint mouth.

She could beckon Annie too. Those bundled wildflowers tucked among her clothes, the way she counted fifty strokes of her hairbrush. *Big sister. Who paid for your burial? And does your grave have a marker with a sweet remembrance on it?* Annie liked such gestures, fell hard for them. She saved things, too, ticket stubs, purchase receipts. Raylene had witnessed as much, and … and … it now occurred to Raylene that the shock of Ray's self-reckoning had changed her fury at his broken promise regarding Annie's valise. What remained was simple disappointment. Though she did not regret her choices, she had in recent days been Ray's pawn. She was not pleased, though, that he had broken his word more than once. *Let the scavengers have his bones.*

Night was full upon her when she returned to Ray's truck and the van to which she had tied Kota for his own safety. The heavy-duty rig would have at one time passed to Thomas, but with no one else to claim it, it was hers now. She gave Kota water and a handful of oats and led him around the clearing before loading him once more. Then she returned Ray's bedroll and the remaining blankets to the truck's seat and slapped the dusting of snow from the cartons of canned food before tying the canvas back over them.

The Ford's motor turned over on the first try and she put it into low gear. Snow frosted everything in the clearing, clinging in places to sandstone walls, turning the fire circles into constellations. The slot canyon was a slice of black now, the other openings wide gray holes in space.

As she steered toward the exit, Ray's last words came to her. He had not offered a farewell or word of gratitude for how she had spared his life, but asked about her pouch and claimed credit for her mother's silver ring, and when she had asked about Annie's valise, he had said … She braked the truck and sat with her eyes closed. He had said that she would find the valise under stones. No, that was wrong. Three hours ago, which now seemed a lifetime, her mind had been on the slot canyon and reaching her mother's grave. She had asked Ray if it was hidden there and he had said ... what had he said? Oh, yes. He'd said, *You will find it.*

She sat thinking. His speech had grown less distinct over the last few days so she had assumed the role of interpreter, but in doing so had failed to outthink her adversary — in this case, Ray — only hearing from him what she thought he should be saying. She had wanted to find Annie's valise near her mother's grave, and that's what she had heard in his words.

The truth was, why would finding one of Annie's possessions prove any easier than other challenges Ray had posed? Had he complicated things, or had she? She turned off the truck and got out. From the truck bed she pulled the one lantern and got it going with matches she used for starting campfires. With the open air pricking her face and soundless songs thrumming within her, she walked the clearing's open spaces, the lantern throwing light just beyond her boots. There were no obvious cairns, no soil recently disturbed.

Annie, she thought to herself. *I am trying.*

Just thinking about Annie revived her memories of Annie's affinity for secrets and stashing things. When they were children, Annie had been the first to stash contraband pencils and paper filched from school, and the first to hide scribbled messages inside their turtle doll. One misspelled note had read, "I kissed Danel behind the chappel!" Raylene had not known to whom that name applied — boy, girl, or some made-up creature. Other times, inside the paper wrapping a corn cake she carried for eating on the way to school, she might find the penciled word "sister" or a drawing of a crescent moon, or a stick-figure dog. Once, the word *blahh*. Hiding things was a talent of Annie's.

Raylene looked again at the bed of Ray's truck, previously full to overflowing with firewood jig-sawed into every crevice between and alongside the basics needed for rough roads and rough living. She had reviewed the supplies as a whole before driving Ray to this sacred place of death and celebration. She'd been in a hurry, set on ferrying him to the bad lands, but in the last two days she had pulled lard, coffee, and salted beef from Ray's footlocker and poured water for them and Kota. She had also carried loads of firewood to what had become Ray's last stand. There was nothing to do but untie the cover one last time.

Minus all that cord wood, the remaining supplies looked less ready for a long journey. The bed looked like an impossible place for holding what she sought, but in spite of that and with the lantern close, she began her search. She checked the long guns and set aside the shovel and ax. Two hunks of cord wood were stored behind the rusty metal locker. These she lifted to check that nothing lay beneath them. She climbed into the bed and lifted the locker's lid. Salted beef, check. Cans of lard and flour, check. Coffee and sugar, still there. Fuel cans and water cans she left where they were, and she knew well that Ray's duffel held only spare denim work pants and shirts of ancient vintage.

Disappointment washed through her. She had been so eager to find that Ray's promise would in the end prove true, that he had *wanted* her to find Annie's valise. As she thought about having been fooled, her gaze fell onto the cartons of canned food. Of the two, she had opened the top one and thus far used up three of its cans of fruit. The second carton lay beneath.

Lifting that second carton out, she paused. It was the last place to look. She almost hated to open it and thereby know another failure, but she pulled it closer and wiggled its lid off. There, tucked alongside cans of various produce lay the black, dog-eared valise, flattened into place.

Raylene's breath caught in her throat as she stroked the worn leather of the last link to her sister and their past. The valise was as she remembered it, with tarnished brass hardware. Once more came the fresh pain of losing Annie, who bold as you please had led their way through childhood and at the other end of childhood had followed not their family's ways, but her own heart. That go-her-own-way heart, like a beacon from afar, cast a glow of comfort over Raylene, through the knowledge that Annie's spirit had never been quenched. Possessing this old thing had only yesterday seemed a necessity, but now Raylene doubted its ability to fill the hollow left by a sister gone from her life.

The leather surrounding the latch had been cut into a flap. It would no longer lock. She gave the old thing a shake and felt the knock of objects within, Annie's private things secured in the best private place she could arrange. Raylene would not have eavesdropped on her sister or followed her to see who she went around with. Annie's life was not her life, and yet — a glimmer of Annie's life was before her now if only she would look.

But, its contents ought to wait. The miles back through the bad lands would prove slow, perhaps treacherous. She would need to make camp soon in a protected spot, awaiting daylight by which to steer around drop-offs and ruts that could seize a tire. She should put the handled bag aside for later and drive. But she could not do so now any more than an hour ago she could have walked away from Ray's blazing pyre.

Pushing her bedding aside, she climbed into the passenger seat with the lantern and pried the valise open. Inside were loose sheets of paper and folded sheets with crumple marks, and at the very bottom, a modest notebook bound in red cloth. She held a few of the loose sheets close enough to make Annie's crazy scrawl dance in the lantern light.

Most of the scribbles were but fragments, seeming to beseech an unnamed person for support — "you cant not know"... "when we're together..." "do You care"... "its not as if " ... with punctuation a mess and poor spelling. Three years Annie's junior, Raylene had coached Annie through her school lessons. At least she could decipher Annie's hand. She felt her blood pounding at words that seemed to reference some personal hurt.

Holding the papers to her face, she inhaled their scent. Perfume. Not toilet water or a tincture made from wildflowers, but real perfume. How had her sister afforded real perfume?

Switching to the notebook, she flipped pages of Annie's mashed up scribbles. Some pages held dates with entries that looked to include a bit of record keeping for the saloon, only without dollar figures. Entries from the previous year, 1935, were sporadic; current year notations were more abundant.

April 4 — slow He called- T angry about hang up (Raylene figured T was Thomas, unhappy about a man calling for Annie at work.)

May 9 — Cryed at sappy movie

May 28 steady- 3 cases — Dooney

June 2 — Supper at O'Shea's

Raylene skimmed pages of notes any young woman might record about window shopping and a magazine purchased at the Five-and-Dime and a saloon customer acting too familiar. So much about Annie's city life seemed unassuming. Ordinary. Until she found one scribble in the shape of a ring with a bubble on top. And then a heart shape penciled on a page. Her breath caught and she slowed to read.

July 12 — need to tell (heart)

A heart, thought Raylene, might have made a gift of real perfume to Annie. A heart might, intentionally or not, also cause heartache.

July 17 — Ftr came in and argude with T

What? Ftr came in & argued with T? T was Thomas and Thomas was Father, if that was what "Ftr" stood for. Thomas was Father, their original father. Ray was *like* a father, had embodied the blood and spirit of a father to them, and so had been revered. But here were cryptic clues in Annie's hand suggesting Ftr was different from T.

Ray's earlier declaration rose up before Raylene as she worked to slow her breathing. He had said, "Thomas. Not father."

She cracked a window to the cool October wind as two truths blossomed inside her. First — Annie should not have labeled their father T, not even out of anger over some insult or disagreement. She had always called him Father. During Raylene's last visit she had called him Father. And, second — all of Annie's notations held the same weight. This movie, those shoes. Three cases from Dooney. Ftr came in & argued with T, written as ordinary news.

She mentally massaged the few clues Ray had provided until what appeared was a grainy picture, possibly wrong. If Annie in her personal writings referred to Ray as Father and Ray considered himself Annie's father, then Ray might have been moved to kill Thomas over Annie's unnecessary death, a convolution equal to the best she had read in books — a father who was uncle, an uncle who was father. She herself had already blamed Thomas for not protecting Annie, so how could she blame Ray for acting as protector? He was a principled man who only struck another when wronged. Had he thought Annie wronged by Thomas's actions or inactions?

Thomas would not have poured tainted booze down Annie's throat, but he might have sold it in his saloon where Annie poured herself drinks.

So much for knowing her own family. She would not have thought any of this possible. What else did she not know about her family's lives, or her own? Including whether Annie was Ray's daughter. If Annie *had* been, might she herself also be Ray's daughter? The men were blood to each other and to her, and both were now gone, and not a moment of that which had already passed could be changed. She and Annie had learned and lived with a father and an uncle. Two fathers, actually, and that's what counted.

She shook herself. Reading further through Annie's journal seemed folly. Surely it contained more to confuse and dismay. But Raylene could no more put the notebook aside than she could un-know what she had read thus far. She scanned more pages of entries about collecting scraps for sewing a quilt, buying a button for repairing a skirt, attending "O, Susanna!" at the Maxey Theater, mundane details of her sister's city life, each of which seemed special now that she read them. Paging along, she came to another scribbled heart shape.

August 8 — 4 kegs kc brew, myup (heart) angry

Myup (heart)? What in the world was myup (heart)? The scrap of paper tucked inside their *khéya* doll had read "myup baby." Raylene had read that strange note over and over, hoping it would reveal itself — *myup baby*. She might have asked Ray about its meaning, but her thoughts involving him had at that time been focused on retribution. *Myup ... myup.* She couldn't fathom how Annie, who had completely left the reservation behind, had carried with her a word from the old language. Meeoop. Myoop. Mee oopeh. My oopeh.

This was something begging translation because if anyone had been angry with Annie, the notation citing that person's

August 8th anger might hold meaning even today. She began again. Meeoop. Mee oopeh. Mee oopa. Mee yupe. What did M-Y-U-P mean? Or M-Y u-p. My U-P? My yoo pee. Yoo pee, Where had she heard that? She paused in the lantern's flickering glow.

Yoo pee. U-P... U.P. She closed her eyes to replay in reverse the events preceding nightfall in the clearing where she now sat, back through Ray's raging fire, through the slot canyon and her mother's grave, through driving the bad lands with Ray, and his injured arm and his camp on the Dahlburg, the relay horse race, and Stoney socking her a good one, and Edda's help, the race crowd in Manderson, riding Kota across the miles from Oglala. Stoney and Joseph and Henry and the railroad man, whose business card she'd lifted while in Joseph's house. Her boot knife in the trunk of the detective's car, and his broken arm and shattered eyeglasses. The photo of Annie, now in her own pocket. The detective had mentioned his boss in connection with Annie, but when he spoke about the photo showing Annie wearing fancy jewelry, she'd been thinking about how she'd never held a photograph of her sister, had never even seen one. His words had floated just beyond her then, but they must have stuck because they now expanded to fill her mind: "My U.P. boss." The very words that detective had said, and he worked for — *of course* — Union Pacific.

The lantern on the seat beside her sputtered and went dark, leaving the fogged windshield backlit by sparks of starlight. Methodically, she ran through the possible options. If there could be a U.P. boss, there could be a U.P. (heart); and a U.P. baby. Did her sister's scribbles contain clues of value, or no value? To Raylene they felt ripe with potential for revealing who had been Annie's designated *heart*. Was that someone who knew about her death, and could that person be the detective's boss? Or was it nobody of consequence now that Annie was gone?

The dreamy swirl of the snowy clearing fell away as resolve solidified inside her, sharp as obsidian. *Sister*, she thought. Even if facts declared them cousins, they had lived as sisters and would have chosen each other as sisters. She could not change any of it now, not the last month or the last year. Not the last hour. Each of those moments had passed. *You are forever my sister, gone from this place but not truly gone because I am one who does not forget.*

She could tell now that in this clearing — far from where Annie had died, far from Thomas's last stand against Raymond — she would find no answers to her questions. Not this day but some future day she would uncover that which remained hidden about Annie's life and death, and perhaps about what had really come between Thomas and Raymond. That would be her next goal.

When she dropped the valise to the floorboard it gave an odd clunk, but her thoughts were elsewhere as she searched her saddlebags for the folded paper packet that she had saved for no particular reason. Exiting the truck in broken starlight, she crossed the clearing to the circle of stones surrounding a handful of coals whose orange eyes seemed to watch the sky. Whoever Ray had been — uncle, father, teacher — his life had shaped hers, and so had his death. She wanted to believe that had Ray been able to, he would have saved Annie. He could not have employed the curse of banishment because Thomas was already gone from the reservation. So, Ray had avenged what he saw as Thomas's failure regarding Annie's death.

With the sandstone canyons whispering to her, she opened the folded paper and began to walk the circle, dropping strands of her own shorn hair onto the remaining hot coals. She had not stepped into the flames with Ray, but a part of her had indeed gone with him, and the same for Thomas and Annie. Invoking her faith in the connection between all things, she asked for safe passage to the spirit world for her sister and her fathers. Both fathers. She asked the smoke to carry her heartbeat to them so they would know its strength and walk to its rhythm. Dipping a hand into the warm ashes, she feathered a finger across her cheek and spoke to the blackened bones that remained. "I will find Annie's grave. For all the Yellow Moons, I will find it."

Returning to the truck, she cranked the motor and set the headlamps shining. Slowly, she pulled out of the clearing and followed the road back to the midnight prairie that reflected snowy light upward and outward. Swirls of snow still danced in the air, yet there was the moon's crooked smile. Plenty of people would say that snow from a half-cloudy, half-clear, twinkling sky was impossible, but Raylene knew that few things that *seemed* impossible truly were.

~~~

Acknowledgements

A novel is much like an island crouched upon the shoulders of a mountain just below the water line with the mountain connected to the Earth's core. This one is no different.

My mountain includes Mary Crow Dog's searing autobiography *Lakota Woman*; also *Hard Times--An oral History of the Great Depression*, by Studs Terkel; *The Children Sing in the West*, by Mary Austin; and *American Indian Myths and Legends*, selected and edited by Richard Erdoes and Alfonso Oriz; *Woodcraft*, by Bernard S. Mason; *The Sioux of the Rosebud--A History in Pictures*, with photographs by John A. Anderson and text by Henry W. Hamilton and Jean Tyree Hamilton; *Old Man Coyote*, by Frank B. Linderman; *Renewing the World--Plains Indian Religion and Morality*, by Howard L. Harrod; *The American Heritage Book of Indians* from the American Heritage Publishing Co.; *The Schooling of the Western Horse*, by John Richard Young; *West of Everything*, by Jane Thompkins; *Bury My Heart at Wounded Knee--An Indian History of the American West*, by Dee Brown; and *Wisdomkeepers— Meetings with Native American Spiritual Elders* by Steve Wall and Harvey Arden.

A deep bow and tip of my hat to fellow authors Lisa Mortara and Bill Kuechler (rest in peace) for their unerring support and helpful criticism; beta-readers Deb Lowrey, who also provided K.C. research assistance, Grace Caudill, Charlotte Voitoff, the amazing and ever-generous Angela Sell, author and rancher Johny Weber, Jennifer Driver Mannix, and Elaine Alexander and the Wednesday Book Club; Johnny Z and Adia Abreu Perojo for Spanish language assistance; and

Cathy Nelson, South Dakota journalist and publisher with connections.

Special thanks, as mentioned earlier, to cultural consultants Danialle Rose and Thomas Ghost Dog of South Dakota.

Research assistance was provided by the Union Cemetery Historical Society, and staff of the Kansas City Library; Though this story is set in 1936, I've primarily used the spelling of Lakota language as provided in the modern digital New Lakota Dictionary (NLD), Ulrich, J. (ed), New Lakota Dictionary App., Lakota Language Consortium, Kyle, SD.

To my one and only — Jim Riley—Thank you.

Author's Note to Readers

Some readers will wonder how a non-Native American chooses to write a story populated with Lakota and other Native characters. Here's how I did.

Authors write the most believable characters they can and steer them into challenging circumstances, pushing them from one end and pulling them from the other in order to take readers on some sort of adventure or journey. That's what I've attempted with Raylene and the Yellow Moon cast.

I desired the right heroine for this particular story, and Raylene is right. She's intuitive, strong, and honorable. She overcomes obstacles put in her way. I have attempted to respectfully portray her within Lakota culture, ranching culture, and as a woman in a largely male-dominated white world. Any deficiencies in this regard land on my doorstep and no-one else's.

You have likely figured out that although I've constructed an important male character, I'm not a man. It so happens that I am not of Irish descent. I never worked for a railroad or worked as a railroad detective. I've never been a ranch hand, or lived in Kansas City or the Dakotas at any time, especially not in the 1930s. This is the magic of fiction. In order to construct an immersive world for readers, I have for years researched the details I've inserted into Yellow Moon Rising and Yellow Moon Justice. The rest is my imagination at work.

This is how my Yellow Moon stories came to life. I am satisfied with how they turned out and now hope they find readers. If you've made it this far, you must be a reader, and I thank you for that.

Best always,
JoJo Riley

Pine Ridge Reservation
1936

With the odors of her uncle's fire — scorched bone, poplar, smoldering wool — in her nostrils and hair, Raylene Little Moon drove out of the *makhósica*, the bad lands, and south through the Pine Ridge Reservation towns of Kyle and Manderson before turning west to Oglala. Her cow pony rode securely in the van behind Raymond's truck, her truck now. Her father's twin brother, her uncle Ray, had been her second *até*, her second father. She was still digesting what he had done and admitted to, and what he had said, but because he had talked in riddles at the end, she wasn't certain what she should believe and what she should not. Had Ray been her uncle or her father? How would she ever know

Under skies at one moment blue, the next gray with clouds, she drove with her window half open to cool the heat of her burdened heart. For years, she had led a mostly solitary life, but still, she swallowed hard at the thought of being the last living member of her immediate family.

The dirt roads she and Ray had traveled north were now nearly impassable after two days of sporadic snowfall that turned creek beds into bridges of ice. Jouncing along, she formed the beginnings of a plan in which she uncovered the details surrounding her sister Annie's death. She felt certain now that Ray had blamed his brother for Annie's death, but questions remained regarding who had arranged Annie's burial, and where she had been laid to rest. Discovering names and details should rightly bring a sense of peace about losing her only sister, if there could ever be peace. On the other hand, gaining this knowledge might do just the opposite. It might haunt her. She sent a message to the sky. *Annie, I will not give up until I find you.* First, though, she needed to deliver the hard news about Ray to Wilma Manheart.

The streets of Oglala were damp with lingering patches of snow, but the sky was clearing. This being October, the weather might change again within an hour. Raylene pulled to a stop across the paved road from Wilma's market. Even though on the prairie, death was as common as the cycle of seasons, bringing the news of Raymond's death to Wilma pained her a little. She sensed that the two of them had been close.

She had just set one boot on the street when the market door itself opened and Wilma stepped out, hand on her heart and a stunned look on her face. Raylene crossed toward her as Wilma said, "I saw the truck, but ... it's you. That means Raymond is ..."

"Dead. I thought you should hear it from me."

Wilma dropped her hands. "Just like my dream." She looked down the road left then off to the right, as if somehow the landscape had changed. "Did you and Raymond fight?"

"I gave him no opportunity." Her uncle had said he'd been waiting for her, but he had also called her by her mother's name, so perhaps he had already been reaching for the spirit world. What she did not say was how Raymond had insisted on dying near the place that held the ashes of Raylene's mother.

Wilma squelched a shiver before standing straighter.

"I would like to buy supplies," said Raylene.

The woman turned and Raylene followed her into the market. Rough as its wind-scrubbed exterior looked, it was the only market serving the southwest quadrant of the reservation. It also held the town's postal window and therefore enjoyed the luxury of electricity for lights and cold cases, one for beer and one for soda pop. And a telephone. Wilma crossed to warm her hands at the pot-bellied wood stove. She said, "Did he say my name?"

Raylene thought a moment. Comforting words seemed in order. "He wished for you to be sound and safe." Wilma studied Raylene for any sign of fabrication but Raylene held steady under the woman's gaze until Wilma glanced away.

Raylene turned to the closest shelves to give the woman a stitch of privacy.

"Will you go back to your job?" asked Wilma. She meant the H-bar-H, where Raylene worked as ranch hand, and where the boss had fired her for needing time away to find Raymond, her father's killer.

Raylene selected cans of vegetables, a small sack of corn meal, and another of flour. "My sister's death remains a mystery," she said, crossing to the front counter. The next part was harder to admit: "Ray suggested that she died from drinking bad hooch in our father's saloon."

"Could that be true?"

"Perhaps. But Thomas was as honorable as Raymond, so I am of two minds about it."

Wilma pulled an empty grain sack from behind the counter and began to pack it with Raylene's items, adding a tin of lard and a hunk of bacon.

Raylene caught Wilma's eye. "Did Ray ever tell you that *he* was my father instead of Thomas?" The notion that her mother had married one twin brother while loving the other still caused her confusion. Both had been Father to her, yet Thomas had been an official father while Raymond had often acted as a father.

Wilma pursed her lips and swallowed hard. At last, she shook her head.

Wilma spent more time than necessary penciling her purchase into the market ledger. She knew more than she was saying. And did Raymond's assertion even matter now that he was no longer here to provide more details? Was it Raylene's folly to have listened to a dying man's mumblings, half desiring them to be true while unable to accept them at face value? It occurred to her that Wilma must have loved Ray to have kept his secrets.

Wilma said, "Oh. A letter came after you left. It's been sitting here." She moved to the general delivery slot behind the far end of the counter and returned with a crumpled envelope.

The letter's initials and return address were for Kansas City, Missouri but not the undertaker's location. Raylene dropped the letter into her sack of purchases as if it held no import when in fact its arrival surprised her. For all the wrong reasons, she was acquainted with one person who had those initials. Ordinarily, she addressed her own problems and made her own amends. But she was an outsider in Kansas City, which would not get her very far. A Kansas City insider might help her gain access to those with answers about Annie's death and the letter was from just such an insider.

www.ingramcontent.com/pod-product-compliance
Lightning Source LLC
Chambersburg PA
CBHW031607240626
47153CB00002B/665